THE FARMER RISKS IT ALL

LARGE PRINT EDITION

FARMERS OF GOODRICH COUNTY

SHARON A. MITCHELL

ASD PUBLISHING

ALSO BY SHARON A. MITCHELL

Farmers of Goodrich County Romances

The Farmer Takes a Wife

The Farmer Says I Do

The Farmer's Christmas Duty

The Farmer's Second Chance

The Farmer Risks It All

In Case of Rain (free short story)

Psychological Thrillers

Gone: A Psychological Thriller

Trust: A Psychological Thriller

Selfish: A Psychological Thriller

Instinct: A Psychological Thriller

Reasons Why: A Psychological Story

Mine: A Psychological Thriller

Sanctum: A Psychological Thriller

When Bad Things Happen Box Set: Books 1 - 3

When Bad Things Happen Box Set 2: Books 4 - 7

When a Plan Comes Together (free prequel to Gone)

Young Anna (free short story)

Anything for Her Son (short story)

Autism Novels and Nonfiction

Autism Goes to School

Autism Runs Away

Autism Belongs

Autism Talks and Talks

Autism Grows Up

Autism Goes to College

Autism Box Set

Autism Questions Parents Ask & the Answers They Seek

Autism Questions Teachers Ask & the Answers They Seek

Large Print Paperback ISBN 978-1-7389755-6-3

This is a work of fiction, a figment of the author's imagination. Any resemblance to real people or places is coincidental.

To Derek, who always believed it could be done.
You will be missed forever.

CHAPTER 1

Emma

"Emma, dear, I'd really like an apple."

Emma controlled her breathing and did not allow her eyes to roll the way they wanted to. "They're in a bowl on the kitchen counter, Mom."

"I know, darling, but would you be a dear and bring me one? You know I still don't have my strength back yet."

Right. The chemo treatments had been bad; no one could deny that. After the first month, her mother insisted she could not manage on her own, despite the close-knit community of friends willing to take her to and from treatments. No, Esther needed her daughter.

Hating to let her Grade 3 kids down, Emma had no choice but to apply for a leave of absence at the end of May, letting a substitute finish off the school year with her students.

Spending the next three months with her mother was not enough; her mom needed her. When a teaching position opened up in their town of Goodrich, it seemed a sign that it was meant to be. Applying, and then being the successful candidate, Emma resigned from her job and found herself a tiny house to rent in Goodrich. Only blocks from her mother, she'd be available to help whenever Esther needed her.

Whenever - that was the operative word. Even though all the treatments were long over, and scans gave her mom the all-clear, if anything, Esther grew more dependent on her daughter. After living in her own house less than two months, Esther insisted she needed her only child closer, so Emma moved back in with her mother, back into the house where she grew up. It was different without her dad around, but he'd passed away almost ten years ago.

Emma thought her mother was a relatively

independent woman, confident and competent, with a full circle of friends and activities. More to keep busy than needing the money, Esther worked part time at the local nursing home, organizing activities for the residents and delivering Meals on Wheels.

Somehow, this cancer diagnosis changed the woman. It would scare anyone, and chemo and radiation were no picnic. But the oncologist said she should be back on her feet in no time. The final radiation session was last September; it was now May. They declared Esther cancer-free in late fall, and her body should have recuperated from the treatments. The doctor cleared her to return to work.

Work. Emma believed it would be good for Esther to go back to her job, even just a few hours a week - get out of the house and think about someone other than herself.

And let Emma do her own job. Not that she wasn't but teaching Grade 1 was new to her this year, plus she had one autistic student, another with a cognitive disability, and several with attentional issues. It felt like a full plate.

If only she was in her own house, she could put in the evening preparation hours required of a first grade teacher. But no, Esther said she needed her daughter close by; it was bad enough that Emma had to leave her alone all day.

At thirty, Emma had not lived at home for over a dozen years. Not that she didn't love her mother, and as an only child, she realized her duty to her remaining parent, but she was used to living on her own, having a life of her own. Waiting on a querulous older woman was not part of her plan.

Yet here she was. Back in the town she'd been so ready to abandon and looking after a woman more demanding than the 29 first graders in her care all day.

She taught her students more independence skills than her mother showed now.

Sighing, Emma got up from the kitchen table where she was marking arithmetic papers. Wrapping an apple in a paper napkin, Emma brought it to her mother.

Esther's look was reproachful. "Dear, you know that's not how I eat apples. They're too big for my hand to hold." She rubbed the prominent veins between her wrist and knuckles. "Those IVs did a number on my hands."

"Fine." Emma worked at keeping her voice

neutral and returned to the kitchen. Pulling open the cutlery drawer with more force than needed, she hunted for a paring knife. Carefully, she quartered the apple, removing all the visible core. Placing the napkin on a small plate, she thought of something. "Mom, would you like some cheese with that?"

"You are such a thoughtful girl. Thank you. Some of that smoked Gouda would work well, please. And you might want to add that to your grocery list. Wouldn't want to run out."

No, we wouldn't, especially since it wasn't available in this town and would mean an hour's drive to the city to get more. She brought the plate into the living room, setting it on the table beside her mother's chair.

Esther glanced at it. "Emma. Where is your head? You know I can't eat peel. It gets stuck in between my teeth and my gums are so sore ever since that nasty chemotherapy."

"Mom, it's good for you. Roughage and all that, plus the peel contains nutrients." Even as she said the words, Emma knew they were futile.

Esther said nothing, just used that reproachful expression she seemed to have perfected over the last half year.

"All right." Emma admitted defeat, picking up the plate and returning to the kitchen. Why did she feel infinite patience with her students, yet her mother's demands got on her last nerve? It's not that she didn't care; she did. Maybe she used up all her empathy at school, but it was hard when her mom was always so needy.

Peeling each quarter of the apple, Emma let her mind wander. How had she ended up in this position? As an only child, so yes, she had an obligation to her mother. But since she'd been here, Esther cut off all contact with her former friends, telling them Emma was here now, so she didn't need their help any longer.

A few of those friends saw through that and tried to drop by, to invite Esther out, anything to keep in contact and help their friend return to her life.

Esther would have none of it.

Emma's mind was on the mess her life had become rather than the task at hand, the knife slipped. Emma sucked on the cut in her thumb before remembering to run it under cold water.

But the damage was done. Drops of bright red dotted the cheese and apple slices.

Sighing, Emma turned off the water, emptied

the plate into the trash can, then went to the bathroom for antiseptic and a bandage.

Pulling out the cheese and another apple, she began again.

"Emma, what is taking you so long? You know my blood sugar is low and I'm getting shaky."

CHAPTER 2

Gabe

He waited until the nurse left the room, one of an endless stream of well-meaning but bothersome health care workers. He spoke softly, just in case she was sleeping. "Are you sure I can't take you home, Mom?"

Norma Jean's eyes fluttered open, and the sides of her lips tipped upward just slightly. "No, son. I know you mean well, but it's too much."

"I can hire people to help."

Her head turned from side to side on the pillow. "We're not playing it that way. The easiest care is right here. It might not be a glamorous way to end my life, but we work with what we're given. We always have."

Gabe watched his mother's grimace of pain and reached for the button that would give her a shot of relief.

"No, that will knock me out, so I can't talk to you. We have so little time left together."

"Mom, we've had all my life. Just rest now."

"I have something to tell you. I made a promise I never would, but I think that was a mistake. You have the right to know. It's important."

Her movements became more restless, a sure sign of increasing pain. Waiting until her eyes closed, Abe reached up and pushed the button.

"I saw that." She would have said more, but her words trailed off as she drifted off into unconsciousness.

It had been almost a month after Norma Jean first noticed a lump that she mentioned it to Gabe. She hadn't wanted to "bother" him when he was so busy at work.

Sheesh.

But the oncologist told him a few weeks

wouldn't have mattered, anyway. The biopsy and scans showed the cancer was already stage IV, affecting her liver, spine and brain. If it had been just in her bones, the one-year survival rate was 51%, and a five-year survival rate of 13%. Who knew what advances in treatment may have been made in five years?

But with metastases like she had, she would not be around long enough to benefit from them. They did radiation to shrink the largest tumors; the ones interfering the most in her quality of life, with only minimal success. Norma Jean valiantly suffered chemo without complaint, but Gabe could see her body almost shrinking daily as the anti-nausea drugs failed to help. After only three treatments, they stopped the chemo; it would kill her faster than would the cancer. Where the neck of the hospital gown gaped on his mother's skeletal body, Gabe could see the burn marks from the radiation. Her skin was so thin and frail, much too frail for a woman not even in her 60s yet.

Yet. She would not make her 60th birthday. When the oncologist privately told him that, Gabe recoiled. The doctor didn't know his mother, know her will and how her determination got her through anything.

It had always been just the two of them, a single mom raising her son. Yeah, he knew there must have been a father around at some time, but he couldn't remember him. Norma Jean told him his dad had died when he was just barely walking and talking. If that was true, then why were there no pictures of him anywhere? Nothing. No smiling father tossing his infant son into the air. No wedding photos, nothing of the happy couple.

And no relatives.

But just the two of them alone against the world was just fine. Norma Jean made it so. A boy could not have asked for a more perfect mother. Sure, money was tight most of the time, and he was alone a lot as she worked two jobs. When she walked through their apartment door, though, her son was the focus of her world, her everything.

He'd been around 10 when they moved. His boyish self never questioned where they suddenly got the money to buy a house. Mind you, it was a small place, just two bedrooms in an older building, but in a neighborhood where people cared, even if they had little.

Paper routes and Saturday mornings delivering flyers morphed into better jobs as he turned 15. By 16, he worked 20 hours a week at the supermarket. Half of his net pay went into the household bank account he and his mother shared. That meant she could let go of her job cleaning offices in the evenings. For such a strong-spirited woman, her body was frail, and even a self-centered teen could see the toll the long hours took on her stamina.

He wondered how could he not think about how they were able to purchase a house. Especially now, the what ifs piled one on top of each other. What if his father had not died? What if the guy kicked the bucket, but left some provision for his wife and child? What if his father's family stepped in to help? What if his maternal grandparents had been around? He should have tried harder as a teen, done more, made sure his mom had more breaks. Maybe this voracious cancer would not have taken root if she'd had an easier life.

She never complained. Not once, ever, could he recall her whining about her lot in life. She just got on with it, meeting any obstacle head on and surviving anything thrown at them.

Anything but this. Even he could see now how accurate the oncologist's predictions were.

CHAPTER 3

Gabe

It was the next day.

"Do *not* press that button again. I have things I need to tell you, and not much time to do so."

"Mom, come on. There's plenty of time. You need your rest."

The look Norma Jean gave her son brooked no argument. Even though he was 30 years old, the ingrained instinct to obey his mother, and with that look in particular, was hard to shake. "We're not in the habit of lying to each other or fooling ourselves. We both know my time is short. *I* get to choose how I spend that time."

"Yes, Mom," although Gabe knew he'd press that button in a heartbeat if it meant his mother would suffer less. If she was going to die (and everything pointed that way) he would do everything in his power to make it an easier passing for her.

Not that many years ago, they'd had their faithful old dog put down. She'd been the third member of their family, sharing her life with them for over 15 years. But cancer got her, too. Ironically breast cancer. Even though the vet did the mastectomy as soon as he discovered the tumors, the surgery only bought Bella a few more years with them. When it became obvious she suffered pain, scans showed tumors throughout the canine's body. The veterinarian came to their home to euthanize Bella, with her people, Norma Jean and Gabe, by her side, their hands stroking her coarse fur. It was over in a minute; the old girl just relaxed and was gone. No struggle; no more pain. Why couldn't it be that easy for people? Not that he wanted his mother gone, but he couldn't bear to see her in such discomfort.

"Gabe." Now louder. "Gabe."

He pulled himself back from his thoughts. Geez. His mother was not long for this world; how could he not give her his full attention, the way she had done for him these past three decades? "Sorry Mom. Daydreaming."

"It's no wonder. You've slept in that chair for the last three nights."

He shifted. "It's fine. More comfortable than it looks."

The look she slanted him said she knew he lied. "Gabe. Listen to me. I'm going to tell you some things, then you're going home to shower and sleep. I don't want to see you back here before 11:00 tomorrow morning."

"But, Mom…"

"Gabriel Ottski, don't you 'but Mom' me. You will do as you're told."

"Yes, ma'am."

"I have things that need to be said, should have been said years ago. But I made a promise, a foolish promise. I was young and scared, but that's no excuse."

"It's fine, Mom, whatever it is. Just rest now."

"Do *not* tell me what to do. Just listen." She took in a few deep breaths and asked for a glass of water before continuing. "Your last name, *our* last name, is not what you think. I made a deal to give you that surname, and I had mine legally changed so ours would be the same."

"You took your husband's name."

"I've never been married."

"Pardon?" What was all that about his father dying when he was a baby? "Then what's this you told me about Bruce?"

"Bruce fathered you, and I mean in the biological sense. He was your father genetically, but that's it."

"He died before he could act like a father?"

"He died, yes, but not before he had years when he could have been a father to you." She paused. "And your half-brother."

"Half-brother!"

"Yes. You are not the only son he created."

"Where is this brother, and why am I just hearing about him now?"

"I don't know where he is. I didn't tell you about him, or about your grandmother, because of my promise to her."

"A grandmother! I thought we had no family. That's what you always said."

"On my side, you don't. Like you, I was an only child. My parents disowned me when they found out I was pregnant."

"Where are they now?"

"They died when you were in elementary school. Carbon monoxide poisoning in their home - the home where I grew up. This was before we had detectors in our houses."

"Is that why you were so paranoid about keeping fresh batteries in our smoke and carbon monoxide detectors?"

Norma Jean nodded.

"Why did I never meet these grandparents?"

"That's my fault. Getting pregnant out of wedlock was a sin, something they could not get past. Unless your father and I married, they said I was dead to them."

"It must have been a shock to learn that their only child was going to have a baby. Surely, after they thought about it, they'd calm down."

His mother raised and lowered her eyebrows in a look Gabe knew well. "You didn't know them. Once they took a stance, that was it."

"Why didn't you and my father get married?"

"A wedding would have required two of us being onboard with the idea. I was; Bruce was not."

"Bruce. Bruce Ottski?"

She nodded.

"He didn't like the idea of me?"

"He didn't like the idea of responsibility - any sort of responsibility."

"You mentioned a grandmother. Did she know you were having me?"

"Bruce and I were living together. His parents dropped in unexpectedly. His mother said she wanted to meet her son's girlfriend. Bruce was not good at keeping in touch with his parents."

"Why?"

"He was a free spirit, wanting to go his own way, follow whatever path seemed the most fun at the time. His parents wanted him to settle down. He said there was plenty of time for that later." She looked off into the distance. "He was like a kid who never wanted to grow up."

"What happened when his parents met you?"

"I invited them to stay for supper; it was the least I could do. We didn't have a lot, but I tried to make an enjoyable meal for them. Gabriella was pleasant, defensive of her son, but wanting to get to know the woman Bruce was with.

"She wasn't stupid. She noticed how I almost gagged when cutting up the raw chicken breast for the stir-fry. Then she noticed how little I ate, and when I excused myself from the table several times to use the bathroom. I had horrible morning sickness with you, the kind that lasted all day."

Was he supposed to apologize for that? He felt

bad that his mom suffered while carrying him, but was it his fault? What could he have done?

"Get that guilty look off your face. I know you, Gabriel Ottski. Some pregnancies are just like that. Anyway, it didn't take Gabriella long to figure out I was carrying a child. She outright asked. At first Bruce denied it, but his mother just looked at him. It wasn't my place to say anything, but he finally admitted I was pregnant, but said we'd take care of it."

"Take care of, as in, get rid of me?"

Norma Jean covered her son's calloused and grease-stained hand with her frail one. "You know, I'd never have agreed to anything like that. I loved you and wanted you from the instant I knew of your existence."

"My father didn't feel the same way." This was more a statement than a question.

"Bruce had trouble seeing past his own next bit of excitement. He was all about the thrill, the fun, the good time."

Gabe placed his other hand on his mother's. "And having a child was none of those things for him."

"No. I'm sorry, son, but the truth is, being a father meant responsibility and Bruce and that 'R' word didn't mix. Never did."

"Where is he now?" If he could find the guy, he'd give him words and probably fists for making his mother's life so hard, raising a child on her own.

"There is no seeking him out. He died. Bruce lived life fast and hard. It was inevitable he would meet his demise, and not in a natural way. He was killed in a car accident - driving too fast in poor conditions. Thankfully, he didn't take anyone else with him. He was alone when his car left the road and hit a tree."

Good riddance. "Did he leave you anything? Did he send child support?"

Norma Jean shook her head.

"What about his parents? Why didn't I meet my grandparents?"

"They were not bad people; if we met under other circumstances, I would have liked them, I think. But they were Bruce's parents first and foremost. They'd spent their lives protecting their only son, covering for him, making excuses for him." She held up her hand. "Scratch that last bit. It's just my opinion." She motioned to the plastic jug on the wheeled table. "May I have some water, please?" Lately, water seemed the only thing she could keep down. It's not that she was thirsty, but she needed to wet her dry mouth if she was to get through the rest of what she needed Gabe to hear.

Norma Jean continued. "It was obvious to his parents and to me that Bruce did not want this baby. He was their son, so they supported him. But it bothered Gabriella. And maybe she knew her child well, and guessed he would bolt. When they left that evening, and I got ready for bed, something rustled in my sweater pocket. I found a check for $10,000 addressed to me—not Bruce and me, just in my name.

"I couldn't take their money. I put the check away, planning to send it back to them. We went to bed like usual, but the next morning, Bruce was gone. Not all of his things were missing, but his suitcase, a duffle bag, and most of his clothes. He didn't answer his phone or respond to any of the messages I sent him. I knew he was gone. It was inevitable, or at least a part of my brain knew that, while my heart had hoped he loved me enough to stay together and become a family."

"The guy sounds like a creep."

"He was nothing like you, that is for sure." She turned her head on the pillow to regard him full on. "Have I told you how proud I am of the man you've become?"

"Thanks, Mom, but there's more, isn't there?"

CHAPTER 4

Emma back then

How had her life become this?

Head cheerleader in high school. Prom queen. Always surrounded by friends, dating the quarterback. It had all seemed such fun, the possibilities endless, and the future bright.

The only flaw had been Stan. Good-looking and as popular as her - Emma's ideal boyfriend.

Except in Stan's mind, Goodrich County was the perfect place to build a life. There was no question that after high school he would farm with his dad and older brother, Greg.

Absolutely nothing Emma said moved Stan from that plan. Not even for her would he move to the city to be with her while she attended college. It made her think she was convenient for him, a ready-made date in high school, but nothing special. Not worth altering his life over.

Her dad said she needed to do what was right for her, that there was a big world out there she needed to explore. So, the heck with Stan. If he wasn't willing to give up the farm for her, she certainly wasn't willing to abandon the chance to be independent, to have a career of her own, one far from the tiny town of Goodrich.

Of course, it meant leaving her parents too. An only child, she took their doting for granted. It wasn't until she lived on her own in the city that she realized the security of unconditional love and approval showered on her by her parents. Even apart, there were phone calls and surprise packets of cash. Well, not surprise, really, since they arrived so frequently.

All these things she took for granted until they stopped.

An aneurysm took her dad. At work, in the break room pouring a coffee, he suddenly dropped to the floor. Despite colleagues around, and prompt attention from EMTs, there was nothing anyone could do.

He was young; retirement still in the future. Once their daughter was through college and secure in a teaching job, the funds now going to Emma would funnel into retirement plans.

It happened at the start of Emma's third year of her Bachelor of Education program. Well settled into college life, she'd found a balance between keeping good grades and having a good time.

College differed from high school, where everyone knew her and never questioned her place at the top of the pecking order. First year was an adjustment. Although she still looked the same, and always, always kept up her perky persona, it took time to find a group of friends. Used to being the leader, it was a rude shock that she realized that sometimes she had to follow the ideas of others.

Emma adapted. By the second year, her status rose, as it should for someone named most likely to succeed. It had taken work, but her social life was now closer to where it should be.

Summers abroad in teaching-related exchange programs expanded her outlook, making her even more positive she had made the right decision to escape from Goodrich.

Then the phone call. Hardly recognizing her mother's voice, hardly making sense of the words Esther choked out between sobs.

Gone. Harold Lowry was gone. Just like that, life changed.

The school administration was good about excusing her from classes for a week as she returned home to help her mom, but Emma almost wished she had stayed in her dorm. There, she could pretend things were normal, like they had always been, with a phone call from her dad a few times a week, and a deposit into her bank account.

But back home in the house where she'd grown up, the lack of his presence was everywhere. For as long as she could remember, her dad had walked through the front door at 5:20 p.m. with the same cheesy greeting, then a hug and kiss for her mom and her. He'd get changed, then settle in front of the television to wait for dinner to be on the table promptly at 6.

Now, silence. No Dad, with his faint stubble rubbing her cheek as he gave her a hug. No lingering scent of Old Spice. No basketball on TV. And no dinner.

In the aftermath of his death, Esther seemed to forget to eat, or that others might need to eat. Thank goodness for neighbors keeping their fridge stocked with meals.

Used to being looked after, 20-year-old Emma found herself in the position of caregiver to her numb mother, coaxing her to eat, take a shower, go for a nap - anything other than doing that catatonic thing where the woman sat frozen in a chair, staring at a blank wall.

The kitchen was her mom's domain; always had been. It was almost like Esther forgot all that, forgot her pride in keeping the room pristine. Soiled dishes piled up in the sink, waiting for Emma to do something about them. By the third day at home, it dawned on Emma that maybe, just maybe, her mom was not snapping out of this.

One of the church ladies brought a stack of frozen, individual meals, stowed them in the freezer, explaining they were for her mother. Rather than pitching in and unloading, then loading the dishwasher as other women had done, she chided Emma gently on the state of the kitchen. "It's your job now to look after your momma," she said.

That was news to Emma. They'd always

looked after her. That was the way it was—parents took care of their kid. But Esther made no move to do any of the things mothers typically did.

She left it all to Emma. Planning the funeral, cleaning the house, seeing that they ate. It was all so much.

Being a small town where everyone knew one another, the bank manager came to the house. Seeing the state her mother was in, Mr. Werther guided Emma into the kitchen and sat her down. Step by step, he walked her through what needed to be done about her parents' bank accounts and finances.

Finances.

Money was something Emma took for granted. It was always there for whatever she needed. Now, that was no longer the case. Without her dad's salary, life would be very different.

Thankfully, the house was paid for, but that didn't mean there were no expenses. Taxes. Upkeep. Appliances that broke down - realities of life Mr. Werther told her she needed to prepare for. Right. How?

Esther was too young for Social Security

benefits. To be in her 50s and eligible, she would have to have a disability. While she was certainly disabled right now, the disability had to have been documented prior to the spouse's death.

Without Harold's salary, how were they going to live?

CHAPTER 5

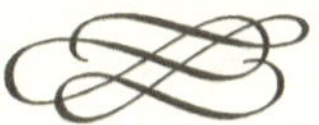

Gabe

"Yes, son, there is more," answered Norma Jean. "I'm not proud of myself when I have to tell you that I cashed the check Bruce's mother left me. At first I didn't; I was sure nothing on earth would make me accept that money. But then, the landlord sent a letter saying our rent was overdue. How could that be? It was automatically deducted from our account, just like my paycheck was automatically deposited. It went in days before the rent was due."

Gabe had a sick feeling he knew what was coming next.

"I went to the back and checked the account. It

had $9.83 in it. I remember than number exactly. My whole previous month's pay should have been in there, as well as savings I'd accumulated, plus Bruce's share of the rent." She motioned for Gabe to pass her the glass of ice chips. "Gone, all of it. It was a joint account between Bruce and me. I never dreamed he would clean me out. Steal from me." She put a hand on the fist Gabe was clenching over and over. "This is ancient history, son, back when I was younger and more naïve. A smarter person would have moved my portion of that money into a new account, one Bruce had no access to. But back then, I was reeling from him leaving me, and coming to grips with being pregnant. That's not an excuse for being stupid, and you better believe I wisened up pretty fast after that. Cashing your grandmother's check was the only way to pay rent and buy groceries that month. I had to try to eat for the sake of the infant I was growing inside of me."

"I'm sorry you were put in that position, Mom. If I could, I'd go after that guy for doing this to you." His voice hardened. "What did you ever see in a jerk like that?" He lowered his voice. "Sorry, Mom. I should have kept that in my head."

"No, you're right to wonder, son. My only

excuse is that I was young. Your father was a handsome man, engaging and flashy. It flattered me to think that someone like that was interested in me. In retrospect, I think he was attracted to the stability I represented. I looked after him, keeping our apartment tidy, doing laundry, shopping and cooking the meals - all those adult things he avoided."

"You did everything?"

"I didn't mind. I was used to it, and it seemed a small price to pay to have someone so exciting in my life. He added spice to everything. I'd always been a plain Jane, solid and dependable, never stepping outside the box. Until I did with an unplanned pregnancy."

"You didn't get pregnant on your own. It was just as much his responsibility as yours."

"A man like you would see it that way, but not Bruce. I think it frightened him; it might mean less fun. He could barely look after himself, let alone a wife and baby."

"Did he move back home?"

"No. Maybe, temporarily. A few weeks later, through mutual friends, I heard he moved in with a woman. He needed someone to take care of him."

"So that was it? You never heard from him again?"

"Pretty much. After I had you, my life changed. I no longer visited the places where Bruce hung out. Couldn't afford it, plus had no interest. My focus changed the instant I saw your sweet little face. You were my world."

"And my grandparents?"

"It's a good thing I kept that apartment. Your grandmother sent me a note - several notes. The first one arrived when I was seven months pregnant. She hoped I was feeling well and asked me to call her. The whole Ottski name was not high on my list of favorites, and I almost didn't reply. But family matters, and I thought she wanted to be involved in her grandson's life. So, I waited a few weeks, then called. She wanted to meet me for lunch. I was almost eight months along then, and the doctor ordered me to begin maternity leave early, so I had time to waddle to the restaurant your grandmother chose."

"What did she say?"

"She was a blunt lady; something I appreciate now, less so then. Gabriella barely asked about my health after staring at my belly. She asked if her son was in touch with me, if he was giving me money. She had such hope in her eyes, as if she expected her boy to redeem himself, and for me to tell her what she wanted to hear. I couldn't give her that satisfaction. What could I do but shake my head?"

"Her expression soured, as if it was my fault. That raised my dander. It wasn't me who had raised a hedonistic son. We had a stilted lunch, and I was eager to get away from her. Just before I left, she asked for my email address. I almost refused, but for your sake, gave it to her. After that, on the first of every month, I received a check for $400."

Gabe scoffed.

"No, son. That doesn't seem like much now, but 30 years ago, it really helped, especially until I could get back to work. Even then, it helped with childcare."

"So she just flung money at the problem?"

"Gabe, honey, don't be bitter. This is all in the past, and we made out just fine."

"You were a great mom, but they could have helped make things easier on you."

"They did, in their own way. They were parents, and Bruce was, and had always been, their focus. They spoiled him, and I think they knew it."

"Your grandfather wanted nothing to do with

us; I think we reminded him of his son's screwups." She realized what she'd said. "I don't mean that you were a screwup; what I mean is that they'd spent decades covering up for their son, getting him out of scrapes, make excuses for him, until even the most closed-eye parent had to realize the child they raised was less than ideal in the adulthood department."

"But they let you suffer because of their kid's shortcomings."

"Divided loyalties, I'd say. They loved their son and tried to support him." She motioned for Gabe to pass her more ice chips. "When I was in hospital with you, your grandmother came to visit. You were in a bassinet beside my bed. Your grandmother Gabriella could hardly take her eyes off you. When I offered that she could hold you, she teared up and said that if she cradled you once, she'd never want to let go. That terrified me - what if she planned to take you? But no, that was not her intention. Bruce forbade his parents to have anything to do with you or me. Neither her husband nor son knew Gabriella was at the hospital. But she had a plan."

CHAPTER 6

Emma ten years ago

Esther Lowry was not destitute; there would be a small monthly income, enough to get by on if she was careful and supplemented with part-time work, Mr. Werther assured Emma.

But not enough to support Emma as well.

"But, but…" started Emma. "What about me?" She hated that she sounded like a peevish child, but, well, that's how she felt. "What am I supposed to do now?"

This was not part of the plan. Her parents would support her through four years of college and until she secured a wonderful teaching job. Dad promised. That's how it was supposed to go.

Thank goodness Daddy had already paid this semester's tuition, books, and dorm fees. She had some breathing room, but what was she supposed to do for spending money for the next few months? For next term's fees?

A look other than sympathy entered Mr. Werther's eyes but was quickly masked. "What other young people do." He waited, getting nothing but a blank look from the young woman. "Move back home to look after your mother and get a job."

Emma's eyes widened.

"Or stay at school and get a part-time job to get you through these last two years of college."

"That's it? You don't have any better solutions?"

"You might quit school and work full time, helping your mom, plus saving so that you can return to school to finish your degree later."

"But we had a plan. Next year was to be my final year, then I'd be a qualified teacher."

He patted her hand. "Plans change, my dear."

No kidding.

They got through the funeral, the barbaric institution that it was. Everyone was looking at her, watching how she handled it, staring at her mother as the older woman's ice finally broke and she fell sobbing into her only child's arms.

All Emma wanted was for everyone to go away and leave them alone. That, and to wake up and this had all been a dream. A nightmare.

When her parents entertained, they expected Emma to put in an appearance, say hello to everyone, then she was free to take refuge in her room, or, more often, to go out with her friends. That's how it had always been.

Not so after the funeral. Her hopes of escaping to her upstairs bedroom were dashed almost immediately. Someone wanted her every minute. People either hugged her or squeezed her hands, saying the same platitudes over and over again until she wanted to scream.

"Look after your mother," was the most common refrain.

Yeah, how was she supposed to do that from over a hundred miles away? Did these people not realize that she had a life, too? That she was on a career path that would grant her a better life than she'd ever found here in this dinky town? Goodrich was fine for some people, but not for someone like her.

"How long are you staying?" Over and over,

people asked that question. Unanimously, silence followed when she replied she was only here for two more days. The person would glance from Emma to her mother, then back again, the reproach clear, even if not voiced. But voice it, some did. Somehow, having known her since she was a child, these people felt they had the right to say whatever they wanted to her.

She was not her mother's keeper. Her mother was an adult. It was only two years ago that her parents were still looking after her; it did not work the other way around. Was it her fault that her mom couldn't get herself together? Was it her fault that her dad had not planned better to support his family? She loved him, but how dare he leave them in the lurch like this when they needed him most?

She had a life to live.

It was only responsible to complete her degree so she could begin a career and support herself decently. Right? Maybe even help support her mom if that became necessary. Emma cringed at the thought, but if she had to, she would. There would be no hope of that if she quit school now and worked at some piddly, minimum-wage job.

Nope, she was returning to school, maybe even a day early. Surely her mom would snap out of it better if she didn't have Emma to rely on. Wouldn't she? The woman had friends; that's what small towns were all about. People would rally around and take care of Esther. Of course they would. They could not expect Emma to put her life on hold, forget her own dreams, just because her mother zoned out. Come on, Mom. Big girl panties and all that.

How humiliating. Having to refuse to join some other students on her floor for a pizza or a latte. Never in her life had she had to think about where her cash came from; it was just there for whatever she wanted. Now, she had to pinch pennies, and it did not sit well. Not at all. Why was life so unfair?

Good thing she'd never spent all the money her dad sent her monthly; that meant she had enough to tide her over for the next few weeks, maybe even to semester break, if she was careful. Before she had to take on that dreaded "j" word, a job.

Jobs were for people who'd finished their career—jobs on a career path as a professional, not slinging hash, waiting on other people, when she was used to them doing her bidding.

But suck it up, buttercup. Watching the funds

in her bank account dwindle alarmingly, she could only pretend to herself for so long.

In two weeks she started at the library. Stocking shelves and showing students how to do research online lacked glamor, but was better than waitressing in the local hangouts, or even worse, serving in the cafeteria. How humiliating that would be.

Emma knew there were people she'd been in high school with who would gloat about her present circumstances. How the mighty had fallen, and all that. Maybe she should have been more sensitive to their situations, but at the time, she'd been too busy maintaining her status. It wasn't easy getting to, then staying at the top of their social circle.

Had it been worth it?

CHAPTER 7

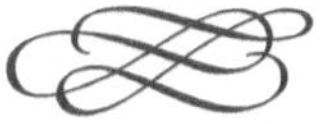

Gabe

"It's about time someone in that family planned something," said Gabe.

Norma Jean tried to make Gabe understand. "Gabriella was in a tough spot—she lived for her son, yet she was going against her son's wishes, and behind her husband's back. It tore the mother in her in two. But she presented me with a deal."

Gabe slanted a hard look at his mother. She made a deal with the devil?

"Hear me out, son. She wanted you to have her son's last name."

"Really? The nerve. She had no right."

"You were Bruce's son and Gabriella's grandson. In exchange for taking the Ottski surname, we would continue to receive $400 a month in child support until you finished high school."

Gabe scoffed. "As if that was enough to make a difference."

"Gabe, it helped. But that wasn't all. She offered to pay our way for one full year, as well as all expenses, as I retrained myself in some sort of career."

"Career? You don't mean your Certified Nursing Assistant Diploma, do you? I thought you had that long before I was born."

Norma Jean shook her head. "No, you were three months old when I started that course."

"Did she pay up like she said she would?"

"Never was even one day late with it."

"Wait! I remember you going back to school around the same time I started school."

"That's right. I heard from your grandmother again when you were in kindergarten. Gabriella stopped by unannounced while you were in school and sniffed around our apartment. She asked to see your room, the only bedroom. Then she wanted to see where I slept, and I pointed to the sofa. She said that she'd been looking into

CNAs and learned that they didn't make much money, at least compared to nurses. She asked if I'd like to be a nurse. Of course, I would - more autonomy, more money and more job choices. She said she'd been saving up and would support us if I took a two-year nursing course. She apologized she didn't have enough money for a four-year program."

"So that's why you and I started school at the same time?"

"Yes. I had to get past my pride to do what I thought was best for both of us."

"And that was it."

"Not quite. She attended my graduation. Then, when you were ten, I heard from her again. A friend of hers had a house for sale. The woman really liked her neighbors, but could no longer manage the house on her own. She had to sell it, but was picky about who it would go to. Gabriella asked me to look at the place. If I liked it, she'd offer me money for half of the down payment. The amount she offered would cover the entire down payment, but coupled with the savings I had, I could put enough down to make our monthly mortgage payment manageable."

"That's when we moved into the house you have now?"

Norma Jean nodded. “I paid off the house, and I returned Gabriella’s down payment money to her.”

“Mom, you didn’t have to do that. She owed us.”

“Did she? I don’t see it that way. Her son owed us, yes, but he would never step up. Instead, his mother did the right thing on his behalf. I felt the child support was warranted, but the rest was above the call of duty.”

Gabe scoffed. “She lied—lied to her family, a lie of omission.” Sort of like you, Mom, he thought, but pushed that aside to contemplate another day. “She snuck around behind their backs instead of being upfront. How was that okay?”

“She wasn’t a bad woman, son, just a woman torn between the love of her son, and her sense of obligation, with a hefty dose of guilt mixed in.”

“With that guilt, did she never want to meet me?”

“Oh, son, she so did. But her son and husband forbade it.”

“And she did what they said?”

“This was another time, Gabe. Things were different a generation or two ago. She defied their wishes as it was.” She paused. “And she saw you—often, but from afar. Did you know she attended your graduation ceremony? And most of your football games? She kept near the back of the stands, but she was there. It got so I looked for her. We'd exchange nods, but the next time I'd glance at where she'd been, she'd have disappeared."

Gabe snorted. "Sounds pretty wimpy to me."

"Maybe, but she did the best she felt she could at the time. Her son and husband are gone now, and she's all alone. She gave me permission to give you her contact information in case you want to meet her."

"That would be the day."

"Don't say never, son. Rule nothing out. I've gotten to know her more in the last decade or so, and she's not a bad person."

CHAPTER 8

Emma today

She stood in front of the mirror—the same mirror where she'd lingered for hours and hours as a teen, perfecting her image. Now, it didn't evoke quite the same emotions as it once had.

She could hear her mother's voice in her head, the admonition she'd grown up with: "A lady must always look her best."

Back then, confidence had oozed from Emma's pores. She had the skills to make herself stand out from the crowd, and parents who had indulged her in anything she wanted to achieve that physical and social perfection.

In high school, appearance held an outsized importance for her, despite a part of her knowing deep down that it shouldn't. Nevertheless, she couldn't shake the feeling that her appearance was a crucial factor in maintaining her social status and reputation as one of the popular kids. The pressure was always on to look a certain way and present a specific image to her peers, one that would ensure she remained at the top of the social hierarchy. Every outfit she wore, every strand of hair she styled, every makeup application she made - all of it had to be just right. In her mind, any misstep could mean a catastrophic drop in status, and she simply couldn't let that happen.

And she never did. Head cheerleader, steady date of the all-star athlete, prom queen. She'd had it all.

Then, after being away from that small town so long, she came back home, for good this time.

Calling it an adjustment put it mildly. But she adapted. Over the past decade of college, and teaching jobs in the city, she'd learned that she could do a lot of things she never imagined.

Moving away to attend university had been one thing, but she was still in a sheltered environment there, shielded from the real world by the safe enclave of the campus, and by the emotional and financial support of her parents.

Until that had all changed halfway through her second semester when that phone call came from home that her dad was in the hospital.

Some of those experiences had made her a better teacher. One of her prof's lectures really hit home. He said that those who sailed through high school did not necessarily make the best teachers.

What? Emma had believed that her experiences as a kid made her ideal for the teaching profession. Had she not been involved in every activity the school offered, not only participated, but the star? No one "got" the varsity experience more than she did.

The prof explained that those to whom school success came easily had a skewed view of what educational institutions were like for many students. Once out in the world with a shiny new B.Ed., neophyte teachers would quickly discover that the children populating their classes were not mini clones of those for whom school came easily. Roughly 15% of pupils in every classroom had intellectual abilities at the lower end of average or below. Perhaps 20% of the classroom population would have some learning disability, whether or not officially diagnosed. Those kids struggled.

It was the teacher's job to teach *all* children, and assuming that every student would pick up the concept the first time, no matter how pretty the lesson was, was opening yourself up to a world of hurt. Without understanding each child's learning style, without presenting the concepts in multiple ways, multiple times, some kids would be left behind. Chances are, those kids would not sit silently, minding their own business. Apart from better serving the students, it was in a teacher's best interests to understand learning differences, rather than fight with frustrated kids all day, every day. That way led to burned out teachers and turned off the students.

Practice teaching had opened Emma's eyes to another world, another way of being. While some of her peers complained about their classroom assignments, Emma learned to relish the time she spent with kids who learned differently. Had such students existed in the rooms where she had been a child? Maybe. They were so far from the young Emma's radar that she hardly noticed. Some she assumed were dumb, or at least that's what those in her tight circle of friends taunted.

Now, when she sat with similar kids, she

found that some of these students were not incapable. They might need things shown to them differently, but once they got it, could take off with the concept and add parts to it that astonished Emma.

It also astonished her to reflect on what a brat she had been in high school. So full of herself. So focused on being the center of attention, of being at the top of the in crowd.

Those last two years of college had taught Emma many things - some she wanted to learn; some she bitterly regretted at the time. Money-management had become crucial once the tap from daddy ran dry after he died. Putting aside fun when work called. (Oh, that had been a bitter one when she'd have to refuse outings with friends because she had shifts scheduled at the library, and really, really needed the money). Obligation. Her mom now needed Emma to act as *her* cheerleader, encouraging every step Esther took out of the shell her house had become. Suddenly, at 20, Emma had become the parent, managing her mother's emotional and financial states.

She also learned compassion, different ways of viewing the world, and, most importantly, the ability to step outside that which she'd known all her life. After all, wasn't that one of her reasons for escaping from Goodrich?

~

But here she was now, ten years later, right back in Goodrich where she began. Her mother needed her more than ever as she was undergoing cancer treatments.

At least she was teaching, something she loved. Being in a classroom brought out the best in her, where she forgot herself and focused solely on the needs of the children in her charge.

Outside of the classroom, she still needed to focus on something other than herself - namely her mother.

Like right now. Even though she would have loved to sleep in this Saturday morning, she was on her way to Alpaca Haven, the store Becca and Stan Wells ran on their farm, selling crafts and products made from the fleece from their alpaca herd.

Emma inwardly cringed at the thought of facing Stan and Becca, after she had presented to them her less than best self when she first returned to Goodrich almost a year ago. To give herself credit, she'd been apprehensive about moving back home. Esther's cancer treatments were too much for her to handle on her own, even with the help of friends. Emma had no choice; her mother needed her, but she feared the town had moved on without her over the past decade.

How would she find her place in this town once again, she'd worried. A pre-emptive strike to restore the status quo she'd enjoyed as a teen, with her and Stan as the stars at the high school fell flat. Stan would have none of it, and made it clear he was with Becca now. Back when they were juniors and seniors, it would only have taken Emma minutes to dislodge Becca from that place, but now her charms no longer worked on Stan. Or anyone.

But they were polite, and their tolerance settled into a truce these past months.

Esther complained bitterly about the cold, despite keeping the thermostat in the house uncomfortably high, in Emma's opinion. In self-defence, Emma tried solutions to keep her mom warm, but Esther bewailed the heavy weight of quilts, the scratchiness of wool, how silk throws kept sliding off when she napped. The one solution came from alpacas. Only alpaca socks kept her mom's feet warm and didn't itch. Only alpaca mittens felt right on her hands. Emma commissioned from Becca an oversized alpaca shawl, and a call last night said it was ready.

So, here she was, about to head out of town in the snow to pick up something she hoped would please her mother, at least for a little while.

Emma turned off the curling iron, examining her image in the mirror. Yes, her shiny locks bounced when she turned her head, then settled back into place, ready to peek out from under her toque. Eyebrow arched just right. Not a line or streak in her well-blended foundation makeup. Eyes enhanced with shadow and mascara. Eye shadow the correct hue to go with the hat she'd put on.

But who was going to see it? Her mom. Becca and Stan. That's it. Still, a lady must always look her best.

CHAPTER 9

Gabe

Texas was never like this. Sure, there was the rare snow flurry in Amarillo and maybe the Guadalupe Mountains, but that was about it. How did people live in a place like this?

His truck tires had not touched actual ground for half an hour - neither pavement nor gravel, nor plain old dirt. Just snow. Were tires even designed to move on this stuff?

Gabe corrected a skid, yet again. Good thing he had experienced driving in areas where the rains turned the ground into slick splattering of sticky muck. It was a fact of life when he looked after cattle and ranching machinery.

But muck differed from snow, especially a foot of drifting snow hiding an ice base. He had to speed up to make his tires churn through the next drift. The curve in the road, coupled with the driving snow coming right at his windshield, made it all tricky. Headlights coming up behind him distracted him just momentarily before he yanked his attention back to staying on the road.

Too late. That split second mattered. With a whirling spray of white, his truck left the road, nosing into the snowbank alongside the road. At least the landing was soft, not like going off the road into boulders.

Reaching over to the passenger footwell where his hat now nestled, Gabe grabbed his Stetson and settled it firmly back on his head. Placing the gearshift into reverse, he attempted to back out of his predicament. The high-pitched rev of spinning tires was the only sound. Okay, try going forward. Maybe he could rock himself out of there. Same result. Maybe he needed to get out and assess the situation.

Just as he was about to lift the door handle, the door was yanked out of his hand.

"What do you think you're doing?" asked a voice, a feminine voice, an annoyed voice.

Gabe lowered his chin and his eyebrows, peering at the speaker. "I could ask you the same thing. Why did you open my door?" He reached for his sidearm, remembering too late that it was in the backseat, in his duffle. This woman didn't look armed, but who could tell for sure with the way she was bundled up? Still, he could overpower any woman if it came to that.

"What is wrong with you driving into a snowbank like that? And who in their right mind would be out here with tires like that?" She pointed in disgust at his tires, new less than a year old, made of rubber to withstand the Texas sun.

Her attitude left much to be desired. He thought people in rural areas were supposed to be friendly. Obviously, *she* didn't get that memo. Gabe did not appreciate being spoken to like that; wasn't used to it. He was a large man, used to respect - well-earned respect, it might be, but people did not talk down to him. He would not put up with it.

Shoving his door the rest of the way open, he used it to push back literally and figuratively on this intrusive female. Stretching himself to his full height, he attempted to tower over her. Attempted, and would have succeeded if his feet had not slid out from under him, the slick soles of his cowboy boots were no match for the effect of frigid temperatures on North Dakota snow.

The side of one of his boots hit the woman's foot. She was quicker than him, and her knee-high, lace-up Sorel boots barely slipped before she righted herself, leaping out of the way of his scrambling feet. Good thing he held on to the truck's door, or he would have gone down with her in a heap. Yep, that would have been the way to put this woman in her place.

"I guess it all fits," she said. "A guy who would drive with summer tires in the winter would also wear boots not made for this climate." Could her disgust be any more clear? "I repeat. What do you think you're doing out here?" She eyed the man. He wasn't dressed like a guy from the city; his clothes showed signs of wear and might be serviceable here in the summer.

"I'm on my way to visit someone, when this snowbank decided to make my acquaintance instead."

"Who?"

That was a little nosey. "I doubt you'd know them."

"Try me. I grew up around here; there's almost no one I don't know or know of."

"Doesn't matter." He was *not* giving out personal information to this person. "If you'll excuse me, I'll extricate myself from this, then be on my way." He tipped his hat to her. "Ma'am."

"How do you think you're going to do that?"

"Do what?"

"Get out of this snowbank. Do you even have a shovel with you? Chains?"

A shovel, no. The last shovel he'd used was when he cleaned out stalls in the barn. Chains, no. Did she think she could tow him out? She wasn't paying attention to him, anyway. She circled three sides of his truck.

"You're stuck."

Well, duh, he knew that.

"Really stuck. You'll need someone with a decent truck to pull you out." She headed back to her car. "Get in."

What? He thought about his weapon tucked into his duffle bag. This woman had to be at least eight inches and a hundred pounds smaller than him. Peering through the snow, he attempted to see if she was alone, or if he was about to be ambushed by a pack of people about to surround him. The woman paid no more attention to him, got behind the wheel of her car, and turned it on.

Good. She was leaving. He swung his door fully open and held on to the frame as he hoisted himself carefully back into his cab, mindful of the slippery ground underfoot.

The woman honked the horn.

Did she expect him to drive out of the way so she could get by? Obviously, he could not do that; give him another half hour, and he might. Besides, there was plenty of room for her to pass, if she was any kind of driver.

She honked again, this time adding an impatient come-here gesture.

He sighed. His mother would insist he be polite to a woman. Gingerly, he picked his way across this sorry excuse for a road, aiming for her driver's side door, catching himself three times as his feet threatened to fly frontwards, sideways, any way but remaining firmly under him.

As he approached her door, her motions grew more pronounced, clearly directing him to the passenger side of her Honda Pilot SUV. Okay, maybe she was uncomfortable with a strange man that close and felt safer speaking to him through her passenger side window.

Switching course at the front of her hood, he

plotted a course for the right side of the car, keeping one hand on the hood for purchase. As he got to the side, the passenger window lowered.

"Get in," the woman ordered.

"What?" Surely, he didn't hear her correctly.

"Get in!" This time she spoke slowly, distinctly, and loudly.

CHAPTER 10

Get into this woman's vehicle? Didn't she know about stranger danger? What sensible woman invited a man she'd never met into the confines of her car?

"Ma'am," he started. A gust came up, skimming his hat off of his head. Shifting quickly to grab the thing before it took off, he let go of his grip on the car. That was all the excuse his feet needed to fly out from under him. He ended up with one foot under her SUV, a bent knee and shin bashed up against her car door, and his head thunking on an icy patch of hard-packed snow.

The suddenness and the impact knocked the breath from his body. He closed his eyes for just a second, trying to calm his heart. When he squinted up, that woman was standing over him, his Stetson in her hand.

"You'd be better off with a toque," she said.

"A what?"

"You say 'what' a lot, you know. This hat," she looked at his highly priced Stetson in disgust, "might be all right in summer, but in winter you need a toque." At his blank look, she tried again. "A stocking cap, a beanie, watch cap. You know, a knitted thing that pulls down over your ears to keep you warm and won't go sailing off in the wind."

"Oh."

"Yeah, oh." She returned to the driver's side of the car. "Get in."

"Why?"

"At least it's a variation on 'what'. Get in if you don't want to freeze to death."

"Thank you for your concern, but I'm fine."

"No, you're not, or you wouldn't be stuck in a snowbank. You're not getting out of there on your own."

"I'll call AAA."

She snorted. "Out here? You'll be a popsicle before they get here, if they'd even come all the way out here. They're great in the city, and not bad on main highways, but where you are now, you're a low priority."

Could she be right?

"Get. In. Stan will pull you out."

"Who's Stan?"

"He and his wife run the store a ways up ahead. That's where I'm heading."

"Does Stan run a tow truck service?"

She thought that funny. "No way, but like every farmer, he has chains and tow ropes, plus a truck with appropriate tires."

"I'll wait here, if you wouldn't mind sending him my way, thank you."

"Don't be ridiculous. You're shivering already, and I'm not sure those things you have on your feet will take you back to your truck."

He straightened, ready to defend his choice of attire, when his feet almost slipped from under him again.

Was that a giggle he heard?

Giving in with as much grace as he could muster, he kept his left hand on the roof of the vehicle, while using his right to open the door. If she wasn't afraid to invite him into her car, who was he to save her from herself? But he couldn't help himself. "Thank you, Miss, but didn't your mama ever warn you about letting strangers into your car?"

"Well, you are a little strange, but I figure anyone who would come out in a winter storm so unprepared can't pose much of a threat."

Was he just insulted? Yeah, he wasn't sure of the extent of the insults, though.

"Where are you from?" the woman asked.

"Bandera, Texas."

"Figures."

What was *that* supposed to mean? A hand thrust into his line of sight.

"I'm Emma. Emma Lowry."

He gave her hand a quick, a very quick squeeze. "I'm Gabe Ottski. Ah, shouldn't you keep both hands on the steering wheel?"

This Emma person slanted him a look. "I've been driving in these winter conditions all of my life."

Still… He'd always considered himself a skillful driver and look what had happened to him.

"What brings you here?" Emma asked, then answered her own question. "Oh, right. To visit some mysterious person you don't want to mention. Never mind. We'll all know about it in a few days. That's just the way things work around here."

And in the small town where he lived, too, he thought. Or had lived. He didn't really live anywhere anymore. He was pondering his present homeless state when he felt their direction shift, and Emma swung the car into an entrance on the left.

"Don't you usually signal your turns?" Gabe asked, instantly regretting he'd not left that thought in his head.

Emma gave him a glare. "Do you see anyone behind us or in front of us on the road?"

She bumped them over a washboard snowy lane, with banks on either side almost as high as the roof of her car. She seemed to know where she was going, never hesitating, and soon a two-storey building emerged in front of them.

Gabe admired the carved wooden sign mounted above the door, announcing they'd arrived at Alpaca Haven.

Emma shut the car engine off and opened her door, preparing to climb out, leaving the keys in the ignition.

"Ah, Miss, your keys..."

"There's no one else here. I don't know where Stan parked his truck or tractor. He might need to move my car if it's in the way of him getting back to your truck."

That was one way of handling things. "Do you think this Stan will be willing to help?" If he wasn't, Gabe needed to come up with a Plan B fast.

Emma gave him a 'duh' look. "That's what people do around here." She pulled open the door to the store and an overhead brass bell tinkled. "Well, are you coming? We're letting in the cold air."

Gabe hurried after her as quickly as his slick boot soles allowed, barely reaching it in time to hold it open for Emma's back.

"Hi, Emma," Becca called. "Wasn't sure you'd make it in this snow. If you hadn't, I planned to bring the shawl to the hardware store tomorrow and taking it to your mom at my lunch break."

"Thanks. That would have been sweet of you, but Mom needed it *now* she said."

Becca shared a smile with Emma. Despite their rocky beginning, and less than pleasant ancient history from high school, they'd become something resembling friends over the past year. Living in a small town, Becca knew Esther Lowry and heard the rumors of how demanding the woman was of her daughter's time and energy. Becca sympathized.

There was a time after her own mother died that Becca's dad had been exceedingly needy. Thankfully, she and her father were on much better terms now, especially since his marriage to Robin, Stan's aunt. Now, the older couple even lived in a house on Becca's farm, and they helped with the alpacas and in the store.

"Is Stan around?" Emma asked.

There was a two second awkward pause, and the past roiled its head between Becca and Emma.

Emma pointed at Gabe. "I found this guy stuck on the road. He drove straight into a snowbank."

Well, it wasn't quite like that. "I hit this icy patch, and the drift caught my tires..." Gabe tried to explain.

Becca looked hard at him, as if studying a specimen. Maybe that's the way these people were with strangers but she saved him from his discomfort. "It's happened to us all, at one time or another."

Emma didn't look like she agreed. "Anyway," she said, "He's going to need a tow."

"Stan's in the back with Dad. One of our commercial washers sprung a leak and they need to get it fixed before we try to wash any more fleece."

"Oh, if this is a bad time," said Gabe, "I'll try AAA."

Both women laughed. "As if," said Becca. "Don't worry. I'll go get Stan."

What did they mean? It was like people here talked in a code.

Waiting, Gabe looked around at an eclectic assortment of… stuff. He had no idea what to call it. Jams, jellies, and honey. Wooden toys, soaps, candles, knitted things… who knew what some of these things were even used for? Still, if they charged these prices and still made a living at it, there must be a market. The only things that interested him were the wood crafts. Those he understood. Not that he was a craftsman himself, but he got the effort it took to make something from scratch, the countless hours learning the requisite skills, then the marketing involved to actually make money of the work you put in.

He only half-listened to the women discussing the alpaca wool items, something about a mother only allowing alpaca wool to touch her sensitive skin. Thankfully, his mother had never been the picky type, always easy to get along with. His only regret was that he hadn't done more for her.

Picking up a toy helicopter, he twirled the propeller with this thumb, admiring how smoothly the mechanism turned. The mechanic in him appreciated the workmanship. Getting the balance just right was no easy feat. Someday he'd like to talk to the guy who crafted such things.

CHAPTER 11

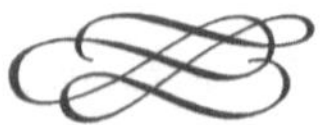

The two women talked in low voices.

"How'd ya find him?" Becca asked.

"Would you believe in a snowbank?"

"Seriously?"

"Yeah. Driving a truck with summer tires. Wearing a Stetson that he almost lost in the wind, and shiny, smooth cowboy boots that went out from under him more than they took him where he wanted to go."

Becca snickered.

"Yeah, I know," said Emma. "I could hardly leave the guy out there to survive on his own. Survive, he wouldn't."

"What's he doing here? He's a long way off the highway."

"Good questions. He says he's here to see someone but wouldn't tell me who. As if it's going to be a secret long if he connects with them."

"He wouldn't say who?"

"No. It was like a city thing, you know, where privacy is a big deal."

"Huh. If he sticks around here for any length of time, he'll get disabused of that notion."

"No kidding."

Stan emerged from the back quarters of the shop. "Hey, Emma. How's it going?"

"Better for me than for that guy." She pointed her thumb toward Gabe.

Stan nodded. "Got it." This wasn't the first city person to struggle with their roads and need help. He approached the stranger who was holding one of Stan's cousin Blair's creations, the man running his thumb over the smooth surface of the wood. "Are you the guy who buried his nose in a snowbank?"

"That's one way of putting it." The guy was a little frivolous about this predicament, Gabe thought, but from the sounds of it, there was little other help around.

"Okay, let's go." But Stan didn't move. Head

tilted slightly to one side, he studied the stranger. "Have we met before?"

"Doubt it. I've never been here before."

"You remind me of someone, don't you think, Becca?"

"Maybe a bit, but I can't think of who," Becca agreed.

"I must have one of those faces, but unless you've been around central Texas, don't think we've run into each other before."

Stan gave another once over to the man in front of him. "Do you have anything decent for your head?"

Decent? Did he know what this hat was—a genuine Shasta 10X Premiere Stetson? The thing set him back almost 500 bucks. Decent?

"The snow's coming down even harder," Stan said. "Becca, this guy needs a hat."

Becca pointed. "Grab a toque from the front display. He looks like he's a large, and those are on the right."

"I don't think…" began Gabe.

From her place near Becca, Emma snorted. "Take the toque," she told him. "You'll regret it if you don't."

When in Rome, and all that. He'd wear a toque. Gabe reached for his wallet.

Becca waved away his money. "You need a hat. We have a hat. It'll keep you far warmer than that contraption you have on your head now."

Gabe removed his 'contraption', not sure what to do with it. He accepted a woolen thing from Stan, resembling what the other man had on his own head, and similar to what Emma wore, but plainer.

"Just throw your hat on the chair by the door," Stan directed.

A man and his Stetson were never parted, at least not during waking hours. A hat protected from the rain and the sun; Texan sun could be brutal.

Sensing his unease, Emma relented. "It's fine. Your cowboy hat will be there when you return."

Guess he had to trust these people. Hooking his hat over the back of the chair, he settled the new cap on his head, expecting the scratchiness of wool. It covered his forehead, ears and a bit of his neck, enveloping his skull in soft warmth. He hated wool; it made him break out in hives, irritating his skin for days. But this felt different. Ah, he remembered the sign as he entered the store - Alpaca Haven. Not that he really knew what alpacas were, but didn't people get wool from them? He followed Stan out the door. “Is this made from alpacas?”

“Yeah. My wife runs a herd of them and uses their fleece to make most of the knit products you see in the store.”

“Nice.” And he wasn’t just being polite. He might buy himself one of these. His thoughts instantly went to his mother, thinking he’d send one to her.

Except he couldn’t. Even though part of his brain knew she had passed away, his heart was slow to catch up, and he often forgot she was no longer with him. She’d been such a vital presence all his life; hard to believe she was gone.

Shoot. The man was saying something to him, and he’d been lost in his own head, missing some of it. “Sorry. Would you mind saying that again?”

“I asked what kind of vehicle you have. I need to know if my truck will be enough to pull you out, or if I should bring a tractor.”

“It’s a Dodge Ram 1500 TRX.”

“Four by four?”

“Yeah.”

“Did you get any traction when you tried rocking it?”

“Nothing.” At least for the few minutes he’d tried.

"Tractor it is, then. Might be a bit snug getting there, but we'll cuddle up for warmth." He snickered.

Gab looked at the guy. Was he joking?

Stan stalked off around the side of the house, calling over his shoulder. "You can come with me, but I don't know how those things on your feet will do in the snow. If you want, you can wait here, and I'll bring the tractor around in a few minutes. It's already warmed up since I was moving bales just a while ago." He gestured toward the store. "Go back inside to wait, if you want to keep warm."

Back inside with those two women? What kind of wuss did the guy take him for?

Stan read his mind and laughed. Obviously, he guessed just what kind of wuss. "They don't bite, or at least not bad enough to leave marks."

Funny. Thrusting his hands in his pockets, Gabe braved the snow and the cold. The buffeting wind would have made it challenging to keep his Stetson in place, but this toque thing held on nicely. Despite the wind chilling his cheeks and nose, the rest of his head remained comfortable.

Soon, Gabe heard the distinctive sound only made by John Deere tractors. Good. At least something he was familiar with. This was a John Deere 4840, one of the more popular work horse yard tractors—small enough for maneuverability, at least compared to the larger 400 and something horsepower field machines, yet powerful enough for most applications.

A drawback to the 4840 was the cab. The larger JDs had spacious cabs with two seats; not these smaller ones. Yep, it would be cozy for two guys, strangers, no less.

Stan brought the tractor to a halt by Gabe and threw open the door. "Get in," he yelled.

Gabe started forward, picking his way carefully so as not to land on his butt in front of his rescuer. "Hey, steps," he said. He'd never seen a tractor like this without a ladder to climb in.

"Yeah. Removed the ladder and installed these steps. My father-in-law helps out with chores, and these are safer for him."

For me, too, thought Gabe.

"Watch where you put your feet," warned Stan, pointing to the tow chain coiled on the floor.

Just how bad of a klutz did this guy think he was? "Got it." Reaching behind, Gabe pulled the door closed, planting his feet on either side of the chain. He braced himself with one hand on the cab's back window, and the other near where the roof met the glass at the front of the cab. That way he could stand, rather than perch on the armrest, uncomfortably close to the other man's personal space. This was bad enough.

"I see you've been in one of these before," observed Stan.

"Used one many, many times. It's a good tractor."

"Let's go put it to the test."

CHAPTER 12

"So," Stan spoke to the man looming over him to his left. "What brings you do these parts?"

"Just looking around."

Stan slanted him a look and waited.

"Scouting things out."

"Why?"

Why? Was he one of those suspicious rural people? "Don't like strangers?"

"Depends on what the stranger wants." Stan kept his eyes on the road in front of him. "Around here, we look after each other. We take care of our own."

"Good to hear. I mean no harm." He felt the need to give up some information about himself, if only to tamp down Stan's speculation. "I'm from a small place, too."

"Oh yeah? Where's that?"

"You wouldn't have heard of it. Although I grew up in San Antonio, for a number of years now, I've lived and worked around the town of Bandera, Texas."

"What sort of work do you do?"

"I'm a heavy-duty mechanic, working mainly on agricultural equipment, but like anyone in a ranching community, I've done my share of work with cattle. When there's a problem, every able-bodied man pitches in."

"Problems crop up often?"

"What do you think? We work with livestock and machinery. What's not to go wrong?"

The atmosphere in the cab lightened just a bit, but Stan was not going to let this go. People in this community mattered to each other.

Up ahead, the flashers from the back of Gabe's pickup truck gleamed in the falling snow. "Wow, a white pickup," said Stan.

"So? Are white trucks rare here?"

"Yeah. Most of us know not to get one."

"Why?" Were these people prissy enough to not like mud splatters on their vehicle?

Stan pointed through the windshield. "For

precisely that reason. Look how your truck blends into the snow. Hard to see in a blizzard."

Good point, one he'd never considered. He reached for the handle behind him to open the tractor door.

"Hold on a minute," Stan told him. "Let me turn this thing around first."

It was more like a six-point turn than the ideal three-point one, but with the bale fork mounted on the front, high snowbanks on each side, and the tractor's 15-foot length, it was a tricky maneuver. But Stan made it; that came from hours and hours in this cab, under all sorts of conditions.

Once they faced back the way they'd come from, Gabe hopped out, grabbing the heavy linked chain as he went. He might not have the right colored pickup, the right tires, shoes, or headgear, but at least he knew how to use a tow chain.

Turning his chair so he could watch out the back window, Stan observed this Gabe character. Other than having trouble keeping his feet under him with the ridiculous boots he wore, the guy seemed to know how to hook up his pickup to the tractor all right, then he hopped into his truck to steer. Hopped was a generous description; lurched was more like it. He knew to put his truck into neutral and handled things decently. Maybe he'd been telling the truth about having farming experience.

With the power of the tractor, it didn't take much to extricate the pickup from its nesting place in the snow. Stan watched Gabe do a walk-around his vehicle, checking for damage. Good. The guy looked after his things.

Gabe stood back out of the way, in case the tractor slipped as Stan backed up the machine to put some slack in the chain. Unhooking the clevis and hook ends from the chain, Gabe coiled the length around his palm and just above his elbow, opening the tractor to stow the loops back on the floor. "Thanks so much, man. Appreciate it."

"No problem. See you back at the store. You wanna go ahead? You'll drive faster than me." Then he added, "But not too fast, huh? Don't want to have to pull you out again."

Gabe had a feeling that if he spent any length of time around this town, he'd never live this down. Tempting as it was to just drive off, he needed to collect his hat and return this borrowed one to Becca. Although, he just might buy it from her now that he knew how comfortable and warm it was.

In less than ten minutes, he turned into the parking lot of Alpaca Haven. Having taken his time on the treacherous road, Stan and the tractor were not far behind him. Emma and Becca watched from the picture window as he parked, then entered the store.

"All good now?" Becca asked.

"Yes, thanks to Stan and his tractor."

Gabe pulled off the borrowed toque, batting it against his thigh to knock off the clinging snow. "Thanks for the loan. It's a good hat. May I buy it from you?"

Becca waved her hand at him. "Keep it, it's yours. I can't sell something that's been worn, and you look like you really need a toque."

"But…" Gabe began.

Stan came in through the back of the store, overhearing the last part of the conversation. "Give it a rest, man. Don't argue with my wife. I can tell you from experience that you'll never win."

"Thank you. I appreciate it, and hope to one day repay your kindness." He turned to Stan. "What do I owe you for the tow?"

"Forget it. Glad to help." He stuck both hands in his pockets. "I think I asked before, but I must have missed the answer. What brings you all the way from Texas to here?"

CHAPTER 13

Gabe felt three pairs of eyes on him. They weren't going to let his go, even if it was none of their business.

Still, he owed them some kind of explanation. How to say something without really saying anything? Growing up, he and his mom had been a tight unit, used to closing ranks around the two of them, insular against the rest of the world. He might have lost his mother, but not the instinct to keep his business private.

Now, it was even more important. Who knew what he'd discover when he looked into this half-brother he supposedly had? If their only connection was the blood they'd inherited from

Bruce, well, then this was likely a bond he wanted no part of.

He loved his mother wholeheartedly. She'd sacrificed and been the ideal parent. But sheesh, couldn't she have timed her revelations about Bruce and his grandmother, Gabriella, better? Like not wait until just two days before she died? They'd had thirty years together. Did she think the right moment would never come up? Still, if that was the worse sin she'd committed in her life, he could forgive her. Mostly.

Her death hit hard, and why wouldn't it? She was his only connection, the stable force in his life. Sure, he was grown and responsible, but in the back of his mind, Mom was always at home, there in the place she'd lived for 20 years. Their home, the place representing love and security; the place holding the essence of Norma Jean.

But no longer.

Packing up that house seemed a betrayal. How did you disseminate two decades of living into the number of boxes he could hold in his pickup? What did you keep? What should he give away, what should he toss out?

Sure, neighbors and friends of Norma Jean volunteered to help, but he refused all offers. This was *his* job, his duty to his only parent. He knew her best. He owed it to her.

Intrusive as it felt, he'd opened every one of his mother's drawers and boxes, all of her mail. She'd done some cleaning up once she received her diagnosis, but by then she'd been too weak to tackle a lifetime of accumulated odds and ends.

It was when he sorted through the accumulated mail that he discovered the bulky envelope from Gabrielle Ottski. His grandmother. Addressed to *him*.

Not now. This was not the time to get lost in his own head, something that had happened all too often since his mom's death.

In the meantime, three people stood waiting for his answer. He must look like an idiot, daydreaming in front of them.

"Sorry," Gabe said. "I've spent too many hours on the road, with too little sleep."

"You mentioned you're scouting things out. What sort of things are you scouting?"

Gabe thought quickly. He knew how small towns were; he should have had this thought through. "I've spent all my life in Texas. It was just me and my mom, and she recently passed away. So, I thought now was as good of time as any to see a bit more of the country."

"And that involved coming to North Dakota in the middle of winter?" Emma could not believe it.

"Believe me, I knew y'all got snow up here, but I did not know it was like this."

"Why North Dakota?" Stan was still suspicious.

"Y'all have cattle. And farms. I know how to work on farm machinery and how to work with stock, plus I can fix anything. Seemed like I might find something to fit me here."

"Maybe," Stan agreed.

Becca stepped in. "Now that your pickup's free, what are your plans?"

"Thought I'd drive into town and find a hotel."

The other three laughed.

"What?" Gabe asked.

"You thought you'd find a hotel in Goodrich?" Emma could not believe the guy.

"Or a B&B. I meant to look online, but cell coverage has been spotty."

"No kidding, it is, especially along the road."

"Can you direct me to a hotel?"

"Not much chance of that."

Becca explained, "There are no hotels or B&Bs in Goodrich."

"The next closest town, then."

"No such luck. While you and Stan were extricating your truck, Emma and I heard on the radio that they've closed the highway to Watford, the nearest city."

"How far is the next one?"

Becca shook her head. "You can't get there; the highways are closed and when they say 'closed', they take that seriously."

"If they think conditions are bad enough to shut down the roads, you do not want to venture out on them," Stan said as his eyes flicked toward where Gabe parked his truck. "Especially with tires like yours. Even if you had chains for them, I wouldn't recommend it."

Chains for tires? That was beyond anything in Gabe's experience. "So. It looks like I'll be bedding down in my truck. Mind if I keep it parked outside your store?"

"What do you have in your truck for winter survival gear?" Stan asked.

Gabe hesitated. Survival gear? He knew to take plenty of water when venturing into the desert, but he didn't think something to drink was what Stan had in mind.

"We're in the process of renovating this old house, and only have minimum done," said Becca. "Otherwise we'd offer you a spare bedroom. But we don't have any. We could probably set something up for you on the floor of the store here…" Her voice trailed off.

"Oh, for goodness sake," said Emma. "He'll have to come with me."

"Will your mother mind?" Becca asked.

"She might enjoy having someone else to talk to. We have a spare room, and there's really nowhere else in town for him to go. You don't want to rap on his truck window tomorrow morning to find an icicle-shaped man. That's never good for business."

Stan and Becca laughed. Gabe didn't.

"You're inviting me to spend the night at your house?"

"Inviting is not really the word I'd use. Maybe once again rescuing you would describe it better."

Gabe glanced from Stan to Becca and didn't see them coming up with any better ideas. In fact, they seemed to agree with this Emma woman about that being the only option.

"Call us when you get home, Emma," Stan told her. "We want to make sure you get there all right." He gave Gabe an assessing look before turning back to Emma. "And call us, me or Blair, if you need anything, anything at all."

What was with these people? They were

alternatively suspicious of him, questioning his intelligence, then taking him in. Did this make any sense? He turned to Emma. "You're inviting me into your house?"

CHAPTER 14

"Emma, the weather's not getting any better. Maybe you should get on your way." Becca handed her the wrapped parcel containing Esther's new shawl. "Hope your mom enjoys this."

"She loves anything made from alpaca fleece." Emma sat on a chair to pull on her boots.

Gabe thought he recognized a pattern on her socks similar to the hat he'd worn. Underneath all that winter outerwear hid an attractive woman. Emma caught him staring at her feet, his gaze moving upward.

Way to go, Gabe, especially when the woman had just offered him a place to stay. Trying to recover, he asked, "Are those alpaca socks?"

"Yep. Warmest, softest things ever." She nodded to Becca. "She made them."

Gabe raised his eyebrows. He didn't know there was anyone under the age of 80 who knew how to knit socks.

"Not just me," explained Becca. "There are a few other people, like my mother-in-law, who pitch in and knit some of the things we sell. Still trying to recruit Emma's mom, but no luck yet."

"Keep trying, please," Emma said. "She needs more to do."

Gabe hurried out the door, turning to hold it open for Emma. Bad move. Didn't know where his brain was at, but he should have remained inside, stretching his arm to hold the door. Outside, the fresh skiff of snow clung to the steps, making his footing treacherous. Slipping, he had to grasp the doorframe to keep upright. Luckily, Emma was quick on her feet and leaped out of the way.

"Chivalry comes with a price," called Stan. "You might want to pick up a better pair of boots."

Better? These were top quality cowboy boots. Gabe watched Emma stalk with no hesitation toward her car. Maybe Stan had a point. The soles on his boots were no match for these weather conditions.

The least he could do was open Emma's car door for her. But mincing his way through the drifts took time, and she was already seating herself by the time he got there. "I'll follow you," he told her.

"What?" Emma got out of the SUV to hear him better.

"I said I'll follow you to town."

"Are you crazy? You'll end up back in the ditch, then Stan will need to pull you out again." She jerked her chin toward her passenger seat. "Get in."

Then Stan was beside him. "Leave me your keys, will ya? I might need to move your pickup if I have to plow the parking lot." He sensed Gabe's hesitation. "You weren't thinking of driving yourself to town, were you?"

"Yeah. My plan was to follow Emma."

"Man, the snow's worse now than when you dove into the snowbank earlier. You'll never make it."

Although he tried to suck it up, something about this insulted his manly pride. They assumed *he* didn't have the driving skills to navigate these roads, yet they had faith that this Emma woman could. What was wrong with this picture? He'd always been capable—able to get himself and others out of any scrapes. Until today, that is.

"If you're going to spend any time in these parts, you've got to get yourself decent tires, and winter boots. You have a toque now, but warm mittens and socks wouldn't hurt."

Hat! "I forgot my hat in your store. Sorry about that; didn't mean to litter your place."

"No problem. I'll throw it in your truck for you. You won't need it in this weather, anyway."

Emma honked her horn.

"Think you'd better hop in," Stan told Gabe.

"Are you sure she's okay with taking in a stranger?"

"Emma does what Emma wants. Mostly. She's taken on a lot since she came home to look after her mother. She gives in to her mom, but other than that, she's pretty definite about what she will and won't do." Stan clapped Gabe on the shoulder. "Don't worry, you'll be safe with her." He started back to the store, calling over his shoulder, "You going like that, or do you need to grab a suitcase from your truck?"

Right. That detail had slipped Gabe's mind. By the time he picked his way over to the truck and clicked open his door locks, Stan was back with his Stetson. "Thanks." Taking it, he settled the hat on the pickup's backseat, where the privacy glass would hide it from any prying eyes. As he hoisted the strap of his duffle bag over his shoulder, he gave Stan a look, certain the man was going to offer to carry it for him.

Stan backed off, holding up his hands, palms out, with a grin.

Silence fell in the car as Emma concentrated on driving. Her Honda Pilot fish-tailed somewhat as it plowed through the worst of the finger drifts spreading across the road, but Emma deftly hung on to the wheel, keeping them in the middle of the road. And she was in the middle. Under other circumstances, Gabe might have said something, but since there was no other traffic in either direction, he kept his mouth shut. He was in no position to criticize anyone else's driving. Besides, this woman had a prickly streak he didn't want to incite.

CHAPTER 15

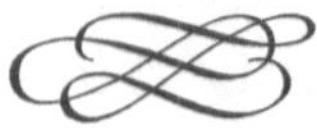

"Mom, I'm home."

"Hurry and shut that door, Emma. You know how I hate it when you let in that icy breeze."

Emma rolled her eyes at Gabe. *He* was the reason for the delay.

He climbed the front stairs timidly, in a fashion that did not sit well with him. "Want me to shovel these steps for you?" he asked.

"Sure, knock yourself out," Emma said. "Shovel's by the railing. First, you should meet Mom, though."

Toeing off her boots, Emma placed them on the boot tray. "Stick your boots here," she told

Gabe, then motioned for him to follow her action.

There was not a boot jack in sight. Using the toe of one boot against the heel of the other might successfully peel off the type of footwear Emma had on, but that approach did not work for cowboy boots. No chair, either. Gabe was not about to ask Emma for a hand tugging off his boots; he'd suffered enough humiliation already today. Bracing his back against the wall, Gabe raised one foot, crossing it near his knee, and used both hands to tug. An awkward angle, the boot did not give up his foot easily. If boot jacks were not common in these parts, he'd have to buy or make himself one.

Emma poked her head into the hallway. "Are you coming?" She watched him struggle with the second boot. "Why anyone would wear such things is beyond me."

Abrasive woman. But, his task done, he straightened, wiping his hands on his jeans. At least his pants seemed to fit in with what other people wore around here.

"Mom, I brought a guest." Emma stood aside so Gabe could enter the living room. "This is Gabe..." How could she have forgotten to ask the guy's last name?

"Ottski, Ma'am. Gabe Ottski." He entered the living room with his hand outstretched. "Pleased to meet you. Thank you for inviting me to stay in your home."

Esther Lowry cut her eyes toward her daughter, but her rural hospitality righted itself. "You are most welcome; we're delighted to have you, aren't we, Emma?"

As if, Emma thought. "We could hardly leave him to sleep in his pickup in a snowstorm."

"Certainly not." Turning to Gabe, she asked, "How long will you be staying with us, Mr. Ottski?"

"Just overnight, then I'll be on my way."

Glancing out the front window, Emma wondered about that. It was snowing harder now, harder than it was when she left for Alpaca Haven this morning. Storms like this sometimes lasted days, and they'd be snowed in, the roads impassable. "Come on," she said to Gabe. "I'll show you to your room and where you can place your stuff."

Slinging the duffle bag's strap over one shoulder, he followed Emma down the hall and up the stairs.

"You walk a lot better in your socks than you do in your cowboy boots," she observed.

The guy said nothing as she led the way into the office they'd turned in to a spare room after her father passed away. Now, it was a mix of her schoolwork, her mom's craft projects begun but never finished, and a place for visitors to stay. The duffle bag made a heavy thunk when he set it down on top of the desk. What did he have in there? Hopefully, not more of those ridiculous cowboy boots. Who would think of wearing those in the winter?

"I'll let you get settled in while I make some lunch. Bathroom's down the hall, on your right. Come downstairs when you're ready."

Mom was picky. Always a good cook, she had high standards. Since she'd abstained from culinary efforts after widowhood, life was tricky. Esther still expected to eat the sort of meals she'd always provided for her family, but Emma had not inherited the cooking gene. Maybe if she'd paid more attention growing up, but there was always so much to do with all the social activities that occupied her every minute. Plus, Esther considered the kitchen her domain and didn't like anyone else messing it up. Like now.

Organized in her job teaching first graders, somehow that skill didn't carry over into the kitchen. In the classroom with 30 little bodies, there was no choice but to be on top of everything. When it came to cooking, though, there never seemed to be enough counter room, or stove burners, or…

"Emma, dear," Esther called from the other room. "Is lunch almost ready? Our guest here must be starving."

"Oh, no, Ma'am," countered Gabe. "I'm just fine. Don't worry about me."

"Nonsense," Esther told him. "Punctuality is important, and we need to eat on time. I'm always reminding Emma of that."

Her back to the living room, Emma rolled her eyes. Right. Punctuality. How many times had she been almost late for school because of her mother calling her back to do 'just one more little thing' before she left for the day. Why Esther couldn't get up out of her chair and do it herself was beyond Emma. Beyond the doctor, too; he could give no physical or cognitive reason for Esther's semi-invalid state.

In her job as a teacher, prep work mattered—without it, you were doomed, and the classroom ran amok. Try coming back from that if you let it happen even once.

Managing this kitchen was even more challenging. Sure, she could feed herself just fine

- maybe better than just fine. But pleasing her mother was a whole other story.

Meals quick and easy to throw together after work rarely met her mom's exacting standards. How good could food be when you'd only given the ingredients half an hour of your attention? When you were a stay-at-home wife and mother, sure you'd have time for creative dishes. It was different when you were gone from the house between eight and five every day, then faced hours of marking and preparation work after supper, and when you had a demanding mother craving your attention full time.

From the living room, she heard the quiet rumble of a male voice responding to her mother's conversation. It didn't sound like he needed to say much, as Esther was more than willing to carry the burden of chat. Esther was lonely; Emma got that. But what was she supposed to do? She needed to work—they needed her to work as her salary carried them both.

Esther wanted Emma to get another job, one that wouldn't require her to bury herself in books each evening. But that was all part of teaching, and it was one of the better paying jobs to be had in a small town. If she quit, she'd be lucky to get a job waitressing or in a store, for less than half her current salary. Then where would she and her mother be?

Happier, Esther would say. Once upon a time, Emma would have described her mother as a sensible and practical woman. No longer. Losing her husband knocked many things out from under Esther - she lost not only her best friend and supporter, but the economic and social stability in her life.

Esther changed from an outgoing person involved in the community with a wide network of friends to being a recluse. Those friends still existed, Emma was sure, but Esther spurned their attention and efforts, saying Emma was all she needed. Oh, goodie, Emma told herself.

But this Gabe character brought out a side Emma feared Esther had buried with her husband. Was that a giggle? From her mother? Over the last decade, that sound became more and more rare, until Emma thought it had gone forever.

What had Gabe done to resurrect that side of Esther? And *why*?

CHAPTER 16

Despite Esther's pronouncements that it was cheating, Emma relied on her slow cooker. Esther would not have such a contraption in her house when she was in charge, but Emma brought hers with her when she moved back home.

Yes, it wasn't exactly the same as a loving hand stirring the pot every twenty minutes all day long, but what could you do? When that pesky work thing kept you out of the house most of the day, you had to come up with something else, and who said shortcuts were a bad thing? There was a reason they were invented.

Before leaving for Alpaca Haven this morning, Emma cut up and browned beef cubes in a skillet, then dumped the meat into her slow cooker. Melting butter and mixing it with canola oil, she braised slivers of onion and garlic until golden, then added them to the cooker. Next, she placed cubed potatoes to the pan to sear. That wasn't totally necessary, and if it was just herself, she'd likely not bother, but Esther noticed when she skipped steps like that. Much as she hated to admit it, Esther was right - the spuds were more attractive with browned edges. The potatoes joined the chopped celery and carrots already in the slow cooker. Pearl barley, thyme, pepper, and bay leaves followed, along with beef broth. No salt, though - Esther would complain.

Esther also complained about the quantity Emma made, saying recipes were better in small batches tended with loving care. Right.

In Emma's world, you took what you got. Esther didn't know Emma cooked in large quantities so she could freeze portions for quick meals later on. A self-preservation trick. Esther no longer ventured down the stairs into the basement where the chest freezer sat, so she did not know the number of containers Emma squirrelled away there. An example was the lasagna they'd have for supper.

Oh! The frozen portion sufficed for two

women; the addition of Gabe made a difference. Setting the empty soup bowls on the counter, Emma opened the door to the basement to bring up a second lasagna container.

"Emma," Esther admonished as she entered the kitchen on Gabe's arm. Turning to Gabe, she said, "That girl is always dashing off. A little organization would save her a world of time. Time when she could be dishing up our lunch."

Emma jogged back up the last few steps, shutting the basement door with her back.

Gabe looked from Esther to the packaged and labeled freezer container in Emma's hand and gave the younger woman a smile before turning back to her mother. "Where do you prefer to sit, Mrs. Lowry?"

"Esther. You can call me Esther, young man."

"Miss Esther, then." He led her to the head of the table. "Is this your chair?"

"Oh, goodness, no. That's where my Harold always sat."

Gabe pivoted to the other end of the table. "Would this be your seat, then?"

"You're so clever." Esther positively simpered.

Clever. Huh. Since they'd pushed the fourth chair tightly between the wall and the table, the guy had a 33% chance of guessing Esther's chair correctly. He blew it on the first try, so his next odds were 50-50 at getting it right. Not even 50-50, as he could guess that the parents might sit at the head and foot of the table.

Seating Esther with care, he turned to Emma at the counter. “Can I dish up the soup for you? It smells great.”

“Sure.” He might as well make himself useful, although keeping Esther entertained was being more than useful. She pulled the ladle from the drawer, passing it to Gabe. Their hands touched, making Emma’s skin tingle. She rubbed the back of her hand on her jeans, erasing the memory of that casual touch. He must have built up some static electricity as Esther shuffled her way across the living room carpet, hanging onto his arm.

Then she remembered. “Watch out for the…”

“Bay leaf?” Gabe asked.

She nodded. Esther would reject the entire meal if she discovered an errant bay leaf Emma had forgotten to scoop out. Maybe this guy knew a bit about cooking.

With the three bowls full and ready, hesitating, Gabe wondered how to pull the table from the wall without disturbing Esther. There was no way he could slide into that space without moving the table.

Seeing his hesitation, Emma motioned to her dad's spot.

Catching Emma's action, Esther chimed in. "Please, Gabe, sit in Harold's place. He'd be honored to have you there."

With a quick glance Emma's way to see if she agreed, he slid into the chair at the head of the table.

Opening the microwave oven, Emma placed the frozen lasagna inside, hitting the defrost button. If she thawed it partway, after lunch, she could add it to the other portion to bake on low in the oven for the afternoon.

"Emma, you're not," said Esther, turning up her lip at the microwave. "You can't use that thing when we have a guest. You need to make something decent from scratch." She shook her head and looked at Gabe. "Young people these days. They're all about the easy way out."

Gabe shot a quick look at Emma before answering Esther. "Microwaves are one of the greatest inventions of this last century. I used to work in a high-end restaurant; you'd be surprised just how much they use microwaves in creating top quality food." He took a second bite of his stew. "This is delicious! Seasoned beautifully. Perfect for a wintry day."

Esther dipped a spoon into her bowl but said nothing.

"You're baking bread today?" Gabe asked Esther. "I noticed the dough rising on the counter. My mother loved to bake bread."

"There was a time when no one in this house ever ate store-boughten bread," Esther told him.

Well, that wasn't exactly the way Emma remembered it.

"Lucky family," Gabe told her.

"Emma can do a decent job with bread when she puts in the time the way I taught her. But oh, no, she's all about the shortcuts. Artisan, she calls it, but it's really just an excuse for not taking the time to go through the kneading and risings."

Gabe turned to Emma. "Artisan, like in a cast iron pot and a hot oven?"

Emma nodded.

"Love that stuff. It's one thing to make the traditional sandwich-type bread, but the bread with a crispy crust and soft inside is the best."

Emma allowed herself a half smile. Maybe this guy was all right.

CHAPTER 17

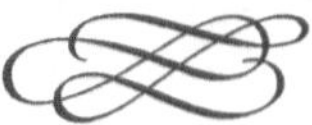

As soon as Esther set down her spoon after finishing her soup Gabe jumped up to clear the table. "May I?" he asked, pointing at the dishwasher.

"Have at it," Emma told him. Keeping her back to her mother, she pulled clean freezer containers from a cupboard and began portioning out the rest of the slow cooker's contents into containers.

"Smart," commented Gabe.

"Shh," Emma warned him. "Don't let my mother know what I'm doing."

"Got it." Gabe positioned his broad shoulders between Emma and the table, shielding Emma from her mother's view. After rinsing their dishes and placing them in the dishwasher, Gabe straightened. “Can I give you a hand with anything else?”

“No, that’s good, thanks.”

“I’ll have a go at your front step, then.”

Emma looked him up and down. “What size are your feet?”

“Pardon?”

“Your feet. What size shoes do you wear?”

“Eleven.”

“Look in the front closet. I think that’s what my dad wore. There should be a pair of his winter boots you can use.”

When Gabe hesitated, she added, “Better than breaking your neck in those cowboy things you had on.”

Overlooking the slight to his favorite pair of boots, Gabe conceded her point. “Thanks, if your mom won’t mind.”

“You’ve won her over already. She’d be pleased if you borrowed my dad’s boots.”

He hated to admit it, but Emma was right. Keeping his balance in the snow in these boots was a lot easier than with the flat slippery soles of his cowboy boots. They were warmer, too.

Whoever had shoveled this porch the last few times only removed the surface snow without delving down through the layers. Packed snow masked icy patches, making it not safe for Emma, and especially not for Esther. It took considerable chopping, but he slowly made his way down to the concrete on both the porch and the steps. A wonder one of these women hadn't slipped and broken her neck. It crossed his mind to wonder what would become of Esther if something happened to Emma. Although not that old, Esther had a frail, needy aura about her.

Esther differed from his mother; Norma Jean had been independent to a fault, rarely asking for help, even when she needed it, and he'd been ever so willing to provide it whenever something needed doing. That was the biggest reason he'd never ventured too far from where he'd been raised and where his mom lived out her last years.

As annoyed as he got with Norma Jean for not accepting his help, how much worse this must be for Emma, with a mother who felt her daughter never did enough for her. Two very different mothers.

Norma Jean. Cagey woman, keeping secrets he'd never suspected all those years.

Hiding things and sharing only partial truths. She'd never been married. A man who deserted them. A grandmother who tried to help. Sort of.

A grandmother who'd spied on him from afar. Something creepy about that.

He'd made it to the bottom of the stairs and cleared the walk between the steps and the sidewalk. But from the look of the crusted snow, that was not the path Emma took from her driveway to the steps. Sometime earlier in the winter, it seemed like she'd cleared a path to walk, but as the snow accumulated, she abandoned that task, only shoveling where her mother might walk. Throwing his back into it, Gabe opened up a three-foot wide walkway from the bottom of the stairs to the front door of Emma's car.

Never shying away from physical work, it gave him time to think. And Gabe had more to think about than he wanted.

Grief was a funny thing. It snuck up on you. You'd be going about your day, thinking everything was fine, when a scent, a memory, even if just a whisper of it wiggled into your brain, stirring up all sorts of remembrances of things past - things done and not done. Before she died, Norma Jean told him there were to be no regrets, but that was far easier said than done. Yes, she knew he loved her; they were tight, the two of them. Even living in a different town, they still spoke almost daily. But could he have done more? Yeah, oh yeah, and he should have.

You should look upon your dearly departed with fondness, not resentment, yet Gabe felt that negative sentiment festering. How dare she keep the truth from him? She'd lied about his father - a ne'er-do-well who ran out on them. A lie of omission kept him from knowing about his grandparents. True, he doubted if he'd have wanted anything to do with them, but he'd never even had the choice. That was so unlike how Norma Jean raised him.

Then, while cleaning out his mother's house, he found the letter from his grandmother. A letter addressed to him.

~

Whack! Something connected with Gabe's head, sending a shock of coldness through his scalp. Icy slush trickled down the nape of his neck, making his skin tingle with goosebumps.

As he spun around to see where the projectile had come from, he caught a glimpse of Emma's wide grin, her rosy cheeks and nose contrasting sharply against the white winter landscape. Her mittened hands were already shaping another snowball to add to the stack beside her knees, the snow crunching beneath her mitts as she packed it tight.

"You didn't!"

Her grin was his only answer.

He'd heard of snowball fights, seen them in movies, but never molded this white stuff before.

Turns out it was an acquired skill because his efforts were less than pretty. It took a few tries before he blended the snow just right until it stuck together when he lobbed it at his attacker.

And attack, she did. Emma took no prisoners in this snowball fight.

Both of them wet, with sodden hair, and reddened faces, Gabe didn't notice as she decreased the distance between them. Suddenly, she was right there, only a foot away and this time, her arm didn't throw an icy ball.

Instead, her mitt came up with a loose handful of snow and rubbed it in his face.

Gasping, Gabe stepped away, his knees catching on the snowbank he'd built alongside the walk. Ending up sprawled on his back, gaping up at his attacker.

"What? Never had your face washed with

snow before?" A smug Emma smirked down at him.

Maybe not, but he gave as good as he got. Before she could move away, Gabe wrapped one hand around her arm, and swung his other behind her knees, catching her as her feet went out from under her. As soon as she was on the ground beside him, he reached for a handful of snow. Leaning over Emma, he mashed the cold, wet stuff on her face, but more mercifully than she had done with him.

She lay there, gasping, and look up at him with wet lashes, her eyes shining in the late afternoon sun.

What a woman of contradictions. She helped him; she humiliated him. She looked after her mother, yet she played with him.

Play. It felt like a long, long time since he'd done anything like this. Maybe never, and certainly not with a woman as complicated as this.

Their laughter stopped and the air stilled between them. Gabe became aware of their proximity—he was almost laying half on top of her, his hands braced on either side of her head. Removing one of his gloves, he gently brushed a clump of melting snow from one of her cheeks, her skin chilly but soft, so soft.

Emma stared up at him, this self-assured woman suddenly vulnerable.

Without conscious thought, he started to lower his face toward hers.

She scrambled out from under him, but not too far away. “Ever made snow angels?” she asked. Grabbing his hand, she pulled him nearer the middle of the yard. “We need fresh snow.”

Suddenly, letting go of his hand, she flopped onto her back, pinwheeling her arms and legs in the snow. “There,” she said. “Now help me up.” She held up her hands for Gabe to grasp.

As he hoisted Emma to her feet, they stared down at the angel. He didn’t let go of her hands, marveling at this woman’s ability to play, as much as the angel she’d created. His thoughts on what she’d done these past fifteen minutes, rather than on what she was about to do, Gabe felt hands on his chest shove him into the snow. Throwing herself beside him, Emma took his hand, waving it up and down with hers, making angel wings.

“Your legs, too,” she said. “Sheesh, didn’t you watch how I did it?”

Oh yeah, he’d watched quite a few things about her.

Emma declared their pair of snow angels beautiful.

Gabe repeated, "Beautiful" but he wasn't looking at the images they'd created on the ground. His eyes never left Emma's face.

Suddenly self-conscious, Emma realized what a mess she must look. What had she been thinking? She probably had mascara all over her cheeks now, makeup and shadow smudged.

As she looked up at Gabe, she saw his eyes widen slightly, and she knew that he must have noticed her appearance. Mortified, she took a step back, feeling exposed and vulnerable. Without another word, she turned and almost raced into the house, her heart beating rapidly as she tried to shake off the feelings of embarrassment and shame threatening to consume her. "I better go check on Mom."

CHAPTER 18

Resentment was a new emotion for him in connection with his mother. Part of his brain tried to tell him she had her reasons for the deception, reasons to do with honor. Maybe that was true, but did she not trust him enough with the truth? He could see it when he was a kid; that it might have been too much to handle, but he'd been an adult for a long time.

What if she had not told him about his father and grandmother? She'd left it late enough—two days more and the decision would have been out of her hands; maybe even one day more would have been too much. We never knew how much time we had. That was the thought spurring him on to find out more about this mysterious half-brother who likely didn't even know *he* existed. Would he want to know him?

Norma Jean was all about autonomy, and true to her nature, left what he'd do about all this in his hands.

What was he going to do? There was the grandmother thing, and there was the half-brother thing. Obviously, since he was here in Goodrich County, he'd chosen to seek his brother, rather than a grandparent he doubted he'd like.

A brother. Growing up, he'd envied the other kids who had brothers, sisters, and cousins. They might fight and annoy each other, but they had each other's backs.

Christmas and other holidays wouldn't have been such quiet affairs with more than just the two of them. Of course, Norma Jean always tried to make it special for him, and invited other people who were alone to share meals with them. But it wasn't the same as having other kids to play with, kids tied by blood.

Did it matter? From his point of view, yeah, there was a difference between friends you gained and genetic ties that were just there.

Would this half-brother feel the same?

Rich aromas filled his senses upon entering the house.

These borrowed boots toed off easily, and he set them on the boot mat beside Emma's, and his second-class-citizen cowboy boots.

"Anything I can do to help?" Gabe asked Emma as he approached the sink to wash his hands.

Torn, Emma hesitated. If he kept Esther company, that would be a great help, but, on the other hand, if her mother got too used to being entertained, life would become even more difficult for Emma when he left. Selfishly, she made her choice.

"Sure. If you wouldn't mind grating this Parmesan, that would be great." She set the grater and cutting board on the counter beside the hard block of cheese.

Donning oven mitts, Emma leaned into the open oven to pull out the lasagna oozing with melted cheeses. Gabe's eyes on her made her nervous, although she had no idea why. Rising too quickly, she banged her exposed arm on the oven's upper rack. Barely keeping her grip on the tray, she slammed it on the stovetop.

Gabe was by her side instantly, taking her injured arm in his hands, guiding her to the sink, and running the burn under cold water. "Is that feeling better?" he asked.

She could only nod.

Turning off the tap and carefully drying her arm with a clean paper towel, he held it closer to his face to inspect the damage. "Not too bad, but it might leave a scar. Still hurt?" He pulled her arm closer to his mouth and blew gently on the welt.

Emma shivered.

"That hurt? Sorry. I was trying to help."

No, it didn't hurt. It did… something.

"Do you have any antibiotic ointment?"

Emma nodded. "Under the sink, in the bathroom upstairs." What an idiot—that was their only bathroom. "Band-Aids are there, too," she called.

"Band-Aids?" Esther's voice came from the living room. "Did you cut yourself *again*? How many times have I said you need to pay attention to what you're doing?"

"I'm fine, mom." Amazing that she'd been such a self-confident teen. How could a mom who had so little belief in her now have raised such a self-assured kid?

Back then, she'd felt the world was her oyster, a belief instilled in her by both her dad and her mom. A dozen years ago, Esther had believed in her. What had changed how her mother viewed her daughter? All she'd done was go to college, then use that education to get a job. She'd *thought* she was doing well. Obviously not, according to her mom.

Then Gabe was back by her side, taking her arm gently in his hands, squeezing ointment onto his thumb, then brushing it onto her burn, watching her face to gauge her reaction.

What was her reaction? She had no way to describe what went on inside her. His touch near the burn site didn't really hurt, but did funny things to her, things she didn't want to examine. She made to pull her arm away, but he hung on.

"We need to treat this now, so you don't have problems later on. Burns can be nasty for infection. I think we caught it right away, so you'll be fine, but I'm worried about it leaving a scar."

"On my arm? Who cares? It's not like anyone would see it."

Gabe ran his forefinger around the area surrounding her burn. "It would be a shame to put a blemish on this skin."

Emma stared at the movement of his finger,

her brain whirring to find a response. Nope, none came to her rescue. “I’m fine, thanks.”

This time he let her arm go, but only long enough to peel the first piece of adhesive from the bandage. Grasping her arm again, just below her elbow, he applied the bandage, tenderly smoothing the edges, and checking that it fully protected the burn. Then lowering his head, he placed a kiss on it. “My mom always did that,” he said. “Makes it heal better.”

Emma stood, torn between yanking her arm back to the safety of her own personal space and following the instinct to press herself closer to this man who was taking care of her. When was the last time anyone had acted as caregiver to her?

That thought snapped her back to reality, tugging her arm to herself, dropping it to her side. It was not her lot to be a helpless female looking for a male protector. No, her role was as a caregiver, not a receiver of care and attention.

She needed to change the atmosphere. “Supper’s ready.” She reached for the bread knife, crumbs spewing as she cut chunk of crusty bread from the loaf she’d baked.

“Can I do anything for you?” Gabe asked.

Oh, he’d done enough.

CHAPTER 19

Taking the same places as they had at lunch, the three of them settled in. Almost like a family.

Scratch that, thought Emma. This guy was only here for one night, or so he'd said. Just because this table had always held two people didn't mean it should be that way now. No point in her mother getting used to it. Or her. It was nice to have someone cushion her from her mother's complaints, someone who recognized her efforts, who almost stood up for her.

Not that Esther was a mean mother - no way, never would be. In fact, she'd been a great mom, whenever Emma thought back to her earlier years. It's just that losing her husband had changed Esther in ways Emma never imagined. What did *she* know about the effects of losing a dearly loved spouse?

Yet, she saw other people, widows and widowers, ones who suffered, but continued their lives. What was the difference between them and Esther? Initially, Emma believed it was time. Those first few months of raw pain, trying to get used to a life never imagined. But Harold had been gone for over a decade. Surely the worst of the wound would scab over by now, allowing you to carry on.

The only part of herself Esther retained was her attention to her appearance. She never left her bedroom in the morning without being fully made up, her clothing spotless and pressed. Pressed by Emma, at her mother's insistence. If she didn't iron a sleeve or a collar just right, Esther would not rest until Emma did it all over again. But dressed up for what?

Harold wouldn't recognize this current Esther; maybe wouldn't even like her. Esther had never been clingy, needy. She'd had interests of her own, friends, activities, community involvement. Some would even say she'd been a community leader, so involved was Esther in the goings on of Goodrich. All those things came to a screeching halt when her husband died. Was this what Harold would have wanted?

Did it matter? It was what it was. She had no power over her mom, try as she might.

Gabe complimented her on the lasagna. Over and over, asking Esther if she didn't agree. Begrudgingly, Esther confirmed Gabe's opinion, telling him he was right, without actually praising her daughter.

Fair is fair. How many times had Emma thought to compliment her mom's cooking as she'd been growing up? Good food was just always there; she'd taken it for granted, just as she'd taken her parents' love and support. Maybe that was what Esther was doing now with her daughter.

Gabe hesitated, a piece of crusty bread in his hand. "Would you consider it rude if I dipped the bread into some of this tomato sauce? It's so good."

"Be my guest." Emma reached for a new hunk of bread and did the same, herself.

"Gabe," began Esther, "I think Emma called us for dinner just as you were about to tell me what brought you to Goodrich."

Emma watched Gabe hesitate. Was he fudging?

"My mother recently passed away," he said. "I'm an only child, but two days before she died, she told me I had a half-brother. A shared father, who hadn't stuck around for either of us. She knew little about this brother, but I tracked him down to this area. Our grandmother had kept an eye on each of us from afar, but the details are sketchy."

"Does he know about you?"

"I've no idea. I've not talked to him. This is my first day in the area, and I thought I'd scope things out before trying to contact him. I don't even know if I have his correct last name.

"What surname do you have? I was born and raised in these parts and know most people," said Esther.

Gabe paused. Did he really want to bare his soul to these people? He still wasn't sure he wanted to contact this half-brother. He looked from Emma to Esther, as they waited expectantly. What did he have to lose? He could always just drive away. "Norly."

"Norly? I know the Norly girls - Phoebe, Lark and Robin, went to school with Robin, the youngest," Esther told him. "Which one do you mean?"

"I don't know."

"What *do* you know?" asked Emma.

"Other than that last name, the only name I have is Blair."

"Blair?" said Emma and Esther in unison.

"That would be Robin Norly's son. I thought Blair's dad was Ron. But Robin's the only Norly girl with a son named Blair. Lark's son is Reid, and Phoebe had two boys, Greg and Stan."

"Stan?" Gabe asked. That wasn't such an uncommon name. Likely had nothing to do with the guy who'd pulled him out of the snowbank.

"Yes, that Stan," confirmed Emma. "Stan Wells, married to Becca, who knitted your toque."

"Stan is a cousin to Blair Windstrom," added Esther.

"There's more," said Emma. "You'll find in a small town that lives are intertwined. Stan and Blair are cousins, and Blair's mother is married to Becca's dad, Keith."

CHAPTER 20

Blair. Wasn't that the name he told Emma to call if she needed anything - to call him or Blair? "Is Blair's last name Norly?" Gabe asked. Obviously not Ottski, like mine, or they would have made the connection before.

Esther shook her head. "Norly was his mother's maiden name. When she married Ron, she took his surname, Windstrom. But we all thought Blair was Ron's son."

"He raised him, so he was his son, in all the ways that count." Emma had a different way of looking at it. Gossip. The Esther of old would have been on the phone by now, sharing this tidbit with her circle of friends. For Blair's and

Robin's sake, maybe it was good that she'd cut herself off from people and was no longer that person.

"What's Blair like?" Gabe asked.

"He's a farmer and married to Beth. She works with me and is the school counselor. They have two foster daughters. He's a good guy."

Although he'd only known Emma for less than a day, she seemed like a person who said what she thought—at least she'd never pulled any punches with him. Would she be open with a stranger about her thoughts about Blair?

How to ask this. "Is he a family sort of guy?" That sounded sort of dorky.

"He's tight with his cousins—Reid, Stan, and Greg. They all hung out together as kids. Greg's the oldest, then Blair and Reid. Stan's a year younger than those two."

Esther broke in. "Emma and Stan were quite the item in high school. Prom king and queen, always together, the leaders in their school, a beautiful couple. They were the ones everyone looked up to and anticipated that the two of them would end up together forever." She turned her gaze towards her daughter, a hint of sadness and regret evident in her eyes. "Their love story would have been a fairy tale ending if only this young lady hadn't decided to go away to school."

"Hard to be a teacher without going to college, I'd imagine," Gabe said. "Did you get your degree, then come right back here?"

"Oh, no," Esther answered for her daughter. "She wanted to see other things, so got a job teaching in the city. A good job, too."

"I'd imagine." To Emma, he asked, "What made you finally give in the lure of home?"

"That was me," Esther said. "I got sick, and since my dear Harold was no longer with us, I needed someone to look after me."

"I hope your health has improved, Miss Esther."

Emma nodded that it had.

Esther shook her head. "I wish that were true. Sadly, it's not the case. These health issues tend to drain the body, leaving one far from their former vigor. You know how these things go—they take so much out of a person that you never get back to where you once were." She sighed, her eyes betraying the pain she had endured. "But let's not dwell on that."

Emma grimaced.

Ah. Gabe thought he got it.

"Excuse me, if you don't mind." Esther got to her feet.

Gabe stood, waiting until the older woman left the room. "I don't mean to pry, but your mother doesn't seem ill."

"She's not. She had cancer and all those nasty treatments, but she's in remission, has been for almost a year. Ages ago her doctors said she can resume all her previous activities."

"Like?"

"Cooking, cleaning, visiting with friends, helping out in the community, working part-time."

"She does none of those things now?"

Emma shook her head.

What to say about that? He was saved from coming up with a response as Esther shuffled back into the kitchen, beaming.

"You're in luck! I just talked to Robin, and she hadn't left the hardware store yet, since she and Keith were taking inventory. They'll be right over." Pleased with herself, she assured Gabe, "You'll get to meet Blair's mother in just a few minutes."

~

"Mom! You didn't!"

Gabe stood. "What did you do?"

Emma asked, "You weren't committed to this?"

His face gave the answer.

"Now you are." Esther patted his hand. "Don't be afraid; Robin is a nice woman. I've known her forever."

Without conscious thought, Gabe's feet took him toward the front door. He needed to get out of here right away. So far, this had been just a vague notion, almost an adventure, solving a puzzle, tracking down a long-lost relative—a relative he didn't know if he even wanted to meet.

He needed time, time to think, time to plan, time to decide if he wanted to take this next step.

Plus, what he had to say could turn their world upside down. For all he knew, this Blair fellow was content, just fine with cousins, a mother, and a wife; he didn't need a brother.

He'd made it to Goodrich County. He could leave and come back another day once he'd given this more thought. How did you even approach a guy and say, "Hi. You don't know me, but I'm your brother"?

He reached for the snow boots he'd used to shovel the walk but put them down. No, if he was leaving, he couldn't take off with someone else's boots. He needed to throw his belongings into his duffle, then put on his cowboy boots, slippery as they were.

He could hear Emma in the living room, chiding her mother for taking such a step without first checking with their guest. In less than two minutes Gabe was back downstairs, his duffle bag over his shoulder.

Emma leaned against the doorway into the living room. "Going somewhere?"

"Yeah. I need to get out of here before this Robin gets here. What if she doesn't want to meet me, doesn't want anything to do with me, or a reminder of the man who fathered her son? Does Blair even know that the man who raised him was not his birth father? Maybe Robin never wanted him to know. Who am I to burst a secret like that?"

"How are you planning on leaving?"

That stopped him. Good point. His truck was at Alpaca Haven. The snow had been falling all afternoon, it was now dark, and the roads would be even worse. He could not ask Emma to drive him all the way to his pickup, couldn't endanger her that way.

It's not like he could call a taxi or Uber way out here.

The decision was taken out of his hands.

There was a knock on the door, then it opened without Emma attempting to take even a step.

CHAPTER 21

A pleasant-looking woman in her early 60s entered the house, bringing with her snow flurries and a man with glasses and a slight stoop. "Hello, Emma, dear. How are you?" She gave the younger woman a light embrace. "Your mom asked me to come over, said she has someone for us to meet." She glanced at the young man frozen at the foot of the stairs, a khaki duffle bag slung over his shoulder. "Is this him? Your boyfriend? He looks…" Her voice trailed off.

No part of Robin's body moved but her eyes, studying Gabe's face with an intensity that had him squirming. "Who are you?" she demanded, searching every inch of his face. "Forgive me," she said. "For a minute there you reminded me of someone, someone I haven't seen in a lifetime." She collected herself and extended her hand. "Nice to meet you. I'm Robin Feldman." She pointed over her shoulder. "This is my husband, Keith. And you are?"

With a thunk, Gabe's right hand released the duffle slung over his shoulder, clunking to the floor. Was there any way out of this? His eyes flicked to Emma's, hoping for a rescue—yet another rescue today. But there was no escape route in her eyes; he'd need to go through with this. Well, the worst that could happen was they'd kick him out for disrupting their lives. He'd been about to leave, anyway.

He took a step forward. "Ma'am, my name is Gabe. It's a pleasure to make your acquaintance." He shifted his gaze to the older man. "And you, too, sir."

Now that he was fully in the hallway, instead of the shadow of the stairwell, Robin stared even harder at him. Her hand dropped to her side without shaking his. The friendly smile left her face, replaced at first by a blank look, then incredulity. She stretched a hand behind her, reaching for her husband. He was there in an instant, wrapping one arm around her shoulder.

"What is it, Robin? Are you all right?" The man asked.

"Keith," was all Robin said.

Keith rubbed her shoulder, glaring at Gabe. "Who are you?" he asked the stranger. Anyone who upset Robin didn't belong in his world.

There was nothing but to get it out. "Gabe, sir. Gabe Ottski."

"Ottski!" whispered Robin and slumped just a bit.

Keith drew his wife closer to his side. "What is your business here, Gabe Ottski?"

"I don't mean to cause trouble."

"Well, it looks like you are." He turned Robin to face him. "Should we leave, honey?"

Robin took a few seconds to lean into her husband, then straightened. "No. I need to have a talk with this young man." To Gabe, she said, "How did you know where to find me?"

"From a letter my grandmother Gabriella sent me. She left clues, and I tried to figure it out."

"Gabriella. Never thought I'd hear of her again. Hoped I'd never hear from any of the Ottski's again."

Gabe winced. "Sorry, Ma'am."

"You're Bruce's son?"

"So I've been told."

"You don't know?"

"No. I never met the man."

"Is he dead?"

"Yes, to the best of my knowledge."

"I take it he didn't stick around to raise you?"

"Not at all."

"Did you live with Gabriella? She tried to clean up Bruce's messes."

"That's what my mother told me."

"Who is your mother?"

"Norma Jean Ottski."

"Ah, Bruce married her. Maybe he stepped up after all."

"No, Ma'am. He didn't marry her, and he didn't stick around. From what I hear, he ran soon after learning my mother was expecting me."

"Then the Ottski thing?"

This was an unpleasant part of the story, but this woman deserved to know. "Mom made a deal with Gabriella. In exchange for giving me the Ottski surname, Gabriella would provide Mom with child support. Not much, but a little. Then Mom changed her own last name so that ours would be the same." Gabe raised his chin slightly. This didn't put his mother in a good light, made it seem like she sold out, but these people had no right to judge her.

Robin nodded. “I can see that, especially if she didn't have family to fall back on, the way I did.”

Okay, maybe this woman wasn't too judgey.

“Why are you here now?” This came from Keith. “What do you want from us?”

CHAPTER 22

Gabe turned to face Keith. "Nothing, sir. I don't want anything from you. My mother recently passed away, and two days before she died, she told me I had a half-brother."

"Why now?"

"I don't have a good answer to that. Mom said she made a promise to Gabriella to never tell me about my parentage, but in her hospital bed, she rethought that, and broke her promise." More quietly, he said, "It's the only time I can recall her ever going back on her word."

"I meant, why did you come here now?" Keith asked.

"Mom died about a month ago. It took time to

sort out her house and estate. I asked for a six-month leave from work, and they agreed, so I thought I'd investigate who my half-brother might be. I don't have any other family."

Gabe turned to Robin. "Ma'am, I know this awkward, and I'm a stranger prying into y'all's personal business. I don't know how to say this other than to just ask. Does your son know that the man who raised him wasn't his biological father? If not, just say the word, and I'll leave. Like I said, I don't mean to cause trouble for you."

Robin took a step forward, leaving the protection of Keith's arm. "Young man, you are not the one causing trouble. It was Bruce Ottski; he wreaked havoc wherever he went." She glanced around at the others—Emma standing in the hallway, Esther lurking around the doorway. Did she want to air her dirty laundry in front of these people? If it was just her it affected, then who cared? But this was Blair's life they were talking about.

She decided. "Would you like to come home with us, young man?"

"Robin!" This from Keith.

A muffled, disappointed moan emerged from the invisible Esther on the other side of the living room entrance.

"I trust Emma. She brought this fellow into this house, and she would not risk putting her mother in danger." There was a time when she'd had words with Emma, shortly after the younger woman returned to town, hoping to take up where she'd left off with Stan, and recapture her place in the town's social circle. But Robin saw through Emma's bravado, respecting the way Em stepped up for her mother. Plus, in the classroom, Emma was doing an excellent job with Robin's great-nephew, an autistic child. She could be trusted to keep confidences. But Esther?

Keith tried again. "Robin, we don't know this man, and he's given you a shock. You might want to digest this news before making any decisions."

"Keith Feldman, don't you tell me what to do. This is my life and my decision, and for now, I want time to speak with Gabe." She didn't add 'in private,' but they all got the implication.

Since her return to Goodrich, Emma suffered her share of gossip. "Robin, we respect your privacy. What we've heard stays in this house," she said, then raised her voice slightly. "Right, Mom?"

"Right," came the agreement after a few seconds' delay.

"Thank you, dear. I knew you'd understand."

Robin turned to Gabe. "Looks like you had your bag in your hand. Were you coming or going?"

Good question, Gabe thought.

Emma jumped in. "He came unprepared for our winters and got his pickup stuck on the road not that far from your place. Stan pulled him out, but they closed the highways, and he had no place to stay. Since Becca and Stan don't have room, I brought him back here."

Why did all that make him sound inept? That was *so* not the impression he wanted to make on either Emma, or these people who might be the only family he had in this world.

"Well?" Robin asked.

"Ma'am?" Somehow, Gabe had lost the thread of this conversation.

"Are you staying here or coming home with us?"

Gabe looked from Emma to the older man scowling at him, and to the woman who seemed to get over her shock at learning his last name. "I..." What to say? Either way, he imposed on someone, and *that* stuck in his craw. He hated being beholden to anyone.

Especially Emma. Since they'd met, everything seemed to put him in a poor light, not at all the impression he wanted her to have of him.

Stay or go? A small part of him shied away from not seeing her anymore. He'd enjoyed their conversations, that is, when she was not rescuing or sniping at him. Watching her with her momma, he'd seen a different side to Emma, one less prickly, almost like a little girl wanting the approval she knew would never come her way. This vulnerable Emma was a lot different from the one who'd competently driven him to her house in a storm.

If he left with Robin and Keith, did that mean he'd never see Emma again? No, this was a small town; he could probably find his way back to her house once he had his own wheels. And if he forgot the way, he could always ask at Alpaca Haven. They'd mentioned that Becca had called Emma to say the shawl was ready. Even if Becca and Stan were reluctant to give him Emma's number, they might give her his cell number.

Somehow, he did not want to lose touch with Emma. He was not sure why she so intrigued him, but she did, and he rarely doubted his instincts. Besides, if he left, then returned when he was better prepared, maybe he would not come across as such a dolt.

He raised his eyes to Robin's, aware that everyone watched him. "Ma'am, are you sure?"

Robin nodded.

Keith glared.

"Sir, is it all right with you?" Best not get off on a worse foot with these potential shirttail relatives than he already had.

"If that's what Robin wants." Keith's words said the right thing, but his glower warned Gabe to not hurt his wife.

Gabe turned to Emma. "Thank you so much for your hospitality, Emma. I appreciate that, the delicious meals, and," one corner of his lip turned up, "the rescue so much. I hope I can repay you one day." To Robin, he said, "I thank you kindly for your offer and look forward to the opportunity to talk more with you." The words 'in private' implied.

CHAPTER 23

"Oh, for goodness' sake," said Emma as she watched Gabe reach for his cowboy boots. "Don't be ridiculous. You'll break your neck in those things. Use Dad's boots until you get yourself something decent for your feet."

There she was again, putting him down, and in front of others, too. He'd argue, but she was right. What could Gabe say but, "Thank you. I'll return them as soon as I can."

"We'll fix you up with boots from the store tomorrow," Robin told him. "Keith owns Feldman's Hardware, and we carry a bit of everything."

"*We* own," corrected Keith. He'd come a long way in giving over control to others, mostly with Robin's help.

Pulling his jacket from the closet and shrugging it on, Gabe stepped into the living room, where Esther's face peeped out. "It has been a pleasure to meet you, Ma'am, and I thank you for your hospitality."

"Don't be a stranger, young man. Come back anytime, although I wish you were staying with us."

"I shall return to say hello to y'all again." If nothing else, he felt that his presence gave Emma a break from her mom, a buffer from what seemed like endless complaints.

On the porch, Keith looked around. "I don't see your pickup, young fella."

How *not* to make a good impression on these people. "No sir, it's not here. I left it at a place called Alpaca Haven, after Stan gave me a tow. I don't have snow tires, and Stan convinced me it was better to park my truck there and ride into town with Emma."

"Stan's my son-in-law, and he's a man with a good head on his shoulders." Unlike you, Keith's words implied. "What possessed you to come to these parts with just summer tires?"

Robin nudged her husband, but he ignored her.

"Where I'm from, we don't see snow. Mud, yes, and my tires are fairly new. But, as Stan and Emma told me, their grip is all wrong for snow."

"Darn right. We'll need to fix you up right away."

"In the meantime, you can ride with us," Robin told him. She took her husband's arm, and they made their way to the crew cab Toyota Tundra parked on the street.

Grateful for the soles on his borrowed boots, Gabe hurried ahead to hold open the front passenger door for Robin, shutting it carefully after she seated herself.

They made their way mostly in silence; the Tundra handling the roads with far more ease than had Gabe's pickup, even though they were of similar size. "Would you be able to tell me where I can buy snow tires, sir?"

"Glen might have some in the service station in town, depending on the size you need. If he has none in stock, the nearest place would be in Watford. You wouldn't want to try to make it there with your vehicle until they have the roads cleared and salted. That is, if you want to make it in one piece."

"Right. Got it." The sooner he could equip himself to stop feeling so useless, the better.

Keith drove right by Alpaca Haven. Craning his neck, Gabe couldn't make out his truck from the little he could see of the parking lot. Stan was right; it blended in with the snow.

Just past the store, Keith turned into an entrance and drove up to a small, modern house. Pushing the button on a remote control attached to his sun visor, a garage door opened, and they drove in. When the engine shut off, silence reigned in the cab.

Awkward. He didn't know these people, and they knew nothing about him—nothing but the fact that his face must somehow resemble that of his father, a man who likely brought nothing but bitter memories to the woman seated in front of him.

Robin recovered first, reaching for her door handle.

Gabe jumped out to get her door for her.

Inside, Keith headed to the kitchen. "I'll start a pot of coffee."

"Follow me," Robin told Gabe. "I'll show you to the guest room."

That gave him a few minutes to think of what to say to this woman he'd only just met.

Cowboys certainly moved around, and many agricultural mechanics did, also, depending on the season and the availability of work. So, he was no stranger to plunking himself down amidst strangers. But in those cases, he only had to prove his ability to do the work required of him, and to fit in with whatever was needed.

This, though, was far different.

He followed Robin through the open plan first floor, light and airy, with the entrance flowing into the living area, then to the kitchen and dining sections. Not a large place, but perfect for two people.

Robin led the way up a flight of carpeted stairs. Straight ahead was what must be the master bedroom, moonlight shining through its floor-to-ceiling windows. On the left, the hallway opened to a bedroom and bathroom located above the kitchen area. "Here you go. The bathroom next door is for you. Come on down as soon as you've settled yourself."

Settled yourself. What was there to settle? Gabe set his duffle bag on the floor by the bed. There would be time later to hang up the few clothes he'd brought with him. That was the thing with jeans and t-shirts - they didn't require much care. Just as well, because he wasn't a pressing-your-clothes kind of guy. He plugged in his phone to charge it, then left to face the woman who gave birth to his half-brother.

CHAPTER 24

How had he not noticed the aromas emanating from the first floor? Shows how distracted he was. Good thing he'd already eaten at Emma's, or his stomach would be rumbling and champing at the bit to sample this fare.

From the rich scent, it had to be a roast beef. Keith stood at the sink peeling potatoes. Or maybe hacking at the potatoes would be a better description.

Robin caught Gabe wincing as Keith lobbed off a sizeable chunk of potato. "Keith is new to working in a kitchen," she explained. "Can you tell?"

Keith scowled at his wife, then at Gabe.

"Think you could do any better?" he asked the younger man.

Glancing between husband and wife, Gabe opted for honesty. "Yes. My mother had me helping in the kitchen ever since I was little."

Without a word, Keith handed the paring knife to Gabe, then stalked to the couch, picking up the remote control and turning on the television.

Quietly, Gabe asked, "Did I insult him? That wasn't my intention."

"Ignore him; that's just Keith's way. He's relieved you offered to take over. His first wife never allowed him in the kitchen. Me, I'm not possessive about this room, especially when it comes to prep work or cleaning up."

"I'd be happy to clean up after the meal, Ma'am, if you'll trust me."

Robin beamed. "Thank you for the offer, but only if you share that duty with Keith. We haven't been married that long, and I'm still training him. If I do most of the cooking, he does most of the cleanup."

"I'm sure he's happy about that deal."

"Not so you'd notice, but it's one of the things we've worked out. If *you* do all the cleaning up, he'll get out of the habit, then I'd need to start all over again when you leave. He'll appreciate sharing the chore with you, though."

Gabe washed and peeled potatoes, plopping them into the pot Robin showed him, happy to have something to do with his hands. Somehow, with them each concentrating on their tasks, conversation came easier. "Would that be Yorkshire pudding you're making?"

"I'm surprised you recognized it."

"The batter, along with the smell of what's coming from the oven, was the first clue; it has my stomach jumping for joy."

"Not everyone's familiar with this dish."

"My mother's mother was from England, and it was a common Sunday meal in her family."

"Did you know your grandmother?"

"No, she and my grandfather passed on before I was born."

"Cousins? Aunts and uncles?"

"No. My mother was an only child. Her extended family is in the UK, I understand, but her parents lost touch with them ages ago."

"So, you have no relatives."

Gabe hesitated. "Maybe a half-brother."

Robin gave Gabe a sideways glance and set down her measuring spoon. "I think there is little doubt you and Blair are related. You resemble your father."

"I feel like I should apologize to y'all for that, Ma'am."

"Nonsense. It is not your fault. You never asked to be born to that man."

Turning away, Robin gave her attention to the electric mixer, switching it from low to high, making conversation impossible.

Good. Gabe needed a few minutes to regroup. This was like trekking an arroyo in search of lost cattle ahead of a flash flood. Maybe he'd find what he sought; maybe he'd lose big time.

Robin pulled a heated pan of drippings from the oven, then turned off the mixer. The pan sizzled as she poured in the batter. She removed the roast from the oven, replacing it with the pan.

"Do y'all toss these potato peelings in the trash, or compost them?" Gabe asked.

"Compost. Some of our kitchen scraps go to the alpacas as treats, the rest we compost." She gave Gabe another glance from the side of her eye. "Not everyone would have asked about composting."

"My mother was big on it. We didn't have much, but we ate well. She always kept a garden. Even when we lived in an apartment, she grew edibles in containers. Then, when we had a house, she devoted half of the yard to growing vegetables."

"She did, or you did, too?"

"Both. With my mom, getting out of helping wasn't an option. Didn't hurt me, though. While I can't say I never weeded without grumbling when I was a kid, I grew to appreciate digging in the dirt, and growing what we ate."

"A farmer at heart."

"I don't know about that, but I can respect growing things."

Robin tented the beef with tinfoil and set the timer on the stove. "We have about 15 minutes until things are ready. Come sit down; I have something to show you."

Robin sat on the couch beside Keith. Other than extending his arm around his wife's shoulders, Keith didn't acknowledge their presence.

Gabe took a seat in the chair kitty corner to the couch.

From the shelf under the coffee table, Robin pulled out a thick photo album.

Starting from the back and flipping through the pages, she searched for what she wanted. "There." She scooted a little closer to Gabe, positioning the album on the coffee table between them. “That’s our wedding.”

“Lovely, Ma’am.” What did you say about someone’s wedding photos?

Robin gave him a wry glance. “Thank you. I see your mama raised you right. But that’s not the point.” She rested her finger on the picture of a younger man standing beside Keith. “That’s Blair —your half-brother.”

CHAPTER 25

They'd never be mistaken for identical twins, but there was a resemblance; Gabe could see it. Eerie, like coming face to face with a doppelgänger—not quite but enough that you'd take a second look.

Standing beside Robin in the wedding picture was Becca. "Our kids stood up for us," Robin explained.

"Who are the girls?" Gabe pointed to two kids, dressed differently, but standing just slightly behind Keith and Robin.

"Friday and Randine."

Gabe wondered if he'd heard the names correctly.

"Yeah, I know. Long story. They're Blair's and Beth's foster daughters. Great kids."

"Even if Randine almost lost your wedding ring," grumbled Keith. With a look from his wife, he added, "But she recovered nicely."

"Emma mentioned she works with Beth."

"Yes, Beth's been around this area for a few years now. She's the counselor at Goodrich School, plus a few others in the district."

Robin flipped through more pages, pointed out various pictures of her son. Quickly, she noticed her finger wasn't needed; Gabe's eyes easily sought images of his brother.

As they moved back in pages and time, Gabe noticed something. "Is Blair a guy who hates having his picture taken, or did you get him to smile more in later photos?"

That made Robin smile. "Yes. He was a solemn man for far too long. Beth's been good for him, Beth, and the girls. He's lighter now, happier."

Gabe noticed a lot of the photos showed rural settings. "What does he do?"

"He's a farmer, like his dad, my late husband."

Ah, the elephant in the room. Ignore the implication, or let it go until a time when he knew more about these people? But who knew how long he'd be around? Maybe he should glean as much information about his sibling before someone asked him to leave.

Weird. He'd grown up with just his mother; it had been good, just the two of them. He was an independent guy, just fine on his own, yet now that the possibility of family was within reach, it seemed important, felt like something within him called to learn more about the people who shared blood ties. *Might* share blood ties, he reminded himself. This was not a done deal.

Maybe he could edge into this. "What kind of farming did your late husband do?"

"Grain and cattle, with an emphasis on the cattle. That was his chief love, growing enough crops to feed them, and to tide us over when cattle prices slumped."

"I understand about that, Ma'am. I've worked in ranching all of my life, dealing with the vagaries of weather and prices and government regulations—all things beyond our control."

"That is exactly why I wanted my girl to take over the hardware store," interjected Keith. "It would have been a sure living for her. Instead, she insisted she had to live on a farm and raise alpacas."

Robin patted his knee. "Keith," her tone a

warning. "Becca followed her heart, and it's paying off for her."

"That's true. She's doing all right for herself."

Gabe could tell Keith hated to admit it.

"Keith is never happy when people don't fall in with his plans," Robin explained to Gabe.

"That's not right, and you know it Robin Norly Windstrom Feldman."

Robin smirked. "Bit of a mouthful, isn't it?" To Gabe she said, "I mostly go by Robin Feldman now, but having grown up here, people still call me by any of the last names I've put on."

"I get it," said Gabe. Although he sort of didn't. Growing up in small places, he understood people's long memories of local history. But until just a month ago, he'd believed his mother's surname had always been Ottski.

"What about you, dear?" Robin asked. "Are you married?"

"No, Ma'am."

"Ever been?"

Gabe shook his head.

"Ever came close?"

He hesitated just fractionally, then said, "Never seemed to meet the right person, someone who clicked." But he wondered if he had only yesterday.

There had never been a woman to stick in his mind the way Emma stitched herself into his memories, his being. Maybe it wasn't just Emma; maybe it was that he usually came across as competent to people, totally unlike his experiences since flying into the ditch in Goodrich County. Likely, it was just an ego thing, meeting an attractive woman, all of it tied up with the uncertainty of finding a brother.

How to steer the conversation back to that brother?

"Did Blair always farm with his dad?"

"No. Well, growing up he did, like any farm kid; there was no choice. But when he finished school, Blair went off on his own."

"Just like my Becca did," added Keith. "Never knew why staying home wasn't good enough for some of these kids."

"Where did Becca go, sir?"

"Europe, of all things. It was like she couldn't get far enough away."

"But she came back, sir."

"Yeah, but that was her mother's doing. Izzy asked her to when I broke my hip and was out of commission for a while."

"Says something about your daughter and how you raised her, that she came home."

"She's all right, my girl. But if it had been just me, I don't know if she'd have done it."

"Keith!" Robin said.

"You know it's true, Robin." To Gabe, he explained, "There was a time when if I said the sky was blue, Becca'd argue it was pink."

"And vice versa," added Robin. Nestling into her husband, she told Gabe, "Those two are so much alike."

"Huh!" from Keith.

"They are, you'll see."

Gabe hoped he'd have the opportunity.

"But they get along much better now that Keith stopped trying to make her into what he wanted."

Keith feigned interest in the ball game on TV.

"Once he gave up the dream of having a third generation own Feldman's Hardware, things eased between them, and they can work together all right."

Gabe looked questioningly; he thought Esther had said Keith and Robin were at the store doing inventory.

"Oh, Keith still works there; we both do, but just part time. There are four owners now - Keith, Becca, me, and Mona. Mona is my nephew's, Reid's, wife. She works at the store full-time, but the rest of us cycle through to do our part. You'll meet Mona tomorrow when we fix you up with boots."

Back to what he really wanted to know about—his brother. "So Blair succumbed to the lure of the farm and returned home?"

"Not exactly. Ron, my husband, died. I couldn't manage the farm on my own, so Blair stayed on after the funeral and carried the farm."

"Working the land and animals gets into your blood. He must love it."

"The land part, yes. Not so much the animals."

"At least he kept cattle. Sensible stock you can do something with. Not like alpacas," grumbled Keith, his eyes never leaving the television screen above the mantle.

"Becca gave me an alpaca toque to wear. It's okay, far better than anything woolen I've tried before. She has a lot of alpaca items in her store."

"The girl knows how to diversify." Keith seemed torn between pride and derision for the path his daughter chose.

"She's doing very well, considering the store's only been open less than a year. We're proud of her, her and Stan, for what they've accomplished."

Keith squeezed his wife's hand that rested on his knee. "Robin helps there, too. She minds the store, knits some products they sell there and helps with the spinning and carding of the fleece."

"New skills for me," said Robin. "I knew how to knit, but this fleece is different to handle. Keith made Becca and me custom knitting needles that make it so much easier."

"Custom needles; that would take some skill."

"My husband is good at things like that."

"Not nearly as good as Blair," Keith added. "He's the real craftsman when it comes to wood."

"I noticed some wooden toys at Alpaca Haven." Could his brother have made them?

"Yes, those are Blair's handiwork, along with the furniture and just about every other wooden piece for sale in the store."

"The sign above the door, too?"

Keith smiled, one of the first Gabe had seen from the man. "The boy did a good job with that, didn't he?"

"How does he find time for all of that when he has crops and cattle to look after?" Gabe wondered.

Through the patio doors along one wall, headlights shone as a vehicle approached.

"Looks like you'll be able to ask him that yourself in just a minute," Robin said.

CHAPTER 26

Why did the house feel empty? Nothing changed; it was still just her and her mother here.

Rather than marking student workbooks at the kitchen table to be near Esther, Emma spread out on the desk in the spare room—the room that had been Gabe's for just a short few hours.

Did she think she could smell his aftershave in here? She remembered the scent, a subtle fragrance, yet one that seemed to overwhelm her when Gabe ministered to the burn on her arm. Even now, just thinking about it, Emma's skin tingled from the memory of those touches. What was the big deal? So what if he'd stuck her arm under the cool, running water? He'd applied ointment and a bandage. Blew on her skin. She shivered at the memory of those sensations etched in her consciousness.

"Emma!" The voice came from downstairs. "Emma, where are you?"

For just a split second, it crossed Emma's mind to pretend she didn't hear her mother calling. Sighing, she got up. If she yelled down from here, Esther would chastise her for conduct unbecoming a lady. Somehow it was different when it was her mother's voice floating up to her…

Emma stood in the doorway of the living room, reluctant to venture in too far. Crossing the threshold committed her to whatever her mom had in mind. "Yes, Mom?"

"Where were you? I called and called, and you didn't answer."

Really? "I was working upstairs."

"You work too much. I've told you over and over. Your father never did that. When he came home, he came home, and his focus was on us, as it should be."

Not quite the way Emma recalled it; she thought his focus was on the television once he'd given them each a hug. But what did a kid know?

"You wanted something, Mom?"

"Yes. That wasn't a proper meal tonight, just lasagna and that bread that splinters crumbs all over when you bite into it. Not a dessert in sight."

"What would you like for dessert? Some fruit?"

"A properly made dessert would be nice, but apparently that is asking too much these days. Not like when I made the meals for this family."

"You're welcome to make as many of the meals as you'd like."

Esther waved a hand. She was not into pesky details. "You haven't made any Kuchen in a while. I fancy some of that."

Emma held on to her patience. "We don't have any."

"That's all right; it's better fresh, anyway. Why don't you whip us up some now?"

"Mom, I have papers to mark, and I need to get my lessons ready for tomorrow."

"They are taking advantage of you at that school; I've told you that so many times. Your father never worked day and night. You need to put your foot down."

"This is part of teaching. I need time every evening to get ready for the next day. First-graders don't deal kindly with unprepared teachers."

"Well then, switch grades. I'm sure those high school teachers don't spend as much time as you on these things." Esther's eyes turned shrewd. "Unless this is an excuse to avoid spending time with me."

"Mom..."

"I bet if that nice young man was still here this evening, you would not be holed up somewhere staring at the scribbles of small children."

She might have a point.

"I bet Gabe keeps a nice balance between work and down time."

"Doubt it, Mom. He works on ranches; I think he'd work whatever hours are required."

"That's why your father turned his back on his parents' farm—too much work for too little money, he always said. He chose a better path."

Yeah, the one that left his widow almost destitute. No, that was uncharitable. It was *her* fault that her father left her mother in this financial position; all their spare cash, he funneled to Emma at college.

Best get her mother off this topic. "We have some pears, apples and blackberries. Would you like a fruit salad?"

"With whipped cream? I mean real cream, not that stuff you squirt from a can."

Emma held in her sigh. "No, Mom, we have no fresh cream."

"Put it on your shopping list, then. Goodness, girl, can't you even keep our home stocked with groceries?"

She might say the same to Esther, but she didn't; she never would. It was not Esther's fault that life dealt her such a bitter blow as to take her husband when they were still in their 50s. "I'll be right back." Emma went into the kitchen, pulling fruit from the fridge, adding some cheese and celery sticks to the mix. Surely *some* of it would appeal to her mom.

Washing the fruit reminded her of the last time she'd stood in front of the sink; that time with Gabe's body so close, gently running her arm under cool water. What had he done that was so special? Nothing, really. Yet somehow, the memory lingered, as did the sensations.

She was not naïve. Nor inexperienced. She'd had boyfriends before, gone steady with Stan for two years, and dated while in college. Yet, none of those guys affected her in the way Gabe had, a guy she'd known less than a day.

Enough. She dragged her mind back to the

task at hand. She needed to get this dessert platter to her mother, then get back upstairs to her work.

Was this what her life had become? Would always be? That girl voted most likely to succeed seemed a distant memory.

CHAPTER 27

"What?" Gabe was on his feet. "What did you say?"

"While you were upstairs, I called Blair. That should be him arriving; probably Beth, too."

"Robin," chided Keith. "You're doing that interfering thing again."

"Nonsense. It'll be fine."

"But why?" Gabe asked. He thought he'd have more time, plan out a strategy, decide if he actually wanted to do this. "What did you tell him?"

Robin stood and patted Gabe's shoulder. "Now don't get your shirt in a knot. I just told him there was someone here he might want to meet."

"He doesn't know?" Gabe heard car doors slam. "Shouldn't he be prepared? Shouldn't you have told him and given him a choice if he wants to meet me?"

"Oh, you worry too much. I said it'll be fine."

But what if it wasn't?

Footsteps stomped on the porch mat, knocking off loose snow. The door opened, a man of about Gabe's size opening it for a pretty woman to enter ahead of him.

"Hey, Mom, Keith," the man said. "What's this about?" Not looking at them, he leaned against the wall, removing his boots.

Beth sat on the bench, taking off hers. Then she stood, took two steps and stopped, her eyes riveted on Gabe's face.

Behind her, Blair assumed she'd moved into the living room, bumping into her back where she stood frozen. His hands went to her shoulders. "Babe, what is it? You all right?"

Beth reached up a hand to cover the one rubbing the top of her arm. "Blair," she whispered.

Only then did Blair notice the fifth person in the room, a stranger, one standing suspiciously close to his mother, Robin's hand on his arm, as if to stop the guy from bolting. Blair's gaze went from his mother's restraining hand up to the guy's face. And stopped. What the…. "Mom, what's going on?" He tightened his grip on his wife.

"Gabe, I'd like you to meet my son, Blair, and his wife, Beth." Robin acted like she couldn't feel the antipathy coming from the new arrivals. Even Keith was on his feet now, the television forgotten.

Gabe couldn't speak, couldn't move, couldn't take his eyes from the man who looked so much like him, yet wasn't him. He had to, though. He had to say something, couldn't just stand there like an idiot.

Why hadn't he thought this out better, had a solid plan, had an idea if this brother would even want to know anything about him? Should he leave? It would only take a few seconds to grab his duffle bag and get out of here.

Then what? He was in the middle of nowhere, without means of transportation. No, wait, Alpaca Haven wasn't that far away, certainly within walking distance. But he'd left the keys with Stan. Stan said he and Becca lived above the store, and they wouldn't mind if he knocked on their door and retrieved his keys. Yeah, his tires were lousy, but he'd rather take his chances in the dark with them, then face this man scowling at him.

"Mom?" Blair's question came out like a warning, freezing Gabe's feet to the floor.

Robin didn't answer.

Keith muttered something about interfering women but draped one arm around his wife's shoulders.

Beth took a step forward. "Robin, what's going on?" She reached behind for Blair's hand, feeling that he needed the contact even more than she did.

Now Robin spoke. "Son, I'd like you to meet your half-brother."

~

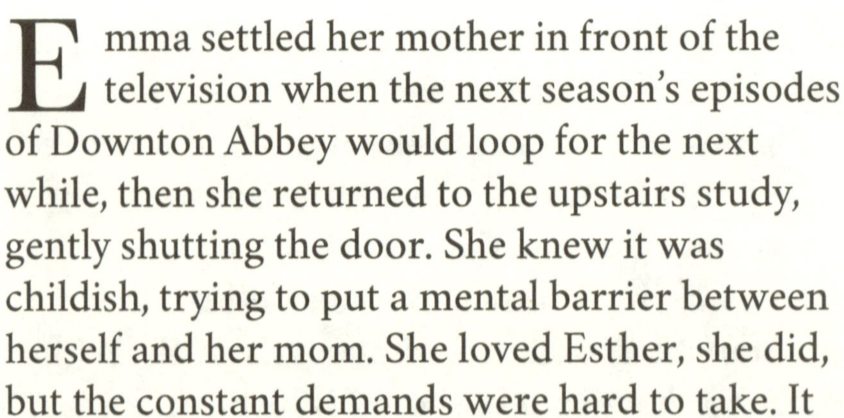

Emma settled her mother in front of the television when the next season's episodes of Downton Abbey would loop for the next while, then she returned to the upstairs study, gently shutting the door. She knew it was childish, trying to put a mental barrier between herself and her mom. She loved Esther, she did, but the constant demands were hard to take. It was almost like having a child, a peevish one at that.

A child. Emma surrounded herself with kids all day and loved it. But they were other people's kids, only loaned to her for ten months at a time. Yet, they all carved a place in her heart.

Especially some of them, the ones who marched to a different drummer. The ones who entered her room like the world was a scary place; children should not have such worries. The ones attracted to every shiny object within sight or sound, interrupting what they wanted to concentrate on. The little bodies not made for sitting still in a chair for hours at a time. Kids who processed information differently.

These were the challenges, the most rewarding parts of teaching, ensuring that each child left her classroom more confident, more equipped to face their world. Sure, it was about teaching reading and writing and math, but kids couldn't tackle these subjects until they felt good about themselves, and understood what they needed to make learning work for them.

One such student this year was Alvin Wells, the son of Greg and Aggie, nephew to Stan and Becca. She'd worked with autistic children before, but never in a Grade 1 class. First grade was special; it could get a child's school experience off to a good start, or a difficult one. Emma was determined this would be a good year for Alvin.

And it was. Oh, she made mistakes, messed up more times than she would like to admit, but Alvin forgave her. And so did his parents.

She kept in touch with them often, especially Aggie. They were nervous, understandably. While kindergarten had been an okay experience for Alvin, Grade 1 classrooms held much more structure. Free play time was scant, with less emphasis on the social skills supposedly learned in kindergarten.

Transitions were tough for kids on the autism spectrum. When making sense of the world didn't come naturally, and took so much extra effort, kids with autism often clung to the known. Change was hard, and kindergarten to Grade 1 was a whole pile of change.

Luckily, this teaching contract wasn't a last-minute thing, giving Emma the summer to prepare. Knowing Alvin would be in her room, she researched the best practices. She took pictures of the classroom, and prepared a pictorial book about how their days in Grade 1 would look. She prepared a visual schedule of how the periods in the day would go.

Calling Aggie in mid-August, she asked if Alvin and his mom would like to come to the school to meet her when it was quiet, with no one else around. That first meeting stretched into three, allowing Alvin time to feel his way around his new classroom. Emma took pictures of Alvin sitting in the desk he'd chosen, putting his lunch bag in his cubby, placing his crayons in his desk, all the things he'd encounter in just a few weeks, except without the pressure of others around him.

Duplicate copies of the booklets she made went home with Aggie, who went over them each night with her son.

Of course, when you deal with six-year-olds, life does not always go as planned. Emma frequently contacted Aggie to let her know when there would be a change to their schedule and emailed her the amended one. Emma went over the change with Alvin at school; Aggie reinforced it at home. Between them, it worked.

Mostly.

One thing that threw Alvin was when Emma was not there. That would happen in a few days when Emma would attend a training session, and a substitute teacher took over the class for the day. Although she always tried to get the same sub, sometimes it was just not possible. This was the case now, so Emma needed to leave as detailed instructions as possible to make the day go better for all concerned.

This was important, and normally she focused well.

Not tonight.

Her snowball fight with Gabe kept entering her mind. What had possessed her to do that? She barely knew the man.

But he'd looked so serious out there shoveling their snow, like he had the weight of the world on his shoulders. His mom had just died; she got that. Even though it had been ten years since her dad passed away, the loss didn't lessen even if the rawness did. For him, the ache would be fresh.

She didn't know how to relieve her mother's pain; never had. But maybe she could lessen this man's, even if just for a few moments.

No, that sounded too altruistic. She needed a break herself, to relive that fun-loving Emma. And, if she was honest, to spend more time with this stranger who intrigued her.

CHAPTER 28

"Half-brother! What's going on?"

Surprises never sat well with Blair. He felt Beth's hand tighten around his.

"Just what I said, son. You share the same father."

"How do you know? This could be some guy off the street." He addressed Gabe for the first time. "What do you want with my mother?"

Finally, Gabe found his voice. "Nothing."

"Then why are you here?" Blair didn't believe him.

Gabe looked from Robin to Blair. Surely there was a better way to have done this. It was done, though; nothing to do but plow on. He took a deep breath. How did you summarize an entire history in just a few sentences to an angry man who looked ready to explode?

"It was just my mother and me all my life. She told me my father died when I was too young to remember him. She got cancer, and two days before she passed away, she admitted she'd lied. The man who fathered me ran when he learned my mom was pregnant. Long story short, she said this was not the first time he'd done that, that I had a half-brother."

Blair never blinked, his stare ferreting out the truth. "What does that have to do with my family?"

"As best I can figure out, the same guy who fathered me was your sire as well." There. He'd said it.

"Get out."

"Blair!" Robin stepped between the two men.

"Mom, stay out of this."

"I will not!"

"Even if it's true, Mom, we want nothing to do with the blood of a man who'd run out on you."

Beth gave Blair a sideways look, but Robin spoke ahead of her.

"Son, that same blood runs through your veins."

Gabe understood, though. His presence was a

reminder of those bad times. "It's all right. I get it. Sounds like you had a good life with your mother and the man who raised you. That's what counts. I'll be on my way, then." He turned to Robin and Keith. "Thank you for the meal and the hospitality. It was a pleasure meeting you."

Robin put a hand on his chest. "Wait. You're not going anywhere."

"Oh yes, he is," countered Blair.

Now Beth spoke up. "Listen a minute, Blair. You might want to think about this."

"I have, and I want this guy out before he disrupts our lives anymore."

Gabe held his hands up. "It's not my intention to disrupt ya'll's lives. Since my mom died, I'm alone and thought I'd look up the possibility that I had a half-brother. Put it down to curiosity."

"What do you do?" Blair asked. "If you think you're getting something out of us, you're mistaken."

"Blair! I raised you better than that."

"No, it's all right," Gabe said. "He's protecting his family, as he should. As to what I do, I'm an agricultural mechanic, working mostly on ranches. But I pretty much do it all—work with cattle, pitch in with whatever needs doing. I took a leave from work to settle my mother's estate, then follow the trail of a possible long-lost half-brother."

"Do you have any proof we're related?"

Gabe shook his head. "Nothing tangible. Just my mother's word about the name of my birth father, that he'd done this with a previous baby, and some letter from a grandmother I never met; my birth father's mother."

Beth said, "Blair, have you looked in the mirror lately? Can't you see it?"

Robin agreed. "The resemblance between you two is unmistakable, plus he looks so much like Bruce."

"Mom, that was over three decades ago. How can you remember what someone looked like that long ago?"

"I see it every time I look at you, son." She nodded at Gabe. "And now looking at this young man."

Blair turned back to Gabe. "Where are you staying?"

"His things are in our guest room," said Robin.

"And you're okay with this?" Blair asked Keith.

"I dislike anything new sprung on me, but this is Robin's doing, so I'll go along with what she wants."

"Well, I don't want a stranger in my mother's

house. We know nothing about this guy, not even where he came from."

"He came from Emma Lowry's house. We picked him up there just a few hours ago," Robin told him.

"You're a friend of Emma's?" Blair asked Gabe.

This was going from bad to worse. He'd hoped to get out of there with at least some of his dignity intact. "Friend isn't exactly the right word; we're new acquaintances. I only arrived in this area this morning in a snowstorm. I've never been in snow before, didn't even know about snow tires, and went into the ditch. Emma came by and rescued me, taking me to Alpaca Haven, where a guy named Stan pulled me out. He and Becca suggested I leave my pickup at their place and get a ride into Goodrich with Emma. She and her mother invited me to spend the night with them."

"What was with Stan's head suggesting Emma take in a stranger?" What was *wrong* with these people, Blair wondered?

"You don't know me, but I can promise you I mean no harm to your family or friends."

"We'll see about that." Blair pulled his phone from his pocket. "For tonight, you're not staying in my mother's house." He turned his back, scrolled through his contacts, and started a call. "Emma, it's Blair. You had a guy who was going to stay with you?" He waited, not taking his eyes from Gabe. "How would you feel about him coming back for the night?" The rest of the call didn't take long.

"Get your stuff," he said to Gabe. "For some reason, Emma is willing to have you return, and she said Esther will be thrilled." He glared. "But this is a small town and we're tight. If I hear that you have put even a toe out of line, I'll come for you."

CHAPTER 29

Traveling light and not unpacking had advantages. In less than a minute, Gabe returned to the living room with his duffle bag over his shoulder.

Looking at his half-brother, he could see the resemblance; yes, it was possible they shared parentage. But that didn't mean they'd ever have a relationship, and from the way Blair'd taken the news, it seemed highly unlikely.

Tension radiated from Blair, the kind Gabe saw in cattle who were spooked or in pain. It never paid to get too close to such animals, nor to appear threatening. Gabe approached his brother in the same wary way he would with an unpredictable animal.

Everyone was still standing, but Blair had his boots on already.

Both Beth and Gabe took steps toward the boot mat; Blair inserted himself in between them, protecting his wife from this stranger.

"Wait," said Robin. "Give me your phone, Gabe."

"Why?"

She gave him that 'mother' look. "Just do it, young man, and unlock the screen."

"Yes, ma'am."

She thumbed through his icons, then added her name and number into his contacts. "I expect you to call me tomorrow morning."

"Mom," began Blair.

"I wasn't speaking to you, Blair, but be sure I will be doing plenty of that in the near future."

Gabe pocketed his phone and waited until Beth had her boots on before moving into that space to lace up his borrowed pair. He turned to Keith and Robin. "Thanks again for the meal. I'm sorry to have caused you trouble."

"You didn't," Robin told him. "If you think *this* is trouble, wait until I give Blair a piece of my mind tomorrow."

Gabe shot a guilty look at Blair. He would not

want to be in his shoes tomorrow but knew Blair would lay all blame on this interloper.

No one spoke as they walked to Blair's pickup. Beth's hand resting in the crook of Blair's arm.

They were about halfway to Goodrich before Blair spoke. "What was in this letter from a supposed grandmother?"

"It's a few pages long. I can show it to you if you'd like."

"No, not that interested. Just give me the condensed version."

"She had just one child, Bruce. She met Bruce's girlfriend once, but the next she heard was that they split. The girl was pregnant and moved back to where her parents lived. She tried to find the girl, but lost track of her. She knew the girl's first and last name, but that's it. The most she could get out of Bruce was that he met her when he interned in some town."

Blair and Beth looked at each other; that fit with what Robin had told him.

"How do you fit into this?" Blair asked.

"My mother lived with Bruce briefly. One day Bruce's parent came over. During supper, the older woman noticed how sick my mother was and suspected she was pregnant. Bruce admitted it but said they'd take care of it."

"Obviously they didn't."

"Bruce felt he did—he took off in the middle of the night."

"Figures."

"Gabriella, Bruce's mother, didn't approve, but her son and husband forbade any contact with my mother. Gabriella went behind their backs and kept in touch with my mom. Well, 'in touch' is a pretty loose term for the occasional contact she had over the years." He didn't need to say more at this point; he might never see this guy again, so he didn't need to know any more personal details about Norma Jean's choices.

No one said anything for the next few miles, the starless night intensifying the blackness inside the truck.

Blair switched topics. "Emma has a lot on her plate these days."

"I gathered that."

"I work with her at the school," offered Beth.

"Yes, she told me."

"Emma and Esther are locals; the town looks out for them."

"Understood." In more ways than one. "I mean them no harm." How many times would he have to say this?

"That had better be true."

All right, this was getting old. Gabe was unused to anyone questioning his integrity. He cut Blair some slack because the guy was in shock over this news, but there were limits to his patience.

Beth put her hand on Blair's arm. "Did Emma sound reluctant to have Gabe in her house?"

"No. Just the opposite, for some weird reason."

Gabe bristled. Brother or not, he'd had about enough.

Beth glanced back at him. "Then have some faith in Emma's judgment. She's not naïve, and she's spent more time with Gabe than you have. In fact, *you* might know this man a little better if you'd taken a different attitude."

Blair narrowed his eyes at his wife.

Great, thought Gabe. Now I'm coming between my brother and his wife. He'd better get out of this town before he did more damage.

When they pulled up in front of Emma's home, Gabe's hand was already on the door handle.

He heard two other doors open, and both Blair and Beth followed him up the walk. Before he could knock, Emma opened the door, a welcoming smile on her face. Wrapping both hands around Gabe's upper arm, she pulled him into the house.

Beth, then Blair, followed. "Are you sure this is all right, Emma?" Blair asked.

"Of course. Mom was so disappointed he left and blamed herself for calling Robin."

"Esther called my mom?" He scowled at Gabe.

That was one thing Gabe would not let the guy lay at his feet. "Not my fault. She jumped to conclusions, then when Emma and I were cleaning the kitchen, she called your mother and told her to come over."

"Now *everyone* knows?" Blair didn't care for himself, but this was his mother's private business, things long buried in the past.

Emma and Beth shared a look. "No," Emma said. "Just Mom and me. I've sworn her to not tell a soul. Years ago, she'd have been on the phone with her friends, but she'd pretty much cut herself off from everyone since she got sick." She kept her hands around Gabe's arm. "This is the first person she's wanted to be around, other than me, in a long time. She's gone to bed now, but she'll be thrilled to see him in the morning."

"If you're sure it's okay," began Blair.

Beth tugged on his arm, pulling him toward the door.

Yes, Emma was sure. What she wasn't sure about was why Gabe's return made her insides glow.

Blair resisted Beth's tug. "Emma, I'm not feeling good about leaving you alone with this guy."

Gabe planted himself directly in front of his brother. Their eyes were almost perfectly level, Gabe's just a fraction higher. "I told you I am not here to hurt anyone. I guarantee I would protect Emma and her mother from me or anyone else." His gaze grew more intense. "I'm not used to having my word questioned."

Emma's eyes narrowed. "Guys, I'm right here and don't appreciate you talking about me." She rounded on Blair first. "Did I ask you how you feel about it? Or about anything? I am not your responsibility, and my decisions are my own." Next it was Gabe's turn. "I'm a big girl and have been taking care of myself for a long time. I rely on *my* judgment, and I don't need looking after by anyone."

That warm, fuzzy feeling she'd had about Gabe cooled fast.

CHAPTER 30

Blair drove out of the town of Goodrich, silent in his thoughts.

"Daydreaming?" Beth asked. "Did you miss our turn?"

"I thought I'd go back to Mom's and talk with her."

"Is now a good time? This is all fresh for all of you. Maybe sleep on it for a night."

Blair shook his head. "I need answers now."

"Have you considered that she might not have those answers? Or feel like sharing them with you?"

"She has no choice. This is my life we're talking about."

"And her life. She certainly does have the choice."

Blair's sideways glance at his wife was less than warm. "Whose side are you on?"

"Beth placed her hand on his arm. "I'm with you, of course, but there are no sides. I'm trying to point out how things might be from Robin's perspective."

Blair drove in silence for a few minutes. "What do you think of this guy?"

Beth shrugged. "We've just met him. I don't have much of an opinion. Robin seems to have taken to him, though, and so has Emma. That counts for something."

"Do you think his claim could be legit?"

Beth gave him a look that said, 'you dolt'. "Stand beside him and look in a mirror if you want an answer to that."

More silence, then they pulled into Robin's and Keith's driveway.

The door was unlocked.

Dancing red and orange flames glowed from behind the fireplace screen, the scents of cedar and birch, the hiss and pop of logs releasing their last drops of moisture into the room.

Robin stood at the stove stirring a pot.

Aromas of cinnamon, nutmeg and citrus filled the air.

"Sit down," said Keith. "Robin's making us some hot mulled wine."

Blair spotted the four double-walled glass mugs lined up on a tray on the counter beside the stove. "You knew we'd be back?"

"I raised you, remember? I knew you wouldn't let this go tonight," Robin told him, carefully filling the mugs.

Blair moved to his mom to take the tray from her. "Beth said I should wait until tomorrow to talk to you, but I didn't want to."

"Your wife is probably right, but that's not you, is it? Come on and sit. Ask away."

Once settled around the coffee table, Blair asked, "Do you believe he is who he says he is?"

Keith took hold of his wife's hand but stared into the fireplace. This was her show.

"Yes, son, I do."

"What makes you so sure?"

"I have only to look at the two of you to see that you share genetics. Plus, he looks very much like his father did at that age—as *your* father did. You resemble Bruce as well, but not quite as much as does Gabe."

"You'd go by appearance alone?"

"If that's all I had, yes, I would. But there's more. How would he have had any idea how to find us unless someone told him of some connection?"

"If his mother knew, how come she never contacted us in all of those years?"

"She must have had her reasons."

"If it's true, and she raised her son as an only child, with no other relatives, she denied him of a family."

"That's true," Robin agreed. "But I did the same thing."

That made Blair sit up straighter. "You *knew* I might have a half-sibling out there somewhere?"

"Not for sure. There was always the possibility."

"Give, Mom. I need answers."

Robin leaned forward to pick up her mug from the coffee table, cradling it with both hands.

Keith put an arm around her shoulders, tucking her into his side.

"I only met Bruce's parents twice. The second time, his mom interrogated me when we were doing the dishes."

"Interrogated! Did she not think you were good enough for her son?"

Robin shook her head. "It was obvious she

loved her son, but it was almost like she was not sure Bruce was good enough for me, like she was warning me." She took a sip of her wine, blowing to cool it slightly. "She told me Bruce was not the marrying kind, although they'd like him to settle down."

"That's not exactly evidence."

"True, but I wondered. Bruce was the type who'd never be without a girlfriend for long. He didn't enjoy being alone, living alone. Responsibility was not his thing; he liked being taken care of. And if he ran out on me, there was a good chance he'd do the same to someone else."

"But you didn't know."

"No, I didn't know. I also didn't care to know. I was too busy wrapped up in my life with a new husband and new baby. The time flew by, and then it was years later. You had Ron and me, your cousins, aunts and uncles. It was a full life and over time, it was like Bruce almost didn't exist in my mind."

"Almost?"

"From time to time I'd be reminded of him—mainly through something you did, the way you tilted your chin to the side, the way you walked, every once in a while you'd remind me of your father, your *biological* father, and I'd wonder if

Bruce had fathered any other children along the way, if he'd finally settled down as his parents wished, and started a family that he stuck with."

"Doesn't sound like he did."

"Not that we know of."

CHAPTER 31

Emma chided herself for opening her door to Gabe so readily. No, that wasn't true—she'd still have invited him into her home, but she might not have greeted him with such enthusiasm.

It wasn't like her. She preferred having the upper hand, holding her cards close to her chest until she sized things up. Spontaneity was not for her; planning and executing that plan was more her style.

But when Blair called to ask if he could bring Gabe back to her house, the little girl in her jumped up and down in delight. Fool.

And she hadn't hidden that pleasure when Gabe stepped through her door. In fact, she'd held on to it, as well as his arm, until he and Blair opened their mouths and squared off. Double fool, she.

Men! They'd talked about her as if she wasn't present, Blair threatening Gabe if he hurt Emma, and Gabe defending himself, defending *her*.

As if she needed defending from anyone. She'd been looking after herself for a long time now, herself and her mother. She was capable of making sound decisions on her own about who she did and did not interact with.

Now Gabe stood in the entryway watching her. He'd not taken off his boots, nor set down his duffle bag. "Emma?" he asked.

The heck with it. Where else was the guy going to go at this time of night in Goodrich, without even a vehicle to take him somewhere? Besides, she felt no physical threat from him at all. A tiny part of her brain wondered about threats to her emotional well-being, though. "I was just about to have some Ovaltine," she said. "Want some?"

Gabe's face lit up. "Ovaltine! I thought only my mom and me liked that stuff. Most people have never even heard of it."

"British grandparents. When I was a little girl, my grandma often made it for me. I grew to like it and always keep some on hand now. It's not easy to find in the supermarket, but I order it online."

"My mother's parents were from England and inflicted the Ovaltine habit on her. Mom passed it on to me. There's something about that malty taste…"

"The milk should still be warm. I turned the burner off when I heard you guys arrive."

Out of habit, Emma had left just the light above the stove on, throwing the kitchen into softened shadows. Gabe automatically took the same chair he'd used twice before at the head of the table. Emma sat in her place by his right.

It was strangely intimate, this sharing of a drink in the quiet, mostly darkened house. Emma kept the television and music off once her mother went to bed. Esther slept lightly, and noises could wake her up, bringing her back downstairs. Thank goodness Esther's room was at the back of the house, and she hadn't heard Gabe, Beth and Blair talking in the entryway.

Emma cherished this time alone each evening —no one complaining, no one expecting anything of her. Just a chance to enjoy solitude.

But she wasn't alone. Normally, she would resent the intrusion, but strangely, tonight she did not. It didn't feel like an impingement; it felt… Well, what did it feel like?

The only description she allowed herself was something tepid, like cosy. Yes, nice felt safe; nice didn't require any presumptions, or digging any deeper.

Gabe interrupted her thoughts. "So, I guess I annoyed you at the door there. Sorry. I didn't mean to question your ability to decide for yourself, or to talk as if you weren't there. It's just that Blair gets to me."

"Sibling rivalry?"

"Animosity is more like it." He closed his eyes and let out a sigh. "It was a waste of time coming all this way. We rub each other the wrong way." He gave a sound between a snort and a laugh. "And to think I thought I might find family at the end of this quest, a brother. I found something all right, but not something I want anything to do with."

"I think Blair is one of those people who doesn't react well to change. You've sprung this on him, and he'll need time to process it. He also leapt into protection mode; that's just who he is."

"It ticks me off that he thinks people need protecting from me. Me! I look after people, always have as soon as I was old enough to see past my own nose."

"Something you have in common."

"All we have in common is blood from a man who didn't know the meaning of responsibility."

"Maybe that's why you and Blair act the opposite from your father."

Gabe studied her in the subdued light. "You believe it? You think we're half-brothers?"

"When I first met you, I thought you reminded me of someone, but I didn't know who. Then when I heard your story, it clicked. Seeing you and Blair side by side clinched it."

"He doesn't seem convinced."

"That's Blair. He's slow to warm up to new things."

Gabe's eyes narrowed. "How do you know him so well?"

"It's a small town; we all grew up together. We weren't in the same grade, but that didn't matter. Everyone knows everyone."

"Were you two a thing?"

"Me and Blair?" She laughed. "Never. I don't think he even liked me very much back then." It hurt to think about it, how she was in high school. "I went out with Stan. Being cousins, all those guys hung out together. They played sports together, and I was at all the games."

"Why wouldn't he have liked you? Jealous of Stan."

Now that was funny. "I wasn't the nicest person when I was a teenager."

"Who is?"

"No, I took it to a different level. I had to be at the top or I wasn't happy."

"The top of what?"

"Everything. Marks, but more important was my social status. Being popular and looked up to mattered above all else."

"Why?"

Good question, and at the time she never gave it any thought. She just *had* to achieve. "Maybe no one would have liked me if I wasn't perfect."

"Come here." Without waiting for her consent, Gabe tugged Emma's chair until it was beside his own. He put his arm around her, tucking her head beneath his chin.

They finished their Ovaltine in silence, the good kind of silence.

CHAPTER 32

Morning came early for Gabe. Although he couldn't have ended yesterday in any better way than spending time with Emma, too many thoughts churned around in his brain to allow him to sleep in. Rising as quietly as he could, he made his way downstairs.

He was not the first one up.

"Gabe! Emma didn't tell me you were coming back. Shame on that girl," Esther said.

"Emma didn't know; it was a last-minute change of plan."

"Doesn't matter; I'm delighted to have you." Her smile turned the opposite way. "That girl of mine. She can't plan to save her soul. I don't know what I'm going to do with her. Now I can't even offer you coffee."

"Do you need me to go to the store to buy some coffee grounds or beans, Ma'am?"

"No, we have lots of grounds. Emma is supposed to set up the coffeemaker each evening, so it comes on automatically in the morning. I don't know where her head was last night."

Gabe knew. Exactly where it should be, nestled on his shoulder. "That's my fault, Ma'am. I distracted her with talk. May I start the coffee for you now?"

"Oh, would you, dear?"

"Sure. I bet Emma will want some before she leaves for work."

"She also fills her travel mug and takes it with her."

"What does she like for breakfast?"

"Depends. My Emma doesn't always leave time for a proper breakfast. When she was a little girl, she and my husband never left the house without a decent breakfast in them. The most important meal of the day, you know."

Yeah, he'd heard that, and that a breakfast cereal company had started the slogan. "What do you usually make for her breakfast?"

"Oh, I don't do that anymore. I haven't been

well, you know, and Emma does our cooking now, you see."

Gabe thought he did see. He held out his arm. "Miss Esther, why don't you and I whip up a scrumptious breakfast for your daughter? And us, of course." He led her toward the kitchen. "Tell me what your favorite start-of-the-day meal was to create for your family."

With his encouragement, Esther started the batter for pancakes, while he set bacon strips on a rack to bake in the oven. Good. The woman seemed to remember how to make pancakes. Perhaps she'd done it enough times over the years that muscle memory took over, despite not doing any work in the kitchen for some time. He wondered just how long it had been when Emma assumed the full role of housekeeper, cook, and companion for her mother, on top of holding down a job.

With the bacon crisping nicely, the eggs ready to be cracked into the frying pan, and Esther scooping batter into the pan for her second round of pancakes, Gabe excused himself to let Emma know breakfast was almost ready.

The carpeted stairs concealed the sound of his footsteps. In the upstairs hallway, the bathroom door opened just as he approached. Emma emerged, colliding with Gabe. His arms immediately wrapped around her to steady her, steady them both. Although he should have let go and step back immediately, he did neither. He couldn't. It felt too good. Her hands on his chest. Her head found its place beneath his chin.

His senses filled with the warmth and softness of her body, the floral and citrusy scents of shampoo and body wash, and Emma. He willed himself to not let his hands smooth their way up and down her back. If he didn't move an inch, maybe they could stay this way for a long, long time.

From the kitchen, a voice wafted up. "Gabe? Gabe, what's taking you so long?"

He moved his hands to Emma's upper arms, holding them lightly as he put distance between their bodies. Looking into her face, he said, "I guess I'm being paged. I came up to tell you we've made you breakfast, and it's almost ready."

"Breakfast?"

He grinned. "Yeah, you know that meal you eat first thing in the morning?"

"I mean, *you* made it?"

"Not on my own. Your mother and I shared duties."

"Mom is cooking?"

"She's doing the pancakes. I'm in charge of the eggs and bacon. Why?"

"My mother doesn't cook."

"She told me how she always made a proper breakfast for you and your father."

"That was ages ago. She has done nothing in the kitchen since I moved back home."

Gabe tried to put a good spin on things. "Just shows how much she likes your cooking better than hers."

Emma wrinkled her nose. Her shoulders slumped. "Yeah. Right."

Gabe tucked a damp strand of hair behind Emma's ear, the tendril silky to his touch. Rather than pull his hand back, he let it hover there, his left hand now mirroring the right, his palms easing their way to cradle her neck, his thumbs brushing softly up and down her cheeks. Soft skin, ever so soft.

Mesmerized, he stared into her eyes, captivated by the scent, the feel, and the essence of this woman. His gaze traveled from her wide ocean blue eyes, lower, settling on her lips.

Those lips parted slightly, and Emma sucked in a little breath.

Slowly, ever so slowly, he leaned down, bringing their mouths only a fraction apart. His eyes flicked back to hers. Did she want this, want it as badly as he did?

For an answer, Emma's eyes drifted shut, and she pressed closer to him ever so slightly. But it was enough.

He touched his lips to hers, just a butterfly kiss, soft pressure and a gentle glide.

She didn't pull away.

He did it again, this time settling his lips more firmly on hers, the touch less hesitant, more reverent, more sensual.

She kissed him back—hesitant at first, tasting, then more sure of herself, sure this was what she wanted. Her hands crept up.

He *knew* this was what *he* wanted; had wanted for far longer than he'd imagined. Maybe this was why he had come on this quest—finding this woman and not a long-lost brother.

Emma's hands rose from his chest up, making little circles as they rested on his shoulders, exploring, taking in the sensations, the textures, the feel of the stubble on his cheeks, playing with the hair at the back of his neck.

Gabe shivered. Lifting his head slightly, his eyes roved over the face so near to his. Her satiny skin now had a faint pinkish hue. Her eyelashes cast shadows beneath her closed eyes. Had God ever created a more lovely woman?

He placed a kiss on each eyelid, then returned to the lips still turned up to his.

"Gabe? Gabriel! What is taking you so long?" The words floated up, words refusing to be ignored.

They heard footsteps from downstairs along the kitchen floor, then the downstairs hallway.

Emma leaned into his hands just slightly, then those lids he'd just kissed flew open, and she jerked back. Her eyes widened, her mouth opened and shut, but no words came out. Her hands went to her face, covering it all but slits for her eyes and she made to dodge around Gabe.

He grasped her shoulders. "What is it, Emma? What's wrong?"

"Let go of me."

"First, tell me what's happened? Are you hurt?"

"You saw me!"

What? "Ah, yeah, I see you." What was the problem? Sure, she wasn't dressed, at least not in daytime clothing. But for a fluffy lilac dressing gown, which fully covered her from neck to calves, with pajama legs peeking out from underneath.

Gabe tried prying her fingers away from her face, but she was having none of it. "Is something wrong with your face?" he asked.

She nodded from behind her hands.

"What's happened?" She seemed fine a few seconds ago. "Emma, tell me, please."

"I don't have any makeup on."

"So?"

"You saw me without makeup!"

He felt like a broken record. "So?"

"No one sees me without makeup!"

This time, when she broke away, he let her. He watched Emma race the few steps to her bedroom. The door shut behind her with a muted snick, cutting off all communication between them.

CHAPTER 33

Breakfast was an awkward affair, despite the decent food. Although the first batch of pancakes was slightly overdone, Esther found her stride, and excelled with the rest.

Gabe's over easy eggs were not his best effort. Somehow, his mind refused to focus on the task at hand, drifting constantly to what had happened in the upstairs hallway, cataloguing every taste, every sensation, memorizing them as if they had to last.

Now Emma refused to meet his eyes.

She'd come downstairs almost a full ten minutes later.

"That girl," groused Esther while they waited.

"She dawdles so in the morning, taking forever to get ready. I tell her to set out the clothes she'll wear the night before, have everything organized. That's what I made her do when she was a little girl, but now, well, I can't tell her what to do." She looked at Gabe to make sure he was in on this conspiracy. "*No* one tells Emma what to do. She might appear to listen, but she goes her own way no matter what."

Gabe longed to say something, to get back on the same wavelength as Emma, to hold on to that closeness they'd shared. It had been shared, hadn't it? He'd thought so at the time, thought she was as into it as he was, but had he misread the situation? Was that why she wouldn't look at him now, only responding to his attempts at conversation with monosyllables? Did she regret what they'd done?

She was certainly trying to get away from him. Emma stood before she'd done more than drag her fork around her plate, cutting food into tiny pieces, shuffling things about, very little making it anywhere near her mouth.

Gabe knew. He watched that same mouth that captivated him upstairs. Now, those soft lips pulled into a straight line as Esther gave her daughter a list of things to pick up for her, admonishing her not to be so forgetful the way she was yesterday.

Emma stood, taking her plate and cutlery to the counter. Opening the cupboard door beneath the sink, she scraped the contents of her plate into the trash can. Turning on the water, she started to rinse her plate, but Gabe was there.

He took the plate from her, their hands brushing slightly. "I've got that. I'll clean up the kitchen; I know you have to get to work."

For the first time in ever so long, she raised her eyes to his. What he saw there made him take a step back. Regret. Sadness. Not one shred of the joy he felt every time he went over their encounter.

"Emma," he tried. Of its own volition, one hand rose to touch the smooth, shiny hair.

Her head wrenched back away from his touch.

Gabe flattened himself against the kitchen counter, giving her the space she seemed to need.

What had he done? This woman had opened her home to him, a stranger, and been nothing but kind. How had he repaid her? By making her uncomfortable in her own home. By making her pull away from him, but how could she escape when he'd invaded her space, the sanctity of the house she shared with her mother? He had to reassure her, let her know he'd get out of her hair, out of her life, anything to wipe away that look on her face.

Emma turned and left the room, her footsteps going upstairs. A minute later, she was back down, a heavy satchel slung over one shoulder, weighing it down.

"Here, let me carry that for you." Gabe hurried forward.

"It's fine. I've got it."

Esther stood in the doorway. "She's constantly toting that thing around. I tell her it's bad for her posture, but does she listen?" Shaking her head, Esther headed back into the kitchen, aiming for the coffeepot.

"At least let me put that in your car for you," Gabe tried.

"I've *got* it, I said."

"Emma...."

"I have to get to school." Then the door shut, and she was gone.

On autopilot, Gabe cleaned up the kitchen. From the living room came sounds of a morning talk show on the television. Emptying, then refilling the dishwasher gave him plenty of time to think, plenty of time to regret his actions, to rue how badly he'd read the situation.

Well, he couldn't stay here. Even if it meant walking to Alpaca Haven to retrieve his truck, anything was better than causing harm to Emma.

Harm. Is this what Blair had worried about? His brother warned him about not hurting anyone and wasn't that just what he'd done? And to the last person in this world he ever wanted to hurt.

On the far edge of the counter sat a tall travel mug. He'd watched Emma set it there as she added milk from the fridge, then filling the container with coffee. Esther had said that Emma took it to school with her every day. But she'd left without it.

Knowing it was futile, Gabe picked it up, and strode to the front door, checking out the sidelight window on the off chance that Emma and her car still sat in the driveway. But she was gone, long gone.

CHAPTER 34

Emma's persona changed. The minute she stepped out of her car in the staff parking lot, her shoulders straightened. Entering the doors of the school, her lips curved upward, masking any signs of her inner conflict. She became the consummate professional, the dedicated teacher her students loved.

As far back as she could remember, they had taught her to do her best, to *be* her best. Always. People liked her when she performed and perform she could. As a small child, her parents brought her out to sing, dance or recite whenever company came over.

Her mother had even run her around to beauty pageants. *That* would have continued, but

Harold didn't like his wife being away so much; he hated having to feed himself.

Knowing what her mother expected of her, Emma had turned on the tears about abandoning any future pageants. When alone in her room, though, she took out her actual feelings, the ones she'd learned to hide so well.

In truth, those pageants terrified her. People tugging and pulling at her hair, coiling it into stiff curls, then filling the air around her head with stinky sprays until her hairdo felt like some stranger's head plunked on her shoulders.

The makeup going on was one thing; the rubbing and scraping to get it off quite another. She made enough fuss that her mother eventually gave her the cotton pads and remover to do it herself. Only once had the young Emma been too tired to remove all the gunk from her face before bed. She woke up to a pillowcase smeared with all manner of stuff, and a lecture from her mother she could still recite to this day.

From it all, she gained some skills useful to this day; Emma could read a crowd. Upon entering a room, she could size up who was in charge, who were the important people to know, to impress. Who was low in the pecking order and not worth bothering her time with.

Still, it was exhausting, always being on.

Only within her classroom did Emma relax. Yes, she was "on" for her kids; performing was part of teaching, as was reading how you were coming across to the children and adjusting accordingly. But with her students, it didn't feel forced.

She wasn't faking it when she showed an interest in each child. And the miracle of teaching was that the kids responded to her. They didn't seem to care what she looked like, or if she ever made a mistake.

That mistake thing had been hard to handle early in her career. The teacher was the leader in the room, always on display, always in control. But no matter how meticulously she prepared, glitches happened. Or the lesson she believed would be flawless fell flat. She accidentally erased some work from the board. She made a spelling mistake in front of all the kids. She got the day of the week wrong.

In her second year of teaching, she had a Grade 3 student she remembered well. Monica was anxious. Who knew small children could suffer from anxiety? Monica did, and Emma'd since learned that this afflicted many other students.

Part of Monica's anxiety centered on a fear of failure. Terrified of getting something wrong, she'd erase and erase her work, rubbing so hard that she'd often worn the paper so thin it tore. Then *that* caused her even more anxiety, until she was a sobbing puddle under her desk, or frozen rigid with fear.

One thing that helped was Monica observing Emma making mistakes. This was so hard to do; it wreaked havoc with Emma's image of the perfect teacher. Yet, perfectionism was doing in little Monica, and for the child's sake, Emma would try.

She could laugh about it now, but back then, she carefully orchestrated her mistakes. As a performer, she knew the value of rehearsing, considering any contingencies and being prepared. She needed her choreographed mistake to get the point across, yet be nothing that would harm the kids, nor harm her own image of herself. That last bit was challenging.

She learned to say, "oops", and laugh at herself. Good thing her mother could not see her. Once wasn't enough for Monica to get the point. Emma needed to show over and over that she could commit an error, without the sky falling, she could even correct the mishap, and carry on as if nothing untoward occurred.

An interesting thing happened. As she got more comfortable with not being perfect, Monica's anxiety lessened—not a lot, but enough to help the little girl function in the classroom. The other thing that happened affected other students. They became better risk-takers, not holding back thoughts and ideas, more willing to try something new, to try out multiple tactics to reach a goal. The kids learned, and Emma learned from them.

It was way harder to apply that lesson at home, though.

CHAPTER 35

Gabe had pretty much assured Blair that he'd gnaw off his arm before hurting Emma, even got in his face about it. Yet, what had he done? Not even 10 hours later, he had hurt Emma. She had certainly not left the house that morning a happy camper, and it was all because of him.

He still was not sure how he'd gotten things so wrong. What felt to him like some of the best moments of his life was most definitely not the way it affected Emma. He stopped in place, reliving that kiss—how she felt pressed up against him, how her soft lips moved against his, the way her fingers twirled the hair at the nape of his neck. At the time, it seemed like they were both into it, yet he had read the situation all wrong. She'd not even been able to look him in the eye afterwards. And what was that about makeup?

He sighed. He needed to get out of here before she got home from school. The least he could do was not make her any more uncomfortable in her own home.

But first, he had some things to do.

Gabe entered the living room, hesitant to interrupt Esther's TV show, but this wasn't something he could figure out on his own, especially with a woman he'd interpreted so wrong. "Miss Esther, what do you usually make for supper?"

"Oh, I don't do that any longer. Emma does the cooking."

He already guessed that. "What does she like to eat?"

"Whatever's fast and easy, from what I can see. When I prepared the meals for this family, we had a schedule. If it was Tuesday, you knew we were having pork chops. Friday was fish, of course. We had a nice, predictable pattern."

"A routine is a good thing," Gabe agreed. "But what would Emma like if you or someone else prepared the meal?"

"Goodness, how would I know? That girl

seems to eat without thinking. I swear, her mind is a million miles away sometimes." When Gabe didn't move, she asked, "Why do you want to know?"

"Emma works hard, and I thought we'd give her a break by making supper for her tonight."

Esther eyed the man in front of her, having caught the 'we'. "There is lots of meat in the freezer in the basement. At least, there should be if Emma kept up with the grocery shopping. Have a look if you want." Picking up the remote, she raised the volume on her show.

Taking that as permission to rummage, Gabe went down the basement stairs. The old chest freezer was easy to find. Lifting the lid, he saw rows of neatly stacked and carefully labeled containers. Ah, Emma's fall-back stashes for those days where she didn't have the time or the energy to cook a meal from scratch.

Well, today she could rest easy and have it all done for her. Rummaging, he found a package of back ribs. Those would do. Before shutting the freezer, he dug around for a second package. Might as well cook in bulk so Emma could freeze the leftovers for another day.

He'd make the ribs two ways—Greek, with lemon potatoes, and BBQ-style with mac and cheese. Comfort foods, both of them. Although he'd grumbled about having to do kitchen duty as a child, now he was grateful to his mother for making him work by her side. More had sunken in that probably Norma Jean ever knew, and now cooking soothed him. Creating good food and sharing it with friends was not a bad thing.

Friends. Is that what he and Emma were? Had it only been yesterday since they'd met? It seemed both only moments ago, and long enough to form a connection, one he wanted to explore, to see how far it might go.

Nowhere was where it was going. One-sided interest would never work.

The least he could do was have inviting aromas simmering in the kitchen when she got home from school.

He got to work.

~

Gabe was upstairs stuffing the last of his belongings into his duffle bag when there was a knock on the front door.

Esther called out, "Who is it?"

The door opened and Robin popped her head in. "Morning, Esther. Is Gabe around?"

Gabe descended the stairs, his bag slung over his shoulder.

Robin looked him up and down. “Isn’t this where we came in last night?”

“True,” Gabe admitted. It was kind of ironic.

“Are you ready?” Robin asked.

“Ready for…?”

“To come to the hardware store for boots. Hurry up. Keith’s waiting in the truck for us.”

Boots. He’d forgotten. That would mean he could return these borrowed ones. Then, would it be too much of an imposition to ask Keith to drive him out to Alpaca Haven to get his truck? That would beat walking or hitchhiking.

Then he could get out of here.

CHAPTER 36

"Have you eaten?" Robin asked as soon as they settled in Keith's truck.

"Yes. Esther and I made breakfast."

Robin and Keith shared a look. "Esther?"

"Yeah, why?"

"You must be a positive influence on her," Robin told him. "I didn't have the impression she did much around the house anymore."

"It sounds like Emma endures the responsibilities, but I asked Esther to help, and she did."

Keith spoke for the first time. "If only life was as simple as that."

Purchasing winter boots at the hardware store didn't take long. There was one style for women and one for men; the only issue was finding the right size.

While Keith rummaged around in the storage room, Gabe wandered the store. One section near the picture window held a display rack with a mini version of the sign posted above the door to Alpaca Haven. Here was a small sampling of items Becca sold in her store on the farm. Gabe picked up a carved wooden airplane, marveling at how smoothly the propeller spun with just the touch of his finger.

"If you go through the doorway at the back on your left, there's another room with crafts. A lot of them are Blair's," Becca told him. "Either Dad or Stan made the metal pieces."

Gabe hadn't spent nearly enough time browsing before Keith was back with two sizes of boots to try on.

Pack boots felt different from what he was used to. Keith assured him they should be a bit snug at first, then the felt would mold to his foot and flatten slightly. Gabe got it; cowboy boots took some breaking in as well. "Can I keep them on now?" he asked before tugging off the price tag. "That way, I can return these to Esther and Emma. They were Harold's, and I need to bring them back."

Gabe's attention shifted to the back of the store when a door opened.

"Leave them here," Robin told him. "If I take them to her, that will give me a reason to visit Esther. She's alone too much these days."

"Who's alone too much?" asked Becca as she hung her coat on a hook in the hallway.

"Esther Lowry."

"Ah. I'd go stir crazy sitting in the house all day like that."

No one said what they were thinking.

"You know..." Robin's voice trailed off.

"What?" Keith asked.

"I wonder if Esther would be interested in putting in some hours working for us here? As it is, we rarely get to take a lunch break because there's no one to cover the store."

Another change. Keith was not a fan. "Don't know how you'd pry her out of that house. Besides, she wouldn't know how to run the cash register."

"She's worked in retail before," argued Robin. "Besides, *you* learned how to handle this payment system so anyone could." She kissed his cheek to let him know she was teasing.

"That would probably help Emma." The words

were out of Gabe's mouth before he thought about them.

The other three looked at him, Robin with her head to the side. "True," she said, still looking at him.

Gabe shuffled his feet. "Look, I hate to ask this, but is there any chance I could get a ride to Alpaca Haven to pick up my truck?"

"Keith, aren't you making a delivery to the Emmerson's out past our place, anyway?" Robin asked.

"Yes, but it's not loaded yet."

"May I give you a hand with that, sir?" Gabe asked.

Twenty minutes later, Keith came back into the store. "All loaded. Are you staying here or coming with us, Robin?"

"You guys go ahead," said Becca. "I've got this for now, and Mona will be here shortly."

Keith signaled his turn as they approached Alpaca Haven.

Gabe leaned forward. "Sir, how far away is the place where you need to deliver this order? Should I come with you and give you a hand unloading?"

"Glen's away at his job during the day, isn't he?" Robin asked. That would leave Keith to unload and stack the material on his own.

"Yeah." Keith looked at Gabe in the rearview mirror. "I never turn down the offer of help with manual labor."

It was almost 45 minutes later that they neared Alpaca Haven again. While Gabe had forgotten about his tire problem, Keith hadn't. "Why don't you check on your tire size, then we can have a coffee at our place while we phone around to see who has tires for your truck?"

Used to being a take-charge guy, Gabe tried not to pace as Robin made coffee, and Keith phoned around about winter tires. It was hard to stand back and let someone else arrange *his* things. But so much about his life had felt out of control this past month.

Keith set down his phone. "You're in luck, young man. Glen has a set of tires in stock that will work on your truck."

"That's great, sir. Can you give me directions on how to get to his shop?"

"No need. Glen's on his way here now. I told him you can't drive your truck in these conditions, so he's bringing the tires out and will change them in the parking lot for you."

Gabe winced. It was one thing to swap out tires with a truck up on a hoist, but something else entirely to use a jack to change all four tires. "I'd better go give him a hand."

"Sit down, Gabe," said Robin. "Glen will handle it. If he couldn't, he wouldn't have said so."

Nothing was easy on his ego since arriving in Goodrich County.

CHAPTER 37

"Cool your jets, son," Keith told him. "This is what Glen does. He'll charge you a bit extra for a house visit, but not much. Enjoy some of Robin's coffee while you wait—it's especially good with Clarabelle's cream."

"Who's Clarabelle?" Gabe had met so many people since arriving in Goodrich County that he'd likely forgotten a name or two.

"That's my cow," said Robin. "My one and only cow."

"Thank heavens, according to Blair," added Keith.

Gabe looked between the older couple.

Robin explained. "We always kept cattle; they were what Ron loved most about farming. When he died, I clung to that herd. It reminded me of my husband and our life together. Blair came back home and dutifully looked after them."

Gabe sipped his coffee, then held the mug away from his face, studying it. "This really *is* good." He sampled the drink again just to make sure his taste buds hadn't exaggerated. "Sorry to interrupt." He really wanted to hear the rest of this story—any little tidbit to learn more about his half-brother.

"Blair did the cattle thing without question. My bad. I hadn't realized how much he disliked the work, not until recently. Blair being Blair, he carried on for my sake."

Interesting. Good to know that about his brother.

"Blair's not a whiner," added Keith. "He does what has to be done."

"But he should have whined, or at least been honest with me earlier on. I think it took Beth's encouragement for Blair to admit to me how much he didn't enjoy tending to our herd."

"He doesn't enjoy farming?" Gabe asked. It wasn't something you could force on a person; you either loved it or you didn't.

"Farming he loves, just not when cattle are involved. He much prefers the crop-growing side of agriculture."

We all had to do things we didn't like; that was part of life. And sometimes the things we enjoyed had downsides that had to simply be gotten through. "He grew crops to feed the cattle?" Gabe asked.

"Yes, but raising cattle is an up and down business. We have no control over prices, and sometimes the farm would have made more money by selling the grain we grew rather than putting it through the animals. Ron knew that; to him it was part of the acceptable losses and over the years, he hoped it would all even out."

"Did it?"

"I don't think my husband wanted to look too closely at that. He'd suffer any losses because he liked having the cattle around. Animals were a big part of his life and his identity; it was what he did and his father before him."

"And Blair?" Gabe wanted—no, needed, to know about his newly found sibling.

"Blair tolerated his work looking after the herd for my sake. Only in the last year have we been honest with each other about it. To me, seeing the animals in the field reminded me of my life with Ron, the way things had always been. I had some difficulty letting go of that, even though I no longer did the physical work. I was mired in the past and my son humored me. To Blair, the cows were an onerous chore, taking time away from things he'd rather be doing. It took time for me to let go of what once was, and for Blair to come clean with how he felt."

"What did he do then?"

"He gradually decreased the size of our herd, not buying new animals when he took some to the auction. He sold the bulls, no more breeding heifers. They all went to market when the time was right."

Gabe understood waiting for the decent market prices before shipping off any cattle. A guy could lose his shirt, otherwise. Margins were tight enough in farming that you needed to pay attention to every marketing decision. "And now?" he asked.

"This spring he'll plow up the pastureland and seed it to wheat, corn and soybeans. He's a happy camper about that. No more pulling all-nighters during a blizzard, checking on calving heifers. He's out of cattle, except for Clarabelle."

"Clarabelle?"

"She's my Jersey cow, the best cream producer

you'll ever come across." The ring of Robin's phone interrupted any further explanation. Glancing at the display, she answered the machine. "Hi, son." She listened. "Yes, he's right here." She smiled at Gabe. She got a knowing look at Blair's next words. "Certainly. We're at home here having coffee. Come right over."

Gabe debated if Blair was coming to learn more about his half-brother, or to protect his mother from anything Gabe might do; the latter, he suspected.

It was like Robin read his thoughts. She patted his hand. "Don't mind Blair. Like Keith, he's averse to anything new."

"Hey!" This from Keith.

"Oh, you know it's true. Blair is cautious by nature; he takes a while to warm up to people. He takes his role of son seriously and protects those he loves."

"That's a good trait. I was that way with my mom, too. Heaven help anyone who did her ill." Including himself. It was so easy for his mind to go to all the things, the little things, he could have done over the years to make her life easier but had never gotten around to. He'd thought they had more time....

Blair hadn't smiled once since entering his

mother's house. The only time his lips curved even slightly up was when he sank his teeth into a piece of the warm gingerbread cake his mom served them.

Even though his mother and Keith seemed relaxed around this guy, Blair reserved judgment. He still had questions that needed answers. "Tell me how you found us," he ordered Gabe.

"I'll show you. I got a letter from my grandmother. *Our* grandmother, I guess." He stood up. "It's in my duffle bag in the truck. I'll go get it so you can read it."

When the door shut behind Gabe, Blair turned to his mother. "You believe him, don't you?"

"Yes, son. I have only to look at him and at you to see the connection."

Keith was a natural skeptic. Blair turned to his stepfather. "What do you think?"

"The resemblance between you two is hard to deny, and if Robin says you both look like this Bruce character, who am I to doubt it? But maybe we'll have more evidence with this letter."

Setting his duffle bag in the entryway, Gabe dug through it. The envelope had seen better days; scrunched between layers of clothes in a soft-sided duffle hadn't helped. Withdrawing the letter from the envelope, he smoothed it out against his thigh before passing it to Robin. He stood out of the way, making room for Blair to sit on the couch beside his mother.

Robin began to read out loud.

CHAPTER 38

Dear Gabriel,

You don't know me and shame on me for that. I am your grandmother.

I don't know if Norma Jean would have allowed us to meet in person, but I took that choice out of her hands. I was abiding by the wishes of my husband and son, although both are now long dead.

Somehow, it's hard to keep a secret.

And that's what you were to me, and I to you—a secret.

Please allow me to explain. This will not put me or any side of my family in a good light.

I don't know how much of this your mother has told you; I suspect very little. That was partly at my request.

Your father's name was Bruce. He was my son, our only child. As much as his father and I loved him, I cannot say I was always proud of him and the choices he made.

Not like you, Gabriel. Norma Jean did a fine job raising you. She was justifiably proud, as am I of you.

I have followed you from afar. You were not to know this, but I was at all of your graduations, and many of your games throughout your teen years.

But I digress. You don't want to know about an invisible old woman. You might have some interest in your father, though.

Bruce, a handsome fellow, had charm and he knew how to use it. He had the gift of language and used that, as well. People wanted to be around him, to do things for him.

His father and I doted on him. Perhaps too much. As he grew older, those ways we thought were so cute took on a more calculated tone.

This does not speak well of your father's character, but the people who raised him shaped that character. That blame falls on our feet.

We spoiled him. We wanted more children, but he was all that came to us, so we lavished all our attention on him. And our hopes and dreams.

The latter was our downfall.

Bruce never became the man we'd hoped. What disappointed me most was my son's inability to take responsibility for his actions.

That's on us. Growing up, Bruce had an easy ride, with his father or I bailing him out of scrapes. At the time, we thought we were helping him, protecting him. Only in hindsight did I see the harm we created.

Mothers may be more intuitive than fathers, or maybe it was more in my nature than in Bill's to admit what was in front of my nose. Nevertheless, Bill clung to the belief that Bruce just needed a little more growing up time. That was at his most realistic; the rest of the time, my Bill sided with Bruce, agreeing that our son had had a string of bad luck. Someone was out to get him, or something unfair happened.

It was never Bruce's fault, you see. Again, that is something he got from his father and me, although I swear to you that was never our intention. We loved our child; maybe too much.

Forgive an old woman for wandering off topic.

You don't want excuses from me—you want facts.

Bruce was with your mother. We met her. Bill was cautious, doubting any woman would ever be good enough for our son. By then I'd known better. Your mother seemed like a lovely young lady, but I feared our son was not good enough for her.

Are you shocked? That's a terrible thing for any mother to think, let alone say out loud.

Your mother became with child. I worried Bruce might not do the right thing and stand by Norma Jean. You see, this had happened before.

I'll get to that part later. For now, what interests you will be your life with your mother.

Your mama was a proud girl. When I offered her money, she would not cash the check. That was fine, as long as Bruce lived up to his responsibilities.

He didn't. As much as it pains me to admit this, he ran.

Over time, your mother and I came to an agreement. If my boy would not provide child support, then I would on his behalf. After all, I was the one who allowed an irresponsible boy to become a man unaccountable for his actions.

I apologize to you for that. The only good thing to come of my errors is that

Norma Jean took them to heart and made sure you never developed such traits.

You inherited Bruce's looks, but not his temperament.

As your mother reared you all on her own, I helped when I could—a little here and there, but never enough, and always hidden in the shadows out of shame.

My son and husband forbade that I have anything to do with you or your mother. It pains me to say that I went behind their backs. I also didn't openly defy them, but kept it shrouded in secrecy. That hurt them, me, your mother, and you. It tells you something about me that even after Bruce's, then Bill's, deaths, I still kept myself hidden from you. Yet another of my shames.

Now that I am alone and ill health keeps me confined to the house most days, I have little to do with my time, but think. And regret.

I missed so much of your life, Gabriel. Things could have been different if I had been more courageous.

You had a fine life with Norma Jean, just the two of you.

But now you are alone. Please accept my condolences on the passing of your mother. She was truly an admirable woman.

She raised you to be responsible and independent. I know you will be fine. But, if by chance you seek some company from a blood relation, and you can find it in your heart to forgive me, or at least speak to me, my door is always open to you.

I know that is a big ask.

Since like you, I am all alone in this world now, I feel for you.

You should know that apart from me, you have other family.

You see, Norma Jean was not the first woman Bruce got with child, then deserted. Sadly, there may be more half-siblings out there somewhere, but this one I know about, or at least knew about.

Not long before Bruce took up with Norma Jean, he had another girlfriend. I met her briefly, and we would have welcomed her as a daughter-in-law if things had progressed that far.

She and Bruce met one summer while he worked on an internship program while at college. It was many years ago, so I don't recall what he did; your father went through many jobs during his life. All I remember was that it was in Goodrich County up north. The girl's name was Robin. She was young, fresh out of high school, getting her first taste of the city.

Only later did Bruce mention they'd broken up. I don't think he ever meant to tell us, but he let it slip that she was pregnant. When I expressed concern, Bruce said it was fine. She'd go back home to her parents, and they'd take care of her, that they'd never liked him, anyway.

I heap shame upon shame in this letter, but you need to hear the truth. I saved bits from my housekeeping money until I had enough to hire a private detective. He traced this Robin and told me she was married and had a son.

I left it at that. From the age of the boy, I knew he must be the child Bruce and Robin had conceived. But she was married now, so I left it at that. What right did I have to interfere in her new life? I burned the report from the detective so my husband would never find out what I'd done.

I know I have no right to ask you to forgive me. The only legacy I can give to you is the knowledge that you have a half-brother if you should choose to seek him out.

Family matters, despite the example I have set.

Please know that you are now and have always been in my heart.

Your grandmother,
Gabriella Ottski

CHAPTER 39

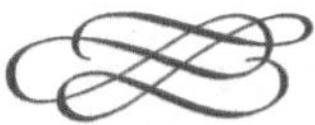

Silence.

In Gabe's mind, the words 'don't anyone move, and no one will get hurt' rolled over and over.

Too late. People had been hurt. So many. These people in front of him. Emma.

Even in these tense moments in someone else's living room, his thoughts wafted to Emma. For someone he'd only met a day ago, how could she occupy so much of his mind? Why did it feel like she should be here with him at this, and all the critical moments in his life? It made no sense that such a new friendship should be his fulcrum. Yet it was. She was.

Movement broke into his thoughts.

Keith pulled his wife to her feet, wrapping his arms around her. "Robin girl, are you all right?" Robin nodded against his shoulder.

That stirred Blair from his reverie. "Mom?"

"I'm fine, son. It's just a bit of a shock to hear Gabriella's side of things."

Now Gabe had second thoughts. And third and fourth. What right did he have to barge into these people's lives, their settled lives, with everything just fine in their world?

He had meant them no harm, just like he'd had no intentions to hurt Emma. Yet he had. With all of them, he'd allowed his own selfish desires to come before their well-being. He tucked away thoughts of Emma to examine another time, a private time.

Three sets of eyes studied him. These were nice people, good people, and here he was dredging up old memories best forgotten. Old wounds when there was no reason to relive those past hurts.

"I'm sorry," he started. But how did you take back something like this? He turned to Blair. "I should never have come. Please accept my apologies for disturbing your lives. I'll be on my way...."

"Have you seen her?" Robin met Gabe's gaze directly.

"Who?"

"Your grandmother."

"No."

"Why not?"

Why? Was there a good reason he should want to see someone who kept in the shadows all of his life? Virtually spied on him. "There hasn't been time."

"Are you going to?"

Good question. "I… I don't know."

Robin turned to her son. "And you? Are you going to go see her?"

"Mom!" Blair ran his hands over his face. "This is all new to me. I've only just heard about this woman who claims to be a grandmother." He glanced at Gabe. "Our grandmother."

"There is no 'claim' about it," said Robin. "She is. Although I suppose the three of you could take DNA tests if you wanted proof."

Gabe and Blair looked at each other.

"Where does Gabriella live?" Robin asked Gabe.

"San Antonio. That's where Mom's house is as well. Was, I mean." He'd sold it just before coming here on this quest.

"Do you know where in San Antonio?"

"There's an address on the envelope." He paused. He'd better admit the rest. "I looked her up in the phone book and the listing there is the same as on the return address."

"So, you were planning to meet her?"

He had not gotten that far in his thoughts. "Maybe. I don't know."

"You need to." There was no doubt in Robin's mind. She turned to her son. "As do you."

"Mom..."

She glared at Blair. "I didn't say you have to invite her to Thanksgiving dinner and phone her every Sunday. But she is your grandmother, and you should meet her. You owe it both to her and to yourself."

More silence.

Blair looked at his half-brother, partly united by who knew what. He opened his mouth to speak.

Gabe's cell phone's ringer cut through the tense air. He ignored it.

"Aren't you going to get that?" Robin asked. "It could be important. Esther is quite taken with you. If she can't reach Emma, she might try you."

Emma. She had his number. He pulled his phone from his pocket. No, not Emma or

Esther. The area code was for San Antonio. Their grandmother? No, oh no, he wasn't up to this.

"Well? Who is it?" Robin wasn't letting this go. A part of Gabe pitied Blair. Growing up, it would have been hard to get anything past this woman.

"I don't recognize the number, but it's a San Antonio area code."

"For heaven's sake, answer it. It might be your grandmother."

Gabe's eyes flashed to Blair's. Was he up for this? No, definitely not.

Blair's nod seemed to encourage him.

Taking a step away and half turning from the group, Gabe brought the phone to his ear. "Hello?" He listened. "Yes, this is he." He only made a few more comments until near the end. "Okay, I'll be there. It's a two-day drive from here, but I'll call your office as soon as I get to the city."

He ended the call and blew out a breath. He needed a minute to gather himself before speaking to the others.

His brother was not a patient man. "Well? Does this have anything to do with us?"

Gabe faced the man who looked so much like himself. "That was a lawyer in San Antonio.

Gabriella Ottski's lawyer. The one in charge of her estate."

"Estate?" Keith asked.

"Yes. She passed away three days ago. Her cleaning lady found her. The lawyer had some trouble tracking me down but got my cell number from my boss."

The other three just watched him.

"I have to go." Gabe moved toward the door and his new boots. "The lawyer says I have been named executor of the estate."

CHAPTER 40

Kiss on the first date? No way, not something she did.

It's not like she done much in the way of dating lately. Or kissing.

Until today.

And oh, man, had she kissed. Emma's face reddened just thinking about how she'd responded when Gabe's lips touched hers. He'd given her plenty of chances to back away, but retreating had been nowhere on her radar. All she'd felt was want, the burning need to get closer to this man, to learn his feel, his taste.

She'd not even been on a date with the guy. This was *so* not like her.

Emma had a few precious minutes to herself,

something that happened rarely to a Grade 1 teacher during the school day. It was recess, and the kids were outside burning off energy. Usually, Emma went out with them, even when it was not her turn at supervision. You learned a lot about students by observing them at play.

Play. It was not only children who played. What possessed her to start a snowball fight with Gabe? She smirked, remembering the look on his face when the first cold, wet mass hit him. That Texan boy hadn't known what hit him. He recovered, rather faster than Emma'd expected, and the game was on.

She smiled. When had she last had fun like that? When had she *ever* had that kind of fun? It had been spontaneous—Emma didn't do impulsive. She thought through every move; strategy was important to get you where you wanted to be. Somehow, with Gabe, she forgot all that.

Her smile faded. She'd washed his face in snow—all fun until he'd turned the tables. A little cold, a little wet. Why should that matter?

But it did, oh, but it did it ever. How could she have forgotten?

She'd carried right on, teaching him how to create snow angels, as if she hadn't a care in the world, as if her face wasn't streaked with rivulets of mascara and blotchy makeup, letting all her skin imperfections show through.

Back in the house, when she checked in the mirror, a garish clown face stared back at her. How disgusting. It's a wonder Gabe hadn't run off down the street screaming.

Yet he'd stayed. Well, not exactly stayed, but he'd come back with Blair and Beth.

Thank goodness she'd scrubbed her face and repaired her makeup by then. Of course, she had; her mother would never let her hear the end of it if she'd paraded around their house without looking her best.

Her best. This morning she had *so* not looked her best. Fresh from her shower, who knew she'd encounter Gabe in the upstairs hallway? Who knew she'd barrel into him, and he'd catch her? Who knew what his arms around her would feel like?

She knew. Or if she didn't know, she'd imagined, but the reality far surpassed anything in her dreams.

She covered her face with her hands. How had she let it happen, let herself get carried away like that? He'd seen her—the bare Emma. Nothing to hide any blemishes, nothing to even out her skin tone, nothing to enhance her eyes. Just her.

But he'd kissed her anyway, and oh, had he kissed her. Tenderly, reverently. She was the one who'd kissed harder, upping the intensity. She couldn't help herself; it just happened.

Thank goodness for her mother's voice. That broke the spell, plummeting Emma back to earth, back to the reality of where she was and how she looked. She wanted nothing more than to impress this man, yet she'd stood in front of him with a naked face and wet, snarled hair.

Way to go, Em.

The bell rang.

Emma pushed back from her desk and rose to her feet, her smile in place. Perfectly composed, perfectly made up, ready to greet her students.

Blair was on his feet. "Where's your truck?" he asked Gabe.

"In the parking lot of Alpaca Haven."

"I'll drive you there."

The two men rode the short distance in silence, a massive silence burdened with too many thoughts.

"You think you blew it, don't you?" Blair finally asked.

Gabe just looked at him. Wasn't it obvious?

"You couldn't have known she was going to die."

"She was old; isn't that what happens to old people?" He didn't like the way that came out but couldn't think of a better way to phrase it.

"You were doing what she wanted you to do."

"She?" What was Blair talking about?

"Your grandmother. *Our* grandmother. She wanted you to find me."

"And now she'll never know."

Blair pulled up beside the only pickup truck in the parking lot and shut off his engine. Tire tracks and footprints around the vehicle, as well as the four tires tossed into the truck bed proved that Glen had done his job.

"Wait! I haven't paid that guy for my new tires."

"Don't worry about it. I'll take care of it."

Gabe just looked at him. That might be something a brother would say, or even a buddy, but they were strangers.

"It's no big deal. You can pay me back if you feel you need to later."

Later. Would there be a later for them? Yeah,

there would be, at least to pay this debt, and maybe that would lead to more. "What's your cell number? Text me the amount and I can transfer the money to you."

How was he going to say this? He hardly knew this guy. "Uh," Gabe said, "There's one more thing."

Blair waited.

This was awkward. "It's about Emma."

Beside him, Blair tensed. "Is something wrong? I warned you…."

"No, she's fine." At least, he thought she was. "She's been… nice to me." How lame that sounded. "I should thank her, but she's at school. I need to get on the road, so I can't wait until she's finished work. Would you, um…."

"Thank her for you? Yeah, I can do that." Blair waited. "There's more, isn't there?"

"No. Yes."

"Well, that's clear."

"I mean no, there isn't more, but…." He let the rest hang in the air.

"I get it. You'd like there to be."

"Maybe," Gabe admitted. "But…" Why couldn't he seem to put together full sentences?

"Don't worry. You'll be back."

How could Blair know that? He colored

slightly and swallowed. "Tell her thanks for everything and I'm sorry for having to rush off."

Before things got any more embarrassing, Gabe got out of the truck, opening the back door to retrieve his duffle bag. What to say to this guy, this stranger who was somehow connected to him? "Thanks" seemed inadequate, but it was a start.

Blair made it easier. "Don't mention it, man." He turned the key in his ignition. "Keep in touch and stay out of snowbanks." With a wave, he left.

CHAPTER 41

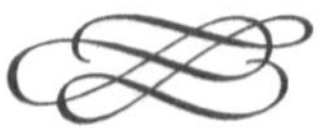

Sitting in the cab of his pickup, the cold invaded Gabe's bones. How did people get used to these winters? Could he?

The needle on the dashboard hadn't budged past that 'C' marking, telling him the engine oil wasn't yet warm enough to properly lubricate the engine. He may not have been born in these parts, but the mechanic in him knew enough to let the truck idle until that needle moved to the right, at least somewhat.

He replayed his last conversation with Blair in his mind. Cringeworthy, at least the parts about Emma had been. What a way to get off on the wrong foot with a newfound brother.

Emma. He needed to talk to her, to explain. To

apologize. He'd planned to leave her house anyway, to save her from any further awkwardness his presence caused. But he would have liked to explain, to figure out what changed her from what he'd thought was a willing recipient in his arms, to a woman frantic to get away from him.

She deserved more than a houseguest sneaking off into the night. It wasn't exactly night now, but he was still scuttling off without first making amends.

There was no way he could phone her while she was teaching. He recoiled from the thought of passing on a message through Esther. Who knew how his words would be delivered? And, right now, Esther liked him; how would she feel if she learned he'd kissed her daughter and made her flee?

He pulled out his phone. Impersonal, but a text message would have to do.

He set his phone on the dashboard. Once he'd been dumped by a text. Not that it had mattered; he wasn't that into her and obviously she felt the same way. No hearts were involved on either side.

But this with Emma? Yeah, it felt like his heart was involved. Impossible. He'd only just met the woman. Sure, they'd shared some nice moments, but that was all they were. Right?

Of all the people he'd met on this trip, some related by blood, why did the idea of not seeing Emma again impact him the most? He'd come all this way to find a half-brother. He'd done it, but also found a woman he could not shake loose from his mind.

He needed to, though. He had to get to San Antonio to take care of things for a grandmother he'd never known. A tiny part of his brain nudged him, asking why didn't he stay in Goodrich a while longer, to see where this thing with Emma might go? Maybe if Emma encouraged him rather than running away, he might have considered it. No, that wasn't true. As much as he might want to, duty called. His mother would have wanted him to do right by Gabriella.

He picked up his phone again.

Emma, it's me, Gabe. I've had some news and I have to leave.
Thank you for your hospitality, yours and Esther's. I appreciate you opening your home to me.
Thank you also for rescuing me, for the loan of your father's boots, and for playing with me.

No. That didn't come out right. His thumb deleted the last phrase.

I enjoyed getting to know you and would have liked to spend more time with you.

There. That sounded better. Not so needy. Emma had been privy to his family's personal information so far; she deserved an explanation for his hasty departure.

I got a phone call. It was from a lawyer in San Antonio. My grandmother died. I'm executor of her estate, if you can believe that. I never even met her! I am on my way there now. Don't know how long it will take to wrap things up.

How to end this? He didn't want to sound sappy, but he wanted to leave the door open to see to her again. He didn't just want to; he *needed* to.

May I call you sometime?
Gabe

There. The ball was in her court. If she wanted nothing to do with him, she could ignore the text. Or maybe she'd reply, but with a polite 'it's been nice knowing you' message. Anyway, he'd tried.

The gauge needle was now about one-quarter of the way to the right. Good enough. He put the pickup in gear and backed out of his parking spot. In his rearview mirror he watched the hand-carved sign above Alpaca Haven's door disappear, maybe for the last time.

CHAPTER 42

Emma was so sick of hearing how much Esther missed Gabe. It was Gabe this and Gabe that. You'd think a finer man had never crossed their entryway.

Maybe that last bit was true.

There was no reasoning with her mother that Gabe had only been with them for a day. There was no reasoning with herself about that either.

He'd said he'd call, or at least that's what his text had said. So why hadn't he? It had been over a week.

Blair had stopped by, telling her that Gabe had asked him to thank her for letting him stay with her and Esther. Maybe that was in lieu of a phone call—send his brother to do it for him, to end things.

End what? In a day, how could you start something?

She was so not an insta-love kind of gal. Not even an infatuation-type woman. Nope, everything she did was planned methodically, designed to achieve a goal.

With Gabe, she had no goal. He'd simply burst into her life, nudging a place in her heart. In her head, she meant. Her head. That's why she couldn't stop thinking about him.

It's the empathy part of you, she told herself. She felt for Gabe's tragic story. He'd lost his only parent, along with his belief that it had been just the two of them in this world. The shock of learning he might have a half-brother was layered on top of the grief of his mother's death. Then the possibility of a grandmother, only to find out she'd died, too.

Yes, that's why the man stuck in her mind. It was his story that got to her, not the man himself.

Still, why didn't he call?

~

And here he'd thought cleaning out his mother's house had been tough. Norma Jean tried to sort through things earlier on in her illness, but soon her deteriorating health sapped too much of her energy. Only now did Gabe appreciate the extent of her efforts.

Norma Jean's tiny house had been orderly compared to what he was in the midst of now.

Upon entering the old lady's home, he was immediately struck by the overwhelming amount of objects and possessions that filled every nook and cranny, making it difficult to even take a step without bumping into something. The space was so cluttered with the detritus of a lifetime that he couldn't begin to fathom how to approach the daunting task of cleaning it up. Gabrielle resided in the home she'd shared with her husband and son for almost 60 years. That's a lot of time to accumulate stuff. He could not think of a kinder word for it than stuff.

A quick walk-through of the house felt like snooping—a voyeur in someone else's life. What was he supposed to do with the place? The instructions in the will were to sell it, but he couldn't sell a home chock full of the debris of someone else's life.

An overwhelming task, he started in the office that was once the haven of Bill Ottski. He'd been gone a long time, Gabrielle only gradually encroaching on what had been her husband's domain. It seemed she layered her things on top of Bill's without removing anything he might have stored there.

On the lawyer's advice, Gabe concentrated on anything legal or financial he might unearth. And financial things he did find. Check books dating back thirty years, along with bank statements, the two carefully reconciled. Bill Ottski kept track of his money. A call to the lawyer assured Gabe that it was safe to chuck any financial information more than seven years old. Soon he filled one trash bag, then a second.

The filing cabinet housed manuals. Every appliance, large or small, the couple ever purchased had its manual in a labeled file folder. Those were too heavy for plastic bags, so Gabe stocked up on cardboard boxes. He ordered a rush on a dumpster; it arrived a day later, had been filled and emptied already.

Each day, as he worked his way through the house, Gabe became less picky. Calling around, he found that the Salvation Army would come pick up items. The clothes were a no-brainer.

Volunteers came and cleared out closets and dressers of Gabrielle's,.Bill's and Bruce's clothing.

When the teenager Bruce left home, it looked like his room had been left as is. Curious about the man who was his father, Gabe resolved to spend more time in that bedroom, but later. He needed to get this house ready to sell.

One volunteer, his arms full of clothes still on their hangers, asked Gabe what he planned to do with the furniture. Good question. He hadn't gotten that far yet.

The first night he'd camped out on a sofa. The crick in his neck the next morning told him he was too old for such things. Stripping a bed in what he thought was a spare room, he ran the sheets and covers through the washing machine and dryer, replacing everything except for the dust. He hated to think about when the bedding had last been washed. At least it was a better place to sleep.

Things in the kitchen looked none too clean either, so Gabe scrubbed and washed at least enough to give himself a place to cook and eat without fear of catching some unknown disease. He suspected Gabrielle had struggled to look after herself for some time, despite having a twice weekly visit from a housekeeper. From the amount of accumulated dust and grime, he doubted his grandmother had been getting her money's worth from the cleaning service.

He was beat, and the day wasn't even half over. This wasn't the most physically taxing work he'd done, not by far. But at least ranching took him outside. Even the agricultural mechanic's work he did was usually done wherever the machine had broken down. Needing a break, but not up for cooking, Gabe ordered in a pizza.

As usual, whenever he had down time and let his thoughts roam, they went in search of Emma. He'd done what he could. There was no point in clinging to a woman he'd just met, one who fled from his embrace, one who didn't respond to his texts. Yet his fingers longed to send her another message. How pathetic was that?

He sat on the sofa, cradling a fresh cup of caffeine, and put his feet up on the coffee table. He wondered if his grandmother would have objected, but didn't care. He just settled comfortably when the doorbell rang. That was fast.

He grabbed his wallet to give the pizza delivery guy a tip and opened the front door.

It couldn't be! "What are *you* doing here?"

CHAPTER 43

Handling new cattle was always tricky. Stressed animals lost their brains; not literally, but they sure acted like it. Cut off from the herd they'd known, moved to a new location with unfamiliar sights and smells, feeding off the fear from other animals—it all added up danger to both the critters and the people handling them.

Buying cattle at auction, you never knew where they came from or their medical history. Stan, Greg, and their father, Jim, had lost too many animals and too much money to risk introducing unknown cattle into their existing herd without first administering antibiotics to the newcomers.

It took time, as well as a great deal of effort. Normally, they only brought in new cows in small batches, but at this morning's auction, such fine groups of steers and heifers presented that they couldn't resist.

Now they had 40 scared young animals to process. That meant all hands on deck, so Stan, Greg, Greg's wife Aggie, as well as their parents Jim and Phoebe, helped unload cattle, herd them toward the squeeze gate, inspect and inoculate each one, before letting them loose in the quarantine holding pen.

Nothing they hadn't done a hundred times before, just not so many at once.

Spring meant muck. Melting snow and fresh rains churned pastures and fields into quagmires, especially when the cloven hooves of dozens of cattle dug in, making the ground treacherous for both man and beast.

Most cows were agile creatures, at least relatively. The same goes for those people who work on farms. They know the risks, how to guess at unpredictable animal behavior, and ways to stay safe.

That's when all goes well.

They'd been at it for hours, skipped lunch, and were bone-weary from wrestling ornery cows, and trying to keep their footing in the sludgy ground. Only half a dozen more animals to process, then they were done.

Aggie might not work the cattle daily, but she'd grown up on a farm and helped whenever needed. She knew cows.

Next to guide through the chute was a bull. Bulls were costly creatures. They had bulls on the farm, but at six years, their favorite was losing his potency. An impulse buy, Greg bid on a young bull, only nine months old, but looked to have good potential. Today's nasty weather worked in his favor, and there were fewer than usual people at the auction, making it easier to win the bid.

A healthy, sturdy bull could breed cows after his first birthday, and Greg had high hopes for this one. He cost more than they'd ever paid for a bull, but farming was a risk. For breeding and bulls, size mattered and the equipment on this animal was impressive, as was his solid frame that would only expand over the next years. For now, he was a solid chunk of muscle. Angry muscle, ready to take his changed circumstances out on whoever was nearby.

Charging down the ramp of the truck, the bull attempted his getaway. His feet slid out from under him, but he caught himself before he hit the ground. Enraged, he turned his attention to the obstacles, yelling and waving arms in his direction. Someone was between him and freedom.

That someone was Aggie.

He lunged toward her. Always aware of her surroundings, Aggie dodged out of the way, Greg barreling toward her. The bull corrected course faster than any human ever could. His left hind leg shot out, catching Aggie in the chest. Down she went, removing the bull's access to the wide-open field.

"Aggie," Greg screamed. Kneeling, he knew to ignore his instincts to gather his wife in his arms before he'd assessed her injuries. "Aggie, are you okay? Where do you hurt?"

Jim was there now, too. He recognized the spasming of the diaphragm when someone had the wind knocked out of them. Removing his grimy glove and brushing Aggie's hair from her forehead, he said, "Easy, there, girl. Just give it a second and you'll be able to breathe again. Easy." His eyes roved over the young woman, but it was hard to determine if she'd been seriously hurt or not, bundled as she was in her bulky jacket.

Aggie closed her eyes, willing herself to relax. She'd fallen out of trees, off horses, the normal rough and tumble stuff any farm kid knew and lived through.

But this, this felt different.

She opened her eyes in response to her husband's frantic pleas. She tried a smile to reassure him. A trickle of something warm came out the side of her mouth.

"Mom!" Greg hollered.

"Phoebe, go get the Suburban," ordered Jim. "Put it in 4x4 and the heater on full blast. Back up here as close as you can get. Bring some towels and blankets." To Stan, he said, "Grab some plywood from the shed. Something big enough to brace Aggie with."

Greg swiped the red from Aggie's mouth. "Don't try to talk. We'll get you to the hospital right away. You'll be fine."

Aggie nodded. She knew she would, just maybe, not right away. She'd close her eyes and rest for just a minute.

Then Phoebe was back with the large SUV, and Stan came running with the plywood. As gently as they could, the four of them slid Aggie onto the wood, then lifted her into the back of the vehicle. Greg and Jim climbed into the back with Aggie, and Phoebe drove them through the mud and out of the pasture, avoiding the worst of the bumps and potholes. Stan, his phone to his ear, called the hospital to tell them what little he knew about the extent of Aggie's injuries and their estimated time of arrival at the emergency department.

Aggie's eyelids fluttered open. "The kids," she said.

CHAPTER 44

"Becca!" Stan's voice was on the phone, but a tone Becca'd never heard.

"Stan, what is it?"

"Aggie's been hurt."

"How is she? Do you need me to come?"

"Greg, Mom and Dad are taking her to the hospital. She got kicked by a bull; we don't know how she is."

"Is she conscious?"

Stan nodded before remembering his wife couldn't see him. "She was. But as they're driving, she said something about the kids. Mom remembered that school will be out soon, and that Alvin and Alice will come home on the bus to an empty house."

"That won't happen. I'll call the school and have them keep the kids there until I can come for them." She checked her watch. Fifteen minutes until school let out for the afternoon. The odds of her getting from Alpaca Haven to the school in that amount of time were slim. Better not risk it. "Tell Phoebe I'll take care of the kids."

Scrolling through her contacts, Becca found Emma's cell phone number. As Alvin's teacher, Emma would know what to do. She pressed the number for the call, but it went to voicemail. Drats. Emma had her phone turned off while she taught, of course.

Beth, then. Oh, but this was Thursday, when Beth worked at the school in another town.

Doing a quick internet search, Becca found the number for the school. "Hello, this is Becca Feldman-Wells. I have an emergency affecting Alvin and Alice Wells. I have to get a message to Alvin's teacher, Emma Lowry. She needs to call me at this number right now. And don't let Alvin and Alice get on the school bus."

Emma frowned at the knock on her classroom door. This was the part of the day both she and her students looked forward to, when she read aloud to them. The kids were so into Rudyard

Kipling's *Rikki-Nikki-Tavi*. The knock broke the spell.

This school honored what took place in the classroom, minimizing disruptions, so if someone was at her door, it was important. Emma motioned to Ezra to come to her desk; as the most accomplished reader in the class, he could carry on while she went to the door.

With a quick glance around her room to make sure everything looked orderly, Emma stepped into the hallway, leaving the door partly open to keep an eye on her kids. In front of her stood the secretary with a note.

"Sorry to interrupt, Emma, but the caller said it was urgent. Becca said to call her right away."

Becca? Had something happened to Gabe? He'd been heading out toward Alpaca Haven. But why would he have Becca contact *her*? Didn't matter the reason, she needed to return this call. "Would you mind staying with my class just for a few minutes while I find out what's going on?"

The two women entered the classroom. Emma pulled her phone from its spot in her purse in the bottom drawer of her desk. "I'll only be a minute."

She returned to the hallway. "Becca, it's Emma. What's going on?"

"It's Aggie. She's injured, and they've taken her to the hospital. There will be no one at home if the kids get on the bus. Can you keep Alvin and Alice at school with you until I come for them?"

"Of course." As she spoke, Emma headed down the hallway to the pre-K room where Alice would be with her class. "What do you want me to say to the kids?"

"Good question. I hadn't thought about that."

They both knew how Alvin reacted to unexpected events.

"Leave it with me," Emma said. "I'll figure something out." This is what she did, excelled at—adapt and plan.

Then she thought of something else. "Why don't I take the kids home with me? Mom would love it, and she'll make a big fuss over them. Alvin trusts me, so it will be okay."

"Would you?" Becca let out a sigh. "In that case, I'll run out and give Stan a hand. They were inoculating a new herd of cattle when Aggie got injured. Now he's trying to handle it by himself. I worry that it's dangerous to be on his own."

"Certainly. You go. I've got this." She had another thought. "I'll give Beth a call; maybe she can stop by here on her way home from Shipley School."

Checking her watch, Emma realized she had little time. A whispered conversation with the pre-K teacher ensured that Alice would play in the room until Emma and Alvin came for her. Then she called Beth.

Unlike classroom teachers, Beth had a private phone line in her office. Thankfully, she was there and picked up.

"Hi Beth, this is Emma Lowry. Look, something's happened. They were unloading cattle at the farm when Aggie got hurt. Greg, Phoebe and Jim are taking her to the hospital. Stan's still at the farm and Becca's going to help him. They're worried about the kids, though. I'll take them home with me."

"Oh, thank you so much, Emma. That helps a lot. I'd have Blair pick them up, but he's gone to San Antonio to help Gabe."

Oh. That was news.

"It'll be after 5:00 before I can get to your house. Is that okay?"

"That's fine. We'll feed the kids."

"Would it help if I sent Friday and Randine to help with Alvin and Alice?"

Yes, it would. Alvin gravitated to the older girls, especially to Friday; the two of them bonded. The more around him that was familiar, the less upset Alvin would be. Still, how to explain this to him? "That would be great if the girls could come. Good idea. For now, do you think it's all right if I just tell Alvin and Alice that their parents had to go to Watford and that you'll pick them up later?"

"Excellent idea. I'll hang up now and text Friday. She checks her phone messages as soon as the bell rings."

"Just in case, I'll have a message sent to their classrooms telling both girls to come to my room instead of getting on the bus."

Ending the call, Emma looked at the time on her phone. She only had a little over five minutes before the last bell rang. She needed to prepare Alvin; changes to his routine did not sit well with him.

A strategy she'd learned in college emphasized visuals; autistic kids often took in information that they saw far easier than that which they heard. Over her years in the classroom, she'd found that the same thing held true for many students, not just those on the autism spectrum. So, using visuals became part of her routine.

Grabbing a piece of paper, she quickly drew grids, using stick figures to sketch out what was going to happen, in comic book fashion. It didn't matter that she was not artistic; as long as she explained what the drawing represented, kids went along with it.

She showed Alvin standing by her as the rest of his classmates exited the classroom. Next, she and Alvin walked together to the pre-K room to collect a smiling Alice, then Friday and Randine joined them. The five of them buckled themselves into Emma's car. She hoped Alvin wouldn't freak out about the lack of child car seats, but they'd cross that worry if it happened. In the following grid, a stick figure represented an older lady labeled 'Ms. Lowry's mom'. The next box had the word Candy Land printed in it. She'd have to remember to get the game from the back cupboard in her classroom and take it home with them. At home, she'd have to draw another story depicting Beth coming to pick up the kids and take them home with her and the older girls.

She made another quick call. "Mom, I'm bringing home company—Greg and Aggie Wells' kids Alvin and Alice. Could you take some brownies out of the freezer, please?" That meant her mother would see all the containers of frozen leftovers Emma had collected, but that couldn't be helped. "Oh, and a loaf of bread, too. We'll make grilled cheese sandwiches for supper."

With only a minute before the bell would ring, Emma made her way to Alvin's desk, kneeling down, so she was at eye level with the child. "Alvin, there's a change to your routine...."

CHAPTER 45

"That's a fine way to greet your only brother," said a bleary-eyed Blair, with a grin so like that of the man standing in front of him. That is, if the other man smiled.

"What are you doing here?" Gabe asked. This made no sense. "How did you get here?"

"I flew, then took an Uber."

"How did you know where I was?"

"Ah, I can read, dummy. You left that envelope and letter on Mom's coffee table. The return address was right there." He fished it out of his pocket. "I brought the letter to you in case you wanted it. You left so fast, you forgot it."

Gabe took the letter but didn't move.

"Are you going to stand there blocking the door, or do I get to come in?"

"Ah, sorry. You surprised me."

A car pulled to the curb in front of the house.

Turning to watch it, Blair asked, "You expecting more company?"

"No. I ordered pizza for lunch, and that must be the delivery guy."

A fellow carrying two flat boxes approached them.

Blair got a whiff. "I'm starved. The stuff they served on the plane was cardboard disguised as panini."

Gabe used his credit card on the payment machine.

Inside the house, the savory aroma of baked dough and melted cheese wafted through the air, making Blair's mouth water. Without thinking, he leaned over to sniff the top of the pizza box, his nose tingling at the sharp and pungent scent of anchovies. He snatched the box from Gabe's hands, lifting the lid to reveal the salty, oily fish piled high on top of the bubbling cheese. "Anchovies!" he exclaimed, his eyes lighting up.

Gabe grinned at Blair's enthusiasm. "Yeah, sorry about that. I thought I was eating alone."

Blair shook his head, his expression turning to

one of longing. "No, man. I love them, but never get to have them. No one else likes them. The girls say they're gross."

"They are, sort of, but the good kind of gross."

Blair hesitated, his gaze flickering between the coffee table and the kitchen table. "Coffee table or kitchen table?"

Gabe led them toward the cozy living room, where the flickering light of a muted basketball game on the television vied with the dust motes coming in from the windows to illuminate the space. He plunked down the other pizza box, settling into the soft cushions of the couch. "Let's do the coffee table. I'll get us some plates and paper towels," he offered, rising to his feet and heading to the kitchen.

They talked little until there were only a few slices left in each box.

"That hit the spot," Blair said. He looked around the room overfilled with knickknacks, doilies, and older-style furniture not ancient enough to be classed as antiques." What have you been up to?"

Gabe groaned and sank lower onto the couch. "You wouldn't believe it. I don't think Gabriella ever threw one thing out." He described how he'd started in the office and what he discovered and didn't discover there. "I had their clothes taken away; that happened yesterday. Even though our grandfather and father died years ago, our grandmother kept their things just the way they were."

"What's next?"

"Beats me. I don't really know how to tackle this mess. I thought I'd root around in Bruce's room, see what I could learn about the guy who sired us."

"Let's go, then."

The two men stood in the bedroom's doorway, their eyes scanning the outdated decor that adorned the space. The room seemed frozen in time, as if it hadn't been touched since its inhabitant was a teenager or a college student in a frat house. An array of posters and pennants of various sports teams and rock bands hung haphazardly on the walls, the vibrant colors and bold designs now faded and peeling at the edges. Trophies and framed photographs lined the shelves, each one representing a memory or achievement from the past. Old furniture cluttered the room, including a worn-out leather armchair, a rusty metal desk, and a squeaky twin bed.

Together, the brothers moved to the framed

photographs. Whereas the pictures downstairs portrayed the baby Bruce to the young man, these were photos chosen by Bruce himself. Pictures of him and his buddies at the lake, in softball uniforms, roasting marshmallows around a campfire. And girls, lots of girls, many with Bruce's arm wrapped casually around their shoulders, sometimes a girl on each man. And in all of them, that same cocky look.

"Yeah, he was quite the guy," Gabe observed.

"Kind of glad I didn't know him."

"True. Although there must have been something good about him; our mothers weren't fools, so there was some appealing part of him."

"Surface only," said Blair. "The man had no sticking power."

Gabe nodded. "Not a guy I'd be proud to have in my life."

They opened desk drawers and pulled boxes from the closet over the next few hours.

Gabe sat back on his heels. "Come across anything you want to keep?"

"Not one thing."

"Do you think your mother would want anything? Maybe a picture of him?"

"I doubt it, but I'll ask her. Do you have any trash bags?"

"I bought a case of them."

"I noticed the dumpster out front. What do you say we chuck everything in this room?"

"I'm all for that."

They'd made good progress when Blair's phone rang. He reached for it on the desk where he'd set it.

Gabe watched as his brother's expression changed from grim stoicism to one of pure joy when he saw the number of who was calling.

"Beth!" Blair spoke into the phone.

"I'll leave and give you some privacy," Gabe said.

"No need," Blair told him. To Beth, he said, "Gabe and I are cleaning out what used to be our father's bedroom, although I use the term 'father' loosely." He listened.

Gabe felt the difference in the air and turned to see what was going on.

Blair tensed, then stood. "How is she? Where is she?" He listened. "How'd it happen?"

Gabe only caught the odd word from the bit of Beth's voice he could hear. Something was obviously wrong, very wrong.

"I'll get the first flight I can and be home. Thank Emma for me, and we'll keep the kids at our place. Love you." He punched off his phone.

Tilting his head back, Blair stood with his eyes closed.

"What? Are your girls okay? Beth?"

Blair shook his head. "No, they're fine. It's Aggie, Greg's wife. You haven't met them yet; Greg is Stan's older brother."

"What's wrong with Aggie?" And Emma. "You mentioned Emma. Is she all right?"

"Yeah, she's fine. She helped us out by looking after Greg's and Aggie's kids until Beth got there to pick them up."

That rang a bell. Gabe remembered Emma saying one kid in her class was Stan's nephew.

"What happened to Aggie?" Then Gabe remembered himself. Who was he but almost a stranger to these people? Maybe this was personal and none of his business.

"Beth said Aggie got kicked by a bull."

Ouch. Gabe well knew the damage that could do to a body.

"Is she going to be all right?"

"They think so. Beth said the doctor's words were 'cautiously optimistic.'"

"Geez."

"They bought 40 cattle at the auction and were unloading and inoculating them when this new bull tried to make a run for it, and Aggie was in his way."

"Did the cattle get out?"

"No, Stan stayed at the farm, and Becca went out to help him."

Blair picked up his phone again and brought up the internet browser. "I gotta get home. I need a plane ticket."

"Make that two tickets. I'm going with you."

CHAPTER 46

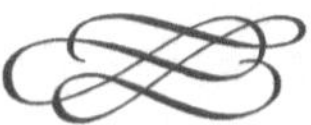

While he and Blair waited at the gate at the airport, Gabe watched for a moment when no passengers cued at the flight attendant's desk. He approached to check on the possibility of upgrading their tickets. Two big guys with shoulders that barely fit in the coach class seats would be far more comfortable in the more spacious area near the front of the plane.

He was in luck. There were a few business class seats not yet sold. And they were at a reduced price since this was last minute. Fishing out his credit card, Gabe paid.

The money was worth it. He worked hard and saved, not owning a lot except for his pickup.

He'd just sold his mother's house, and he was her sole heir. If this wasn't a time to spend some money, he didn't know what was. This was a family matter.

Family.

Apparently he had a family now, a brother who'd come to help him with their grandmother's house, and now a half-cousin needing help with a cattle herd. Well, Gabe knew cattle, and he knew machinery. He could make himself useful to these people.

Returning to the plastic chair where Blair waited, Gabe flashed their new boarding passes. "For once, things are looking up for us. They had a couple of unsold seats in business class going for cheap, so I snagged them."

Blair's look was not one of gratitude. "Showing off, little brother?"

"What? No. It didn't cost much to upgrade. Besides, I just sold Mom's house and what am I going to do with the money? There's nothing I need. But it sounds like there's a lot of work to be done when we hit Goodrich, so it'll help if we arrive rested and with a decent meal in us, rather than being squashed in steerage."

Blair regarded him, unsure how to take this. Finally, he nodded, and took his boarding pass.

Thank goodness for the buffer zone between their seats. If they'd had to sit rubbing shoulders for the whole plane ride, Gabe would have wrenched that cell phone from Blair's hands and lobbed it down the aisle. The man would not stop playing with it, checking his texts and emails over and over, despite having no internet connection while in the air. Yeah, the guy was concerned about Aggie, but sheesh, no amount of wishing would get him information before they touched down. Give it a rest, man.

Who said men can't multi-task? As soon as they landed Blair stood in the aisle of the plane and pulled his case from the overhead bin while checking his messages at the same time. Sitting in the front of the plane, they got off first and strode through the parking lot to Blair's pickup in no time.

Checking his phone while standing, or even walking, was one thing. But while driving? No way; Gabe drew the line there.

He snatched the phone from Blair's hands. "Give me that. You drive and I'll check your messages. I'll read you anything that comes in. Your family doesn't need *you* getting wrecked up in an accident."

"Yeah, you're right. My password is 1204."

"Are those random numbers, or do they mean something?"

"That's when we got married."

"Dude! You do know how lame that is, don't you? Anyone could guess a password like that."

Blair shrugged. "Only someone who knew us, and they'd probably use it to call me to say they found my phone."

Gabe shook his head.

Aggie would be okay—not right away, not even in a short while, but eventually. So far, what they'd learned is that she had a small pneumothorax, small enough not to warrant invasive procedures, just observation and oxygen. With any luck, the air would be reabsorbed, and the lung returned to normal within a few weeks.

The blood that so terrified Greg was caused by a pulmonary contusion that would resolve itself.

Of more concern was the diagnosis of flail chest. Could that be as gross as it sounded? While Blair drove, Gabe used the phone to search the internet to find out what the heck it meant.

Flail chest happens when three or more ribs are fractured in at least two places, hence Aggie's pulmonary contusion. Of greater concern was how the flail chest affected her breathing.

In a text from Greg, he described the horror of watching the sides of his wife's chest move in differing directions, while listening to her short, shallow pants, both things attributed to flail chest. IV fluids, supplemental oxygen, pain medication and splinting helped.

Now she rested more comfortably under sedation, but that didn't alleviate Greg's guilt. "Blair, she could have been killed! Just a little more force, and that kick could have damaged her heart. A little lower and he'd have caught her gut, injuring all sorts of organs. Man, I should never have had her out there. It's dangerous, we all know that. How could I have taken a chance with my wife's life?"

Since his phone was on speaker, Blair went ahead, saying anything that came to mind, anything that might alleviate his cousin's pain just a little. "You did what we've all done thousands of times before, what *Aggie's* done before. You didn't *make* her do anything. You and I both know Aggie better than that; no one can make her do anything she doesn't want to do. And did you even ask her to help you this afternoon?"

Greg described the auction, the shipment of cattle, and how they'd set things up to process the animals.

"The only thing that would have stopped Aggie from being involved was if the kids had been home. But they were in school, so of course she'd dive in to help. Wasn't Mom there as well? Accidents happen; we all know the risk. But Aggie's going to be right ticked with you if she thinks you're beating yourself up about this. That's not what she needs from you now."

CHAPTER 47

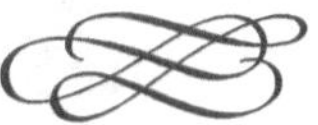

Now that they were getting closer to Goodrich, the logistics took over. "Can you drop me at a hotel?" Gabe asked Blair.

"In Goodrich? You've got to be kidding. Like there is any such thing."

"What's the closest place that has one?"

"Watford. But I thought you were coming here to help. How are you going to get from Watford to the farm every day? You don't even have wheels."

"Guess I wasn't thinking. I should have driven."

"And you'd still be on the road for two more

days. If you meant it about helping, we need you here now."

Returning to Emma's was the first thought to Gabe's mind. Oh, how he'd love to be near her, but that was out of the question, considering how things were between them. She'd never even responded to his text.

"I'd say you should stay with us," said Blair, "But Alvin and Alice are here for the night. Tomorrow, Aunt Phoebe will stay at their place with them, so our spare room will be free. For tonight, you can sleep at Mom's and Keith's."

It was taken out of his hands, like so much of his life lately. He used to think of himself as a methodical guy, weighing options, and choosing the best course. Now his life felt caught in a whirlwind of something beyond his control.

It didn't help that Robin welcomed him with a hug. Keith shook his hand, thanking him for pitching in to help the family. As if there was a choice.

To make it worse, Keith loaned him his pickup while he was here; that he'd hitch a ride with Robin.

"But what about your deliveries?" Gabe asked.

"On those days, you'll take Robin's car, and I'll use the pickup."

They were arranging his life around him. Suck it up, he told himself. It was only temporary, but necessary if he was going to be of any use to these people.

Well, he was back. Back in Robin's and Keith's house, where he'd parked his things, but never stayed the night. He would, now. For how long, he had no idea. Gabriella's house could wait; these people needed his help now.

Placing his winter boots in the entryway closet, Gabe noticed the borrowed ones he'd worn before, the ones belonging to Emma's dad. Straightening them with his hand, he turned to Robin.

"Right, those," said Robin. "I said I'd return them to Emma, but I haven't had time yet." She gave Gabe a look he couldn't interpret. "Now that you're back, why don't you take them to her?"

Great. Just who Emma would want to see—the guy she tried to get away from, the guy whose text she ignored. "I'm, uh, I might be kind of busy this next while, helping out at the farm."

"It's not like Harold's waiting for the things," muttered Keith.

Robin shot her husband a mock glare. "Keith's right; there's no hurry. I'm sure Emma will be glad to see you any time."

Right. Like *that* could be true. Well, he could drop them and go, only bothering her for a minute. Or, he could time things so that Emma would be in school, and he'd leave them with Esther. Yeah, that would be best for everyone.

Now to get to work. "I appreciate the loan of your truck, sir," Gabe said to Keith. "Could I bother you for directions to get to the Wells' farm?"

"No need," Robin told him. "We're coming with you."

"Robin's been cooking all afternoon, making meal packages for Phoebe and Jim, and for Greg's family," Keith explained.

"They'll be exhausted and won't want to fuss in the kitchen. Phoebe says Greg is spending the night at the hospital, but she and Jim are on their way home."

Dressed in what he'd usually wear around the ranch at his workplace in Texas, Gabe ignored his cowboy boots, reaching for his new winter ones instead. Helping Keith pack frozen containers of food into boxes, he carried them to the back seat of the pickup, then climbed in.

Robin motioned for him to get out of the vehicle. "Sit up front with Keith. It'll be easier to see where you're going, so you know the route for next time."

"If you're sure, ma'am."

It was dark when they arrived. The time of day didn't matter when there was farm work to be done. After carrying the boxes into the house where Becca was checking on a roast chicken in the oven, Gabe left Robin and Keith there while he followed the sound of a heavy machinery engine.

Behind the barn, he found Stan revving a tractor similar to the one he'd used to pull Gabe's truck from the snowbank. But this one was a little older, a little more banged up.

Stan shoved the gears into neutral and park when he saw Gabe approaching.

"What can I do to help?" Gabe yelled.

"Ever run one of these?"

"Yeah, often."

"Okay. I need three bales from over there moved into that pasture." He pointed to the south. "I'm a bit late feeding them today, as you can tell by the bellowing. The herd will follow you. They're not that bright about getting out of the way, so you'll need to watch for them. I have to grind some feed, then I'll bring it to the pasture and meet you there." Stan climbed out of the cab, and headed for a machine shed.

As Gabe climbed onto the tractor, leaving the biting wind and stinging snow behind, the crunch of the icy ground beneath his boots rang in his ears. So this passed for spring around here?

He quickly familiarized himself with the machine's layout, his fingers navigating the knobs, buttons, and levers, feeling the rough textures and contours of each control under his touch. Despite the darkness and the swirling snow, Gabe's senses were heightened as he scanned the landscape for any signs of movement. The black Angus cows were difficult to spot in the gloomy surroundings, their dark forms blending into the grayish snow, mixed with the muck on the ground. Maneuvering, Gabe managed to position two bales in place, and by then Stan had the auger churning away, the chopped grain pouring into the self-feeder. The cattle's annoyed bellows changed to contented munching. Despite the sad reason he was here, Gabe felt a sense of satisfaction and accomplishment as he tended to the animals' needs, his body and mind fully engaged in the moment. This was work he loved.

By the time they were finished with the

feeding, a set of headlights turned into the lane and stopped by the house.

After cooling down their tractors, Gabe and Stan climbed out. “Come on,” Stan said. “My parents got home. Let’s find out how Aggie is and grab something to eat.”

CHAPTER 48

"Oh, my!" Phoebe Wells stared at Gabe, her hands on her cheeks. "Robin, he looks just like his father."

Both women regarded him like some kind of specimen.

Gabe squirmed. Since no one here, or likely anywhere, had fond memories of his birth father, he tried not to take offense at the comparison.

"Mom! He just got finished feeding our cattle. Quit gaping at the guy," said Stan.

Jim came forward with an outstretched hand. "Jim Wells. I thank you for your help, and we're real glad to meet you. Robin's done nothing but talk about you this past week."

Now Phoebe came up to him, her arms wide

for a hug. "Forgive me, young man. I didn't mean to be rude. It just took me aback, is all. It's been over 30 years since I last saw Bruce Ottski, but you're his spitting image."

"Gee, thanks." Was it okay to be sarcastic to these strangers?

Everyone laughed, so maybe it was okay.

"Sit," Becca told them. "Supper's ready."

"Oh, you dear girl. Thank you. I wasn't up to having to make a meal. It's not like we did anything much, but hanging around a hospital wears a body out."

"I made some meal packages and put them in your freezer," Robin told her sister. "Some for Greg, too."

Phoebe gave Robin a hug. "Thanks, sis. You know how much we appreciate it."

Talk turned to the accident and Aggie's condition. They'll know more after this first night, but the doctors seemed optimistic about the prognosis. Recovery would not be fast, nor without pain, but she'll survive.

"Greg is beating himself up over this," Phoebe said.

"We were all there. It could have been any one of us who took that kick, or none of us," said Jim. "How often have we done the exact same thing with new cattle and no one got hurt? This was a fluke, and we'll have to drum that into the stupid head of my son."

"I'm always up for bashing his head," offered Stan.

Becca kicked him under the table.

"What time do you want me here tomorrow? Gabe asked.

"I'll leave home around 7:00," Stan told him. "You're staying with Aunt Robin and Keith, right? Why don't you meet me in the parking lot of Alpaca Haven and follow me out here in the morning?"

Almost dozing off in the back seat of Keith's pickup on the way home, Gabe thought about his day. Working on Gabriella's house, the surprise of Blair's arrival, the news about Aggie's accident, the plane ride here, then feeding cattle. Each part was not much, but put together felt like a full day.

He glanced at his watch. Almost 9 p.m. Too late to deliver Emma's father's boots to her—both a disappointment and a relief. Part of him yearned to see that woman again, but part of him dreaded seeing the look in her eyes when she once again tried to put distance between them.

~

"What is *he* doing here?" Greg stormed into the machine shed where Gabe was changing the oil in a tractor. "Why are you letting him near our machinery? We don't know anything about this guy."

Gabe stood, wiping his hands on a rag, then waiting, feet planted firmly apart.

"Cool it, Greg," Stan told his older brother. "He knows what he's doing."

"Yeah? Just last week Blair doubted he's who he says he is. He just shows up out of the blue."

"Greg," warned Stan.

Gabe needed to take this into his own hands. "You must be Greg Wells. Pleased to meet you. I'm very sorry to hear about your wife's accident."

Greg didn't budge.

"As for what I'm doing, Blair told me you could use a hand, so I came along. I'm an agricultural mechanic by trade, and I've spent my life working on ranches in Texas. I know cattle and I know machines." When Greg still didn't move, Gabe added, "But if you're not comfortable having a stranger around your place, I understand, and I'll be on my way."

"Son," interrupted Jim, "I believe you owe this man an apology. He's come out of his way to help us, and after working with him all morning, I can tell you he does know what he's doing. We'll cut you some slack because you're worried about your wife, but Gabe is our guest, and a relative of sorts."

Greg took in a breath, then blew it out. "You're right, Dad. Sorry. I didn't sleep at all last night, just watched Aggie try to breathe." He turned to Gabe. "I apologize. It's just that so much has spun out of my control, then I see this stranger working on my tractor…"

"It's okay," Gabe told him. "I get it." He turned back to the tractor, where the oil had almost finished draining into a pan. "When Stan told me this thing was due for servicing, I thought I'd get at it. I can quit or carry on. Your call." Then he added, "I can show you my journeyman's certificate if that helps, or I can give you my employer's number if you want to check me out."

"Geez, now I feel like an idiot," said Greg.

"Well, that fits. You look like one, too," Stan told him.

Greg threw a grimy rag at his younger brother.

"I just came home for a shower and a change of clothes, and to check up on things."

"We're under control," Stan said, "At least we were until *you* got here."

"Okay, enough, boys." Jim had spent years calming the waters between his sons. "Blair was here for a few hours this morning, then he's coming back later this afternoon. That makes four of us, so we'll get everything done easily. You go on back to your wife and give Aggie our love."

"Mom said she'll move into our place to stay with the kids, and that you might come too, Dad. Thanks. That relieved Aggie's mind."

"Happy to, son. That's what family's for."

"Well, Emma's not family, but she helped out yesterday, too. Don't know what we would have done about the kids with none of us around to get them."

"Becca said Emma didn't hesitate, just took charge, and that when Beth got to Emma's house to pick them up, the kids had eaten and were calm. Even Alvin."

"Emma has a way with him," Greg said. "Aggie and I really worried about how he'd do in Grade 1, but she's been great. Our only regret is that she won't be his teacher again next year."

Emma again. As if she wasn't in Gabe's thoughts enough.

CHAPTER 49

The playground came alive with the joyful screams and laughter of children let loose from the confines of their desks, their tiny frames darting and weaving in every direction, filling the open space with energy and excitement.

Except for Alvin. He sat slumped against the wall of the school.

While he handled the academic side of school well, the social parts came less easily to him. He could join in the play, but rarely initiated interactions. He did best with structured games, when everyone knew and followed the rules. Even games like Red Light, Green Light followed predictable patterns.

It's not that it was imperative for Alvin to always play with a group; solitary activities were just fine. But functioning in a group was a part of life, and he needed to be able to do so when required. For the most part, he could, and seemed to have fun with his peers.

Not today. Too much was different. He hadn't gone home last night; he'd slept in a strange bed. Sure, Alice, Friday, Randine, Aunt Beth and Uncle Blair were there, but they weren't Mommy and Daddy. Talking to Daddy on the phone hadn't helped much, and Daddy said Mommy was sleeping. She *never* went to sleep before he did. Now Ms. Lowry said he'd go home after school today, but Grandma would be there, not Mommy and Daddy. That's not the way it was supposed to be. It was all so wrong.

Emma made one last surveillance of the playground, checking that the adult supervisors were all there, and no crisis was about to erupt. She walked quickly to the parking lot, letting herself into her car. This was one of the few places she could make a call without being interrupted or overheard.

"Mrs. Wells? This is Emma Lowry. I thought you might want an update on how Alvin's doing. Aggie must be worried about him. How is she?"

Normally Emma would never speak to an extended family member about a student; only the legal guardians. But, just like it takes a village to raise a child, Alvin was one autistic boy lucky enough to have a large and engaged family. At the start of the school year, Greg and Aggie gave written consent for Phoebe and Jim, Stan and Becca, and Blair and Beth to pick up Alvin and Alice, and for Emma to contact any of these adults if needed.

Emma answered Phoebe's question. "No, no outbursts. I'm giving him lots of sensory breaks and keeping things routine as much as it's possible with six-year-olds. He's more withdrawn than usual and clutches his fidget toy and wants to sit in the beanbag chair at the back of the room. He's wearing the compression vest and lap weights more than usual, but that's fine. He keeps going over and over the story I drew about you staying with him and Alice tonight." She paused, her eyes seeking Alvin's small frame. He hadn't moved from his spot in the sun, along the wall. "Please tell Aggie he's fine. Confused, but doing all right."

~

Never one to shy away from what needed to be done, Gabe desperately sought an excuse. He'd serviced two tractors and a baler today at the Wells' farm until Jim told him to go home.

Back at Robin's and Keith's house, he'd cleaned up the kitchen after Robin's meal of pot roast with garlic mashed potatoes and string beans, the latter two grown in their garden last summer, and the beef from one of the cows Blair butchered.

Now Keith and Robin settled on the couch in front of the television. Although gracious to him, he was a fifth wheel and knew it. He should get out of the house and leave them alone for a bit.

Leaving people alone was something he used to think he was good at. His mind and his body warred about this one when it came to Emma.

From within the hall closet, Emma's father's boots called to him. Returning them was the correct thing to do, right? Of course it was; his mother would be appalled if he didn't return something he'd borrowed.

Despite knowing that Emma likely didn't want to see him, Gabe couldn't resist the magnetic pull towards her, drawn like a moth to a flame, unable to resist the lure of her company. The thought of leaving the boots with Esther, taking the easy way out, crossed his mind many times, but the mere idea of missing the chance to see Emma, to speak with her, was unbearable. It was as though an invisible force was constantly tugging at his heartstrings, compelling him to seek out Emma's presence, no matter the cost.

He'd spent all of two days in her company, so why the allure?

He opened the closet door, bringing out Harold Lowry's boots, his excuse for paying a visit to Emma.

"Oh, good, you're taking those back. Give our love to Emma." Robin feigned interest in the television, but watched the conflicting emotions wash over Gabe's face.

CHAPTER 50

As Gabe waited after knocking on the door, the seconds dragged like an eternity. Would Emma answer, or had she already caught a glimpse of him through the peephole and decided not to open the door? Maybe he had crossed a line by coming unannounced, but if he had called, what if she told him to leave the boots with her mother tomorrow? Or what if she wouldn't even respond to his call? She'd ignored his text message, after all. Either way, he risked being rejected by Emma. Nevertheless, he stood there, holding his breath with a glimmer of hope that she would let him in.

The sound of light footsteps, a lock turning, then the door opened.

"You!" Emma said.

Not an auspicious beginning, but at least she hadn't slammed the door in his face. He stood there drinking in all the features of her face, as if committing them to memory. He noticed the way her eyebrows arched slightly in concentration, and the way her lips curved up ever so slightly at the corners in surprise. The way the light danced in her eyes as she spoke, the subtle movement of her eyelashes as she blinked up at him, and the way her hair framed her face all came together in a sight that took his breath away, along with any words he should be saying. It was as though he was seeing her for the first time, and yet the familiarity of her face was comforting to him.

"Hey." That was the only word to come to his mind.

"Hi." She wasn't a chatterbox, either.

He stood there like an idiot, just taking in the sight before him.

Emma shifted her feet.

Sheesh. And here he stood gawking at her like some love-stuck schoolboy. "Sorry. I don't mean to stare." That was a lie. "I, ah…" He produced her dad's boots from behind his back. "Here." He thrust them at her.

Emma took a slight step back before reaching for them.

Words, words, he needed words. "Thanks. I mean, thank you for letting me borrow them. You were right, and my cowboy boots were stupid in this weather." He stuck out his left foot. "Keith sold me these. They work much better." He caught himself. "I don't mean better than your dad's did. They were just fine, great even. I meant better than my cowboy boots." Geez, Gabe, babble much?

"I know what you were trying to say." She smiled for the first time since she'd opened the door. "Want to come in?"

Did he? He tried to act cool. "Sure, if it's no bother."

"Let's go into the kitchen. Mom's asleep in front of the TV." She bent to take a pan from a lower cupboard. "Want some Ovaltine?"

And just like that, they were back to that easy camaraderie they'd shared the last time over a hot drink. Except this evening the kitchen was not in shadows. Although dim light added to the atmosphere, it made it harder to catalog the expressions playing across her face.

They talked about Aggie's progress and the

things the family was doing to keep things as normal as possible for the kids.

"I hear your name mentioned a lot when I'm working at the Wells'. They're grateful for all you're doing to help Alvin."

"This would be a tough time for any child, but especially for an autistic child who clings to routine. It helps now that Greg is home at night with the kids."

"And you?" Gabe asked. "How have you been?"

"Me, I'm fine." Emma ran a hand down the side of her head, smoothing out any wayward strands. "How's it going with your grandmother's place?"

"That's on hold for now. Since I'm the executor of her estate, and there are no pressing bills, it can just sit until things settle down here for the Wells' and I can head back to Texas."

"It's good of you to come to help them."

"Not much I can do for Gabriella now that she's dead. I might as well do what I can for the living."

The living and the future. As much as he hated to do anything to dispel the harmony between them, he had to know. It ate at him and he couldn't let it go. "Why didn't you reply to my text?"

CHAPTER 51

"What text?" Emma had scrambled through her phone's message often enough to be positive there'd been no text from Gabe. Nothing in messenger or her email inbox either, no matter how often she looked.

"The one I sent you the day I left here."

He sounded so sure.

"I never received anything from you."

"Are you sure?"

What, did he think she was ghosting him? That wasn't her style. "Gabe, there's been nothing." She set her phone on the table.

Gabe pulled his cell from his pocket. "Look, it's here." He thumbed through his messages until he found the one to Emma, the one he'd read over and over and over again.

Emma took it from him, their fingers touching, doing that sparky thing she'd felt before. How pathetic. Just a brush from the edge of his finger did things to her.

Then she was caught up in his words and the message she'd searched for since the day he left town.

Emma, it's me, Gabe. I've had some news and I have to leave.

Thank you for your hospitality, yours and Esther's. I appreciate you opening your home to me.

Thank you also for rescuing me, for the loan of your father's boots, and for playing with me.

I've enjoyed getting to know you and would have liked to spend more time with you.

I got a phone call. It was from a lawyer in San Antonio. My grandmother died. I'm executor of her estate, if you can believe that. I never even met her!

I am on my way there now. Don't know how long it will take to wrap things up.

May I call you sometime? Would you call me?

Gabe

He *had* thought about her; he hadn't left town without thinking of her. She blinked hard. Why should this make her cry? That was just stupid, but there it was, that stinging sensation at the top of her nose.

She gave a quick look up to find Gabe's intense gaze on her. What must he think of her when she didn't reply? "Gabe, I never got this. See?" She held out her phone to him.

He covered her hand with his. "That's okay. Some quirk of cyberspace." He gave the fist she'd wrapped around her cell phone a squeeze. "I'm just relieved you're not mad at me?"

"Mad? Why would I be mad?"

Gabe blew out a breath. "I thought I blew it. When you didn't reply, I thought you were upset that I'd kissed you."

Emma's cheeks reddened and she couldn't meet his eyes.

"Em?" He put a finger under her chin, gently raising her face so he could get a better look. "You are. I'm sorry. I didn't want to make things awkward between us. I just, well, I couldn't help myself. You looked so beautiful that morning, all fresh from your shower, smelling amazing. You glowed."

Now her eyes flew up to his. "I had no makeup on. I looked awful."

"You were the loveliest thing I'd ever laid eyes on."

"My hair was wet and hanging down. I hadn't even put moisturizer on my face yet!"

"You don't need it, any of that stuff." He gathered both of her hands in his. "Emma, how could you not know how absolutely beautiful you are? Just yourself, without anything else."

Right. Sweet of him to say, but she knew what she looked like, saw herself before and after makeup. She'd seen childhood pictures from her beauty pageant days where she was transformed from a regular little girl into a porcelain doll, admired by all. Anyway, he was here now, and he had tried to text her. Enough. Let's just enjoy the moment.

But Gabe wasn't letting things go.

"Emma, I wasn't sure you'd let me in the door today."

"Why ever not?"

"Because of the way I acted the last time we were together. Please accept my apology and believe me when I say that I don't usually get things so wrong. I don't think I've ever overstepped so badly."

"Gabe, what are you talking about?"

"The kiss. I kissed you when I shouldn't have."

Emma reddened. Couldn't he just leave it alone? This was *not* easy to talk about. "Why shouldn't you have?"

"Obviously, I misjudged and caused you to run away from me."

"I wasn't running away from you because we kissed. You saw me without makeup; that's why I took off."

"I don't get it."

"I was embarrassed at you seeing me looking such a mess."

Gabe squinted at her.

"You don't get it, but it's important to me to look my best."

"Why?"

"Doesn't matter right now." But there was something he needed to know. "I liked that kiss.

Enough that I forgot what I looked like. And it wasn't just you kissing me: I kissed you back. You didn't read anything wrong." She smiled shyly. "I liked it."

Gabe grinned. "Yeah? Think you wanna do it again sometime?"

"Yes, I think I do."

"Now?" Gabe rested his elbows on the table and leaned forward.

For an answer, Emma rose to her feet. Gabe turned sideways in his chair.

Resting her hands on his shoulders, Emma lowered her head while his lifted to meet hers. From this position, Emma had the power, could guide the kiss the way she wanted.

As their lips met, the world around them faded away. The sweetness of the kiss was like the last time, the memories flooding back. His lips were soft and warm, and he tasted like warm milk and the sweetest honey. Emma lost herself in the moment, her heart beating faster.

He held her close, his arms wrapped around her waist as they continued to explore each other's mouths, the kisses slow and gentle. She ran her fingers through his hair, pulling him closer to her as their bodies pressed together.

"Emma!" a voice from the next room.

They parted, the sweetness of the kiss lingering on their lips.

"Emma, where are you? This shawl has fallen off and I'm getting chilled."

Emma put her finger to Gabe's lips and whispered in his ear. "Shh. Don't let her know you're here. I'll convince Mom to go to bed, then be right back."

There would be time for the world to intrude, but tonight she wasn't sharing this man with anyone.

CHAPTER 52

After nearly a week in the hospital, Aggie came home. Greg spent much of each day hanging out with her; in Aggie's words, hovering. Phoebe came to the house in the late afternoons to help with the kids, while Greg joined his father and brother tending to their cattle.

Gabe divided his time between the Wells' farm, doing what he could, helping Blair on his farm, and getting to know the ins and outs of alpaca care with Becca and Stan. Fascinating creatures, although he couldn't quite wrap his mind around keeping animals solely for their fleece that was shorn just once a year. Oh, and for their poop. Astoundingly, the dry pellets they produced were in demand as garden fertilizer. Who knew?

The best parts of Gabe's days were his evenings. Often helping Emma cook dinner, he hung out with her. She and Esther, to be honest, but time with Emma was time with Emma. He'd take it anyway he could.

Was it all smooth sailing? No.

Passed around like a relative who'd overstayed his welcome, Gabe slept some nights at Robin's and Keith's place, some at Blair's farmhouse, and during calving when births were imminent, he stayed with Jim and Phoebe, taking his turn with Jim getting up every few hours to check how labor progressed, and if the cow was in distress. Normally Greg and Stan shared such vigils, but Greg needed to remain with Aggie until her breathing evened out, and Stan spent long hours doing his own work, plus much of Greg's.

Supposedly they were at the tail end of winter.

The days were long, but such was farming and ranching. Much as he knew the Wells family needed the help right now, a part of his brain that didn't do him proud resented the time he missed spending with Emma.

Emma. A complicated woman with many

sides. He liked the relaxed Emma best. When she let down her guard, she was fun to be with.

Smart, too. She helped him look at situations, putting different perspectives on things. Would his relationship with his half-brother be as good as it was without Emma sharing her thoughts on the how's and why's of their interactions?

Emma came most alive when she talked about her students, both past and present. They were important little people to her, ones entrusted in her care, ones she was determined to help become confident, competent children.

Gabe suspected no one had done the same for a young Emma.

While her most animated side shone through when talking about her teaching, a completely different Emma poked out in Esther's company. Somehow, her mother caused Emma to shrink in on herself with her constant complaints. Why? As far as Gabe could see, no one could do more for Esther than Emma did now.

Was that it? Was she doing *too* much? Sometimes when he observed mother and daughter together, it was like watching the color leach out of Emma until only a pale imitation of what she was dredged through her days with her mother.

True, life handed Esther some tough breaks. She lost her husband far too early. Then a cancer diagnosis threw her into a tailspin; he'd watched his mother cope with the news and face the possibility that she might not make it. Esther had, though, and rather than embracing the gift of life she'd been given, she'd shrunken her world to her house. And her daughter. Emma did everything for her. How much was too much?

With the girls upstairs doing their homework, Gabe and Beth tackled the dishes in the farmhouse kitchen. Having done the cooking, Blair escaped to do some woodworking in the barn he'd converted to a shop. When life settled down, Gabe wouldn't mind spending some time out there with his brother, learning the art of fine woodworking. But that was a dream for the future.

On any other night, Gabe would hurry through dishes, then leave to spend the rest of the evening with Emma. Not tonight, though, and it wasn't his choice.

Emma told him not to come, that she had too much school work to catch up on.

Esther constantly complained about all the hours Emma spent on marking and planning.

Gabe suspected that the teacher might use marking as an excuse to escape her mother.

Was she trying to get away from *him*, too? Maybe she needed a break; although he had no problem spending all his free time in her company, she might not feel the same way.

Still, it hurt. So he mentioned his suspicions that school work was an excuse to avoid her mother, and asked point blank if she was doing the same thing to him.

In hindsight, perhaps not the wisest move.

Emma had gone quiet for a very long time, dead air hanging in the invisible phone line between them. Then she spoke slowly and distinctly. "I am a teacher. Teachers teach. But they don't enter a classroom unprepared. I've spent a lot of time playing with you this week, too much time."

Ouch, that hurt.

"Now I'm behind, and I won't do that to my students. It's not who I am. I took on this job and I will be the best Grade 1 teacher possible. That means I need time to prepare."

He'd tried to back peddle. "I get it…"

"There have been evenings when I had a few spare hours, but you were busy with calving, or some such thing." She didn't have to say that she hadn't complained about how he spent his time.

"You're right. I'm sorry. It's just that school seems to take up so much of your time."

"You've been listening to my mother."

"Your mother isn't necessarily wrong about everything."

More silence. "Good night, Gabe."

He couldn't help but put his foot in things. It was because he cared. He didn't want Emma running herself ragged over her job or over her mother. A job was a job, and maybe it did require the kind of hours Emma put in. He didn't know. But he did know that Emma was not getting a fair shake from her mother.

Beth was a psychologist and knew people. She also knew Emma. Would it be disloyal of him to talk to Beth about Emma?

He needed some insights before he said or did the wrong thing again with the woman who was starting to mean so much to him. So much that he didn't want to risk blowing things.

How to broach this? "Have you known Emma's mother for long?"

"A few years."

"Emma implies that her mother's changed,

that she used to be different before losing her husband."

"I didn't know her then, but Robin mentioned that, too. Esther used to be involved in most of what went on around town."

"Now she hardly leaves the house."

"So I've heard," said Beth. "Must be tough on Emma."

"Yeah. She works all day, then does everything around the house."

Beth tilted her head to look at Gabe as he handed her a pot to dry.

Gabe got it. "I know. So do you and every other adult who holds down a job. But this is different. I've been over there quite a bit, and it's almost like Esther lays in wait for Emma to get home to pick at her. Nothing is ever good enough, or done right."

"That would wear on a person."

"You can see it in Emma's face. It's almost like she braces herself for what her mother will criticize next."

"People can get into a pattern of behaving a certain way with each other, whether that's a good way or not."

"I sometimes wonder how Emma puts up with

it." There, he'd said it. But there was more. "I wonder if she *should* put up with it."

"Good question. Does she defend herself?"

"Never that I've seen. I don't think she should have to put up with it."

"Do you think whether she does or not is your call?"

They worked in silence for a few minutes. "Maybe not. Sometimes I think about suggesting to Emma that she move out, get her own place, and leave her mother to fend for herself."

CHAPTER 53

Gabe and Emma finished loading the dishwasher. They'd done it so often together that they worked in sync. Esther sat at the kitchen table, fingers tapping, waiting for them to finish. It was harder for Gabe to steal kisses with her mother sitting there watching them.

"Emma, dear, if you had brought me the Scrabble board before you started cleaning up, I would've had it already set up for us," admonished Esther.

Emma's eyes raised to Gabe's, then quickly shuttered.

"I'd get it for you, Mrs. Lowry, but I don't know where it's kept," said Gabe.

"It's in the corner hutch in the living room," Esther told him.

"Would you mind bringing it to us, then? We'll be finished here in a minute." Gabe ignored the look Emma gave him, keeping his eyes steady on her mother, a coaxing smile on his face.

Flustered, Esther held onto the table for support as she got to her feet. "I suppose I could do that, although it's usually Emma's job."

This was not the first time the three of them played Scrabble, and Gabe learned just what competitive players these women were. Esther was certainly no slouch at the game, but she had high expectations for how her daughter should perform. When her letters allowed Emma only a low word count, Esther would tsk, shake her head in disapproval, or in some way chide her daughter for not doing as well as she should.

Tonight, Gabe had enough. He hated seeing this bright, competent young woman shrinking to herself, second-guessing her every move. This was only a game. He pretended to shift positions, bringing up one ankle to place it over his other knee. In doing so, he jarred the table badly, knocking their tiles all over. "Geez, how clumsy of me. Sorry to have ruined our game."

He stood and reached for Emma's hand,

pulling her to her feet. "It looks like a nice night. Shall we go for a walk?" He didn't give her a chance to respond but led her to the entryway and helped her put on her coat.

"You did that on purpose, didn't you?" whispered Emma.

"Maybe. But I won't tell if you won't."

Emma's smile was reward enough.

The streets were almost deserted, with just the occasional car driving by. It was that slushy time of year, the transition between winter and spring, that never came in a tidy fashion. It's always a trick to know whether to wear sneakers, rubber boots, or stick to your winter footwear. They skirted puddles with just a skiff of ice beginning to form in the night air and crunched through darkened snow, weakened by sand and muddy water. Gabe knew that if he had on his cowboy boots, he'd be struggling to keep his feet under him.

He pulled Emma's hand through his arm, linking their fingers. This felt right.

So much more right than that stifling atmosphere in the kitchen.

What was so wrong with playing a board game with the older woman? It should've been a fun time, something families enjoyed together. But Esther's constant picking at Emma made it hard for Gabe to bear.

Before he could censor himself, Gabe asked the question that had been on his mind for weeks. "Why don't you move out? Get a place of your own?"

Emma walked in silence as they passed the next few houses on the block. "When I first moved back here, I rented a little house. It was nice, it was all mine. I checked up on mom at least once a day, and I'd make enough supper for both of us, putting the leftovers in her fridge for the next day so all she had to do was heat them up."

"Sounds like a plan. Did it work?"

"At first. But then she needed more and more help. The chemotherapy really wore her down, and I found I was doing all the housekeeping and cooking for two places. She just didn't have the energy or the motivation. I get that; she was so focused on conserving her energy to battle the assault to her body that there was little left for the mundane things. Then she started radiation, and it got worse. She was so needy, and this wasn't the mother that I knew growing up. That mother was capable, and independent, organized, always pushing us to be our best, but this mother just slumped in a chair, waiting for me to do everything for her."

"I saw how the cancer treatments ravaged my mother's body." Gabe was inside his own head for a few minutes, remembering. "But your mom looks pretty good now, and you said she is cancer free."

"That's what the doctors tell us repeatedly."

"Em, this is none of my business, and I know I'm poking my nose where it doesn't belong, but please hear me out anyway. What if you got a place of your own again? I imagine it would feel good to have space to yourself; after all, you lived away from home for a long time. You could go back to cooking meals for the both of you, the way you did before, and you could hire a cleaning lady to come in a few times a week to keep things tidy for Esther." How to say this delicately? "Maybe, just maybe, without you around to rely on, do you think your mom would start doing more things for herself?"

"You think I'm not doing a good job?"

"No! You're doing a great job with everything."

Emma's defensive tone evaporated. "I have

wondered about this so many times myself. When I broached Mom about getting my own place again, she got all upset. She clutched her heart and said that I am all she has left now. How could I desert her?"

"She's been through a lot, for sure, and she's your mother, so you have an obligation to her. But I'm not sure what's happening now is good for you, good for either of you."

Emma didn't say anything, just walked with her head down. She didn't pull her hand away from his, though. "When I was little, she gave up a lot for me."

"Isn't that what parents do?"

"No, I mean more than would be expected. She spent weeks and months driving me around the beauty pageant circuit. For months on end, we'd be gone every weekend. She gave up her free time for me."

Gabe tilted his, looking at Emma quizzically. "That's one way to look at it. How old were you?"

"Three when it started."

"Did you ask to participate, for her to take you?" What three-year-old even knew what a beauty pageant was?

"No, of course not. It was just what we did."

"Was it more for your sake or for hers?"

Emma thought of all the times she'd rather stayed home and played with her toys. Yes, it was fun to get all dressed and parade around, having everyone tell you how pretty you looked, but getting to that stage hurt. The stuff they did to her hair, yanking and twisting it, then those annoyed people telling her three-year-old self to sit still or they couldn't get her makeup on correctly. She wanted to be beautiful, didn't she? Then quit moving around, they'd say. It was so clear in her head. How to explain this to Gabe? She couldn't.

Gabe was still talking. "As I see it, it's a draw. She gave up time for you when you were small, and you've devoted your time to her now." He stopped, pulling Emma to face him, taking both her hands in his. "But do you have to pay forever?"

Emma's eyes became luminescent in the sheen of the streetlight.

He gathered her into his arms. "Sorry, Em, I didn't mean to make you cry. It's just that I can't stand to see what's going on. I know your mom isn't happy, but to watch her take it out on you is tough to see. I hate what this is doing to you."

Two words came out muffled against his coat. "Me, too."

Should he push this any further? It was going okay so far.

"Emma, I know she's your mother, but I hate seeing what she's doing to you."

Emma stilled.

"I understand that she's had some bad times and is lonely. But that doesn't give her the right to make your life miserable. It's like she's taken away your spirit, your choices."

Emma stepped back so she could meet his eyes. "No one takes away my choices."

"I know. I just meant it's like she's playing you, and I don't like to see that."

"Gabe, I'm a big girl and have been looking after myself for a long time now. No one takes my choices from me, and that includes you."

"Em, I didn't mean anything by it. I'm not trying to push you."

"That's not what it feels like." She crossed her arms over her chest.

"Selfishly, if you had your own place, I'd get to see more of you without having to share you with your mother."

"I see."

He tried to recapture her hands, but she moved even farther away.

"My mother might pressure me one way, but

you're doing the same thing. I don't appreciate it from her, you, or anybody. I make my own decisions."

"Em..."

"Good night, Gabe. I'll walk myself home."

CHAPTER 54

It was time. Conflicting responsibilities ate at Gabe. He needed to help the Wells family, but it was getting harder and harder to put off the calls from Gabriella's lawyer. The sooner the estate was settled, the sooner the law firm would get paid. Fair enough, and the thought of his grandmother's house hung heavy on his mind.

A grandmother. Who would have thought?

He'd sought out his brother ahead of an old lady. She'd died before he got to her, and he'd live with that choice forever. But in death, he still owed her an obligation. Cleaning out anyone's house was no walk in the park, but when that person was a stranger, it was so much harder.

Or maybe not, as Robin said. If you had no

ties to the person, no shared memories or treasures, didn't that make it easier to simply get rid of everything? There was no family other than Blair and him. Unless it was something one of them wanted, it could all go. When you looked at it that way, why drag his feet?

Speaking of feet, Aggie was now reliably on hers. Certainly not up to wrestling cattle, but capable of walking unaided across her living room, and helping with meals. Greg hovered less, no longer terrified his wife would be unable to breathe. Now he feared her wrath as he got underfoot and on her nerves.

Today, plane ticket in hand, Gabe was ready to fly back to San Antonio. But he wasn't going alone. Blair insisted they purchase two tickets; Gabriella was his grandmother too, so why should Gabe have to do all the work on his own? Or have all the fun, as Robin said.

Yeah, they'd get this done, the two of them. They agreed they'd each keep a picture of Gabriella and her husband, Bill, but neither wanted any reminders of Bruce. Robin wanted no mementos either, so that made the job easier.

The plan was to throw all personal things into the dumpster. They'd call an auction house to sell the furniture on consignment. Since neither of them felt up to cleaning the place, they'd hire a service to attack that chore, then put the house on the market.

The one thing they would bring home was a treasure found in the garage—a 2010 Bentley GT with just over 32,000 miles on her. They agreed that it was a fitting car for Robin.

"At least this way she'll get *something* out of Bruce's family," said Gabe.

"Hey! She got *me*. What more could anyone want?" was Blair's response.

Once again, they flew in premium seats, at Gabe's insistence. "You can pay me back out of your share of the estate," he told Blair.

"My share? She left everything to you, brother. I'm not touching it."

This was an argument they'd been over a number of times already, each digging in harder on his own position. "She didn't know where you were," Gabe insisted. "If she had, she would have split things between us. Since I found you, it only makes sense that we consider this *our* inheritance."

"Not what the will says, so we're not going there." Blair pulled his cap over his eyes, settled himself in his seat, and feigned sleep.

That left Gabe with his own thoughts, and

whenever he wasn't fully occupied with something else, Emma filled his mind.

He blew it. He'd made some headway and should have quit while he was ahead. He knew he shouldn't have pushed Emma, but he had anyway. He knew he'd have to leave soon and detested leaving her alone in the hands of her mother. At least while he was around, he buffered her somewhat.

Now she was ticked with him, thinking he doubted her ability to handle decisions on her own.

Yes, she'd replied to his texts—said it was fine after he apologized, although he was not positive about what he was apologizing for. Was he wrong to speak his mind? Isn't that what you did when you were in a relationship?

Maybe this was all on his side, and Emma saw him only as someone to hang out with, not someone with whom she was becoming more deeply involved. Was it only him feeling this deeper connection?

This was hardly a conversation to explore via text messaging.

He'd let her know he was leaving with Blair to return to Texas and wasn't sure how long he'd be gone.

She'd replied, wishing him well, but that's it. No "I'll miss you", no "Can't wait until you return", nothing you wouldn't say to a polite stranger.

From the seat beside him, Blair spoke. "You're going to wear out your phone if you don't give the thing a rest."

"It's just that Emma…" What could he say?

"You might not want to get too hung up on her."

"Why? What makes you say that?" Part of Gabe really wanted to know, and part of him bristled at some implied criticism in Blair's voice.

"Nothing. It's just that she has a bit of a reputation."

"Reputation?" For playing with lots of guys? He'd never seen her with anyone else or heard of it. "What do you mean?" His fingers curled into his palms.

"Look, she was a piece of work in high school."

"That was a long time ago. I was a jerk myself, then." He looked at Blair. "Wouldn't doubt you were, too."

"Me? Never. Emma dated Stan; hooked onto him was more like it. Smothered the guy, but he didn't seem to notice. He had a pretty girl on his arm for parties, and one who played all the sports he liked. That's as far as Stan's brain stretched. There were about two years there when the rest of us didn't see much of Stan, unless we were playing on the field or court or rink with him. Emma cut him off from everyone she didn't deem important."

"That's not the Emma I know." His blood heated and his teeth clenched. How dare Blair say those things about her?

"Well, that was what Emma was like back then. When she returned to Goodrich, she somehow thought she'd take up where she left off with Stan, trying to take him over again. But by then Stan was totally smitten with Becca, and was working to get her onside with that." He smirked. "Becca really made him work for it."

"I've seen Emma with both Becca and Stan. They seem fine."

"Yeah, they've made a sort of truce, and Emma doesn't pull any of that crap anymore."

"You've got it all wrong. That is not Emma at all. I'd prefer you shut up about things you know nothing about." His fist clenched.

"You might want to watch yourself, buddy." He pulled his cap back over his eyes and settled himself for a nap. "Just sayin'."

CHAPTER 55

The two men worked in different rooms in the house. It was better if they kept their distance since Blair said those things about Emma. Gabe knew his brother had her pegged all wrong and didn't know the sweet, wonderful woman she was now.

Who knew what insecurities drove the teenaged Emma back then, or even if what Blair said was true? How accurately did a teenage boy perceive anyone around him? From what Gabe had seen of his half-brother so far, the guy wasn't exactly Mr. Congeniality or Mr. Sensitive himself. In fact, without Beth to smooth his edges, sometimes he'd barely pass for civilized.

He didn't deserve to be anywhere near a woman like Emma.

Emma.

She dutifully responded to each of his texts—maybe not right away, but at least sometime that day. Mostly. But her responses were those of a polite stranger; the essentials and no more than courtesy required. Gone was the closeness he believed they'd shared, the intimate thoughts about their days. Their kisses.

Gabe tried something risky. He'd ended one text with XOXO. Yeah, juvenile for sure, but he did it anyway.

She replied with just her name, her full name and not the shortened Em they'd used before. Before he messed things up.

There had to be a way to return to what they had, or what he *thought* they'd had. Maybe it was all in his mind, all on his part, and this was Emma's way of politely giving him the brush off.

~

Emma Lowry had a lot on her mind. Part of it was Gabe; well, he occupied a *lot* of her thoughts, she'd admit. But stuff with her mother weighed heavily, too. Sure, she was ticked with

Gabe for trying to push her, but maybe her back was up because he struck too close to home and the darker edges where her brain went when she let herself be something other than the dutiful daughter.

But she'd get to that later.

First, she had a phone call to make.

"Greg? This is Emma Lowry from school." She listened. "No, there's no problem, and Alvin is fine. Or mostly fine."

"Can you hang on a minute, Emma? Let me shut this tractor down so I can hear you better."

She waited. She didn't have that much time before the kids would be back in from recess. From where she stood in the hallway, she looked through her classroom door to check on Alvin. The child was still lounging in the beanbag chair.

"That's better," said Greg. "What's up?"

"Maybe nothing, but Alvin's been sort of listless today. He dragged his heels about going out for recess, so I let him stay in. He's put his head down on his desk several times this morning."

"He sometimes doesn't sleep well, so he's probably tired. He picks up on the tension around here when we worry about Aggie."

"That's why I'm calling. I know Aggie's lungs

are sensitive right now. Alvin's nose has been running, and he's coughed a few times. There are two other students from this class away ill. One of the mothers called me this morning to say her son has the flu."

There was silence as the meaning of that sunk in.

"I don't want to be an alarmist or anything, and maybe Alvin is just tired. I thought I should let you know, though, in case you don't want Aggie to be exposed to anything viral or upper respiratory."

"Geez. That would be just what we don't need. It could throw Aggie right back in the hospital." His voice faded off. "Or worse."

"I'm not saying Alvin's sick. Just thought I should give you a heads up."

"Thanks. I'll talk to Mom. Maybe Alvin should stay with her and Dad until we know if he's got something."

"Let me know if there's anything I can do." Emma hung up.

The sound of high-pitched, excited little voices filled the hallway with noise and fresh air as students burst from the boot room in a vague semblance of order and filed into their classrooms. As usual, Emma stood in the doorway, greeting each of her kids as they trickled in.

In the back of the classroom, Alvin lay sound asleep, curled up in his favorite chair.

~

The pungent, earthy scents of cumin, coriander, turmeric, and garam masala filled the living room with enticing aromas. Gabe and Blair might not agree about Emma, but their taste buds were in sync enough to enjoy the complex, sweet, mild and spicy flavors of Indian food. Now they sprawled on opposite ends of the couch, socked feet on the coffee table, holding paper plates of dal makhani, butter chicken, and samosas, sopping up palak paneer with naan.

Blair's phone trilled.

Gabe had heard that ring tone often enough that he recognized it, even without Blair's sappy grin confirming Beth was on the line.

Gabe gathered up the empty takeout containers, taking them to the kitchen to give the couple some privacy.

After a few minutes, Blair was on his feet, heading into the kitchen, while still talking. "He's here. I'll give you to him, and you can see what he thinks of the idea." He passed his phone to Gabe. Needlessly, he said, "It's Beth."

Gabe rolled his eyes and took the phone. "How are things with you and the girls, Beth?"

"We're good, but that's not why I'm calling. You know you are welcome to stay here with us as long as you want, but I've heard you mention a few times that you'd like your own place."

"I hate imposing on everyone."

"Don't know if this interests you or not, but there's a house near us that may be vacant soon. Jed Olson stopped by just before supper to ask if I knew of anyone who might want to stay in their farmhouse. I didn't give them your name or anything, but I told them I'd ask around and get back to them."

"Thanks, Beth. Can I think about this and give you a call soon?" Gabe handed the phone back to Blair.

After finishing his chat with his wife, Blair returned to the kitchen. "So? What do you think?"

"Renting a house sounds like more than just passing through."

Blair just looked at him.

This was encroaching into touch-feely areas, but it was better to know than get this wrong. "How do y'all feel about me sticking around?"

CHAPTER 56

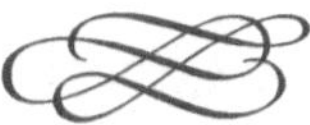

Esther thought Emma'd run back to school for some books she'd forgotten. Yes, Emma suffered through the lecture about planning ahead, but it was tolerable when it might not be for too much longer. So that she didn't tell a lie to her mother, Emma really did stop at the darkened school, using her key to let herself into her classroom. But it only took minutes to pick up her planning book, then return to the car.

From there, she drove to the address given in a text message. It was hard to keep anything quiet in a small town, but Emma tried, unwilling to have people speculating before she'd made up her mind.

There was a house that had become available for rent. Just a one-bedroom older place, but it was close enough to the school to walk. She was meeting the owner there to take a look. If it was decent, she was pretty sure she'd take it.

Pretty sure. That was *so* not like her. She was a decisive person—weigh all the options, create a plan, then bring that plan to life, a thing to be proud of. Whatever she did, she did well. Otherwise, what's the point?

This decision was a big deal. Yes, it had been a major move when she gave up her job in the city to return to Goodrich to help her mom. Then a smaller decision to leave her rental house and move in with Esther. But that had never been a permanent plan, at least not in Emma's mind.

Doing her best, *being* the best, were mantras Esther drilled into her daughter's head all her growing up years. How did people see her, judge her, other than by what she did, what she accomplished? If she couldn't be the best, her image would be tarnished, and that was unacceptable.

She had a career. To keep her edge, to succeed and rise in her field, took time and concentration. She felt both of those things slowly eroding the longer she lived with her mother.

Of course, she loved Esther; the woman had raised her and done so much for her. But this morass bogged her down, both of them really, pulling them under, neither able to breathe or stretch their wings, or just be.

Emma had felt this for a long time, at first refusing to recognize these feelings and looking at them, fearing they were a sign she was not fulfilling her duty. But as the months went on, the quagmire rose, miring her feet in quicksand. If she didn't get out soon, she would go under.

She got that you could get used to anything given enough time, but this life she had now was not one she wanted to keep. Despite the subtle and not-so-subtle pressures from Esther, the bitter truth of her current existence and how the future loomed was not something Emma could bring herself to swallow.

No, she hadn't needed Gabe to stick his nose in and point this out. It wasn't his business, anyway. What right did he have to criticize her, to suggest she wasn't following the best course for her life? What did he know about her history and what went on inside her?

That was the problem, he'd said. He *wanted* to know those things, wanted to know every part of her.

That was too much. She'd never let anyone in that far. It would be harder to maintain your image if someone got a peek at your flaws.

Those flaws would drive him away, and she rather liked having him around. As long as Gabe didn't poke around in her head too much, it was easy to keep up her persona with him; he didn't ask a lot.

But sometimes he did. He even got mad.

There was that time when they'd been together several evenings in a row, throwing off Emma's schedule, and she got to bed late. So late that she'd slept right through her alarm the next morning, having to race to school without her morning shower. Settling on just a quick blow out of her hair, she entered her classroom, not at her best. That couldn't happen again.

After supper that night when Gabe called, Emma said no, she couldn't see him that night.

"Why not?"

"I have to wash my hair."

A black hole's worth of silence filled the air waves coming from Gabe's phone. "You have to wash your hair," he repeated. "Are you giving me that old high school brush off?"

"No! I mean it. I didn't get to wash my hair

this morning, and I need to do a deep conditioning tonight."

Another silence. Finally, he answered with a timbre in his voice she hadn't heard before. "Just so I've got this straight, let me go over it. I've washed my hair thousands of times in my life—takes a few minutes at most. But you're saying you need the whole evening to do this, and that you're prioritizing your hair over spending time with me."

"No, I didn't mean it that way." But had she?

"That's sure what's coming across to me."

"I don't mean it that way, but this is something I have to do. My hair gets unruly if I don't look after it."

"Em, I've never seen you with a hair out of place."

"That doesn't come easy. I've been neglecting things to hang out with you."

"Not sure how to take that, either. You're saying I'm getting in the way of your life?"

"Gabe, don't be that way."

"Back at ya, babe."

Now she didn't know what to say.

"Emma, if you don't want to see me anymore, all you have to do is say so."

"That's not what I'm trying to say." Or was it?

Things were getting a little scary with Gabe, too intense, too out of control. He was not part of her plan, and she hated feeling off kilter.

"Hope you and your hair enjoy your evening." Then he was gone.

CHAPTER 57

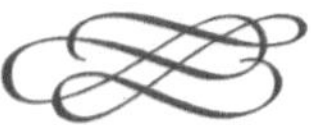

Moving didn't take long. The little house came furnished, so it was just her linens, kitchen things, clothing, and personal stuff to move. Most of that was still in boxes in the garage from when she'd moved out of her previous rental.

Each box was sealed shut and labeled with its contents, as well as a list number. That number corresponded to a spreadsheet Emma kept, detailing each item in that box. It was the most efficient way of packing.

In less than a day, Emma cleaned her new place and moved in. Now, with no packing boxes in sight, she surveyed her kingdom, one that was hers and hers alone.

Her slow cooker and air fryer sat prominently on the kitchen counter, the appliances she used the most. Well, apart from her Nespresso coffee maker. She loved that thing, but her mother hadn't, so it was relegated to the garage's storage area. Until now.

With her usual meticulousness, Emma had planned out how to tell her mother she was moving out. This would not be a discussion, but a telling, no room for guilt-tripping, although she knew Esther would try. The spin she put on it was that this separation would be good for them, that Esther didn't need to be put back in her mothering role. No, that wasn't fair since she'd already raised her daughter. Yeah, it was a spin, but a way of saving face for them both.

Emma cleaned out her mom's kitchen fridge, removing anything old, unrecognizable, or not to Esther's taste. In the nearly empty freezer compartment, she neatly stacked the frozen meals she'd stockpiled in the basement's deep freeze, making them easy for Esther to get, without needing to navigate the stairs. There was enough so her mother could feed herself for almost two weeks.

She stroked her mom's ego with reminders of how much Esther had done all the years Emma was growing up. Now, Emma didn't want to put a damper on her mom's social life; Esther should be free to entertain any of her friends whenever she wanted, without worrying if the company would bother Emma.

Then she broke the script, something she never did. "Mom, please understand. I have to do this, have to trust myself. You always told me that action breeds results. I feel like I have to make this move, that it's right for me."

For just a minute, her mom held her eyes. This was a direct look, woman to woman, with no manipulation or anything other than two people being honest with each other. Esther nodded before fretting once again about what people would think.

And they were back to their regular way of relating.

Emma explained how she told everyone at school how good her mom had been while she got herself settled back in Goodrich, but she was fine now, thanks to her mom's help, and was ready to go back to living on her own.

Spin doctor, for sure. But appearances meant everything to Esther, and this fit the image she wanted people to see. Or at least what she *used* to want people to believe. This fragile, needy woman was not Esther Lowry. Hopefully, this nudge would get her back on her feet. It had to.

This would either push Esther to take back her life or crumple the veneer of living she had now. The choice would have to be Esther's. The problem was that when people broke, they shattered everyone around them. Emma needed to remove herself from that fallout zone.

It felt a bit funny not mentioning her move to Gabe. He sent a text every night, and she kept her replies cordial, but light. She was good at that, being friendly yet keeping people at a distance, giving people what they wanted while not letting them demand more of her than she was willing to yield.

Text messages were not easy to interpret; you missed the nuances decipherable from in-person conversations. Even the few times Gabe called, things were not like they had once been between them, back when a half hour phone call flew by. Now their talk was stilted, with no free flow of thoughts. Did she sense a coolness to his tone? It would be easier if she could read his body language. She thought of suggesting they

FaceTime but wasn't sure she wanted to encourage that level of intimacy.

Instead, their calls dwindled to nothing, and texts to one or two a week. Looked like their little interlude was drawing to a close.

She didn't know how she felt about that, but there was little point in analyzing emotions to death; they were messy and didn't stay in their assigned compartments. A relationship had never been part of her plan, anyway, at least not with a guy who was a total stranger.

She'd reserve judgment until he was back in town. That is, *if* he returned. He had a life back in Texas, and a job waiting for him.

CHAPTER 58

Gabriella's house was in as good a shape as they were going to get it. The cleaners would come in tomorrow; the bills were put on autopay, the overflowing dumpster would be removed this afternoon, and the realtor was taking care of the rest.

There was nothing to pack, other than a few photos they each selected, and the clothes they'd brought with them. Vehicles inspected and full of gas, Gabe stood beside his truck and Blair beside the Bentley.

Gabe studied the air by Blair's left ear. "Ah, I was wondering." He paused. "Before we hit the road, would you like to see the ranch where I work and meet my boss? He's a good guy."

Blair could hear his wife's voice inside his head, coaching him on how to handle this. Much as he itched to get back to his family and his farm, what could another hour or two hurt? "Sure."

Some of the tension left Gabe's shoulders.

"Always interesting to see how other agricultural operations work." There. That took things out of the touch-feely realm, and on a basis within their comfort zones.

Even though it was just after seven in the morning, Gabe knew where he'd find Colin. The rancher always started his workday with coffee, work assignments, and paperwork. "Get the blasted stuff out of the way," Colin believed.

Once out of the city, both men breathed easier, taking in the open spaces, rolling hills, brindled grasslands, and in the distance, limestone cliffs of the Texas Hill Country. The entrance to the ranch was about a 15-minute drive northeast of San Antonio. After driving under the overhead arch displaying the Avery Ranch brand, and following the dusty half-mile lane, Gabe and Blair parked their vehicles in front of a windowed office attached to the side of a machine shed.

Exiting their vehicles, the men gazed at the surrounding fields holding Texas longhorns in the distance. "You miss having cattle?" Gabe asked Blair.

"Nope. Got my fill with Clarabelle. And when I start wondering about my decision to get out of them, I need only go give Reid, or Greg and Stan a hand with theirs. That's enough for me."

The office door opened, and an older man approached, a huge grin on his face. "Gabe! Y'all are back." Colin Avery came forward with his hand extended, pulling Gabe in for a one-armed, manly hug. "Good to see you, boy."

"Good to see you too, sir. But I'm not back, just stopped in to see how things are going and to introduce you to my brother. I'd like you to meet Blair Windstrom. Blair, this is my boss and the owner of this ranch, Colin Avery."

The men shook hands. "That's a sweet ride you have there, young fella." Colin nodded at the Bentley.

"Not mine, sir. It belongs to Gabe's grandmother."

"*Our* grandmother."

Colin looked between the two younger men, their resemblance striking. To Blair, he said, "You must be pretty proud to call this man your brother."

"I'm getting there, sir."

"Well, we're mighty proud of him. The place isn't the same without him here."

"How are things going?" Gabe asked.

Colin scowled. "The fella we hired to take your place didn't work out. He had the same paper qualifications as you, and decent references, but he wasn't the man for the job, at least not on *my* ranch."

"What happened?"

"He might have been an okay mechanic but did the bare bones the job required. He fixed things on a 'good enough' basis, not thinking about the long haul. And he thought routine maintenance beneath him. When there was nothing broken down, he sat and picked his nails, no matter that the rest of us were running around putting out fires, he never pitched in. Said he was a heavy duty mechanic, not some wrangler."

"Sorry to hear that. So you have no one now?"

"Got some ads out, and Tommy said he'd send someone over if we really get in a pinch, but no. That's why I was hoping you're back ahead of your six months."

Gabe and Blair exchanged glances. "Is there anything urgent that needs doing right now?"

"You know how it is. There's always some piece of equipment on the fritz."

"Tell me about it," said Blair.

"You ranch, too?" Colin asked.

"I farm. Used to have cattle, mainly Angus, but got out of that. Now I mostly crop the land but help my cousins with their stock operations."

"Wanna have a tour of the place?"

"Love to, sir." What farmer or rancher didn't like checking out other people's spreads?

Metal on metal bangs came from inside the machine shed, along with muffled complaints. "That'll be Jack. The 5310's down, and he's trying to fix it."

"You have a John Deere 5310?" asked Blair.

"Can't say we do right now, since it ain't working," said Colin.

This machine shed and the shop beside it were as familiar to Gabe as his own living room. Except, he'd never seen the shop in this condition. Tools were all over, the concrete floor littered with parts, and hardly a clear bench surface to work on.

A feeling settled in Gabe's gut, one he couldn't shake off.

Colin continued the tour, pointing things out and responding to Blair's questions.

Everywhere Gabe looked, he saw signs that all was not well on the Avery ranch. Gone were the days when farming mainly required a strong back and a willingness to put in the hours. Modern ranching and farming relied on machinery and that machinery had to be in top running order or work ground to a halt.

Colin had been good to him over the years, and he owed the man. "Sir, I really do need to get back up north—unfinished business and all that, but what if I stayed here a week and tackled some of these repairs for you?"

"Would you?" The relief in Colin's voice was palpable. "There's room in the bunk house if you don't want to drive back and forth from your place."

Gabe turned to Blair. "How about I catch up with you later? I'll see you in a week or so while I give Colin a hand here."

CHAPTER 59

Having accomplished as much as he could in a week, Gabe left the Avery ranch. Pausing before turning onto the road, he sent a text to his brother.

Brother. It felt funny to say that word, but he was thinking he could get used to it.

Just finishing up here and heading your way. I should be there within three days.

He had barely made it onto the road before the reply came back. Pulling over, he read the message.

Stop here before you do anything else. We have something you'll wanna know about.

Gabe immediately texted back a…

?

For a response, Blair sent an emoji:

¯_(ツ)_/¯

Very funny. He sent one of his own:

👊

Gabe waited, but nothing more came from Blair.

While he was stopped, he sent a text to Emma. Part of him wasn't sure if he was doing this out of habit or if he really wanted to connect with her.

> Finished here in San Antonio for now and heading your way. Should be there in three days.

This reply came back almost immediately.

> Drive safely.

Well, what did he expect? It's not like he had

said anything overly personal to her, either. But this polite-stranger-thing was getting on his nerves. He needed to move things forward or back off completely. He didn't think he could remain in this hinterland with Emma. The problem was, he also didn't want to contemplate his life without her.

~

Beth questioned her husband's judgment. "Are you sure you should go ahead and do this without first talking to Gabe about it?"

"Beth, it's a house, just a place to stay. It's not like he's signing a mortgage or making a lifetime commitment. We told the Olsons that Gabe will take their place for a month. They trust that I am vouching for my brother, so they're fine with having him move into their house. After this first month, it's up to Gabe what he wants to do."

"Do you even know that he wants to stay that long?" Beth asked.

"He does."

"He was fine staying with us."

"No, he wasn't."

"Blair!"

"I don't mean I didn't want him around, but

he's a guy used to living on his own. He needs his space and to feel independent. Anyone would."

"You talk like you think you know him."

"I kinda think I do. It's funny. I've only known about his existence for less than a month, but he's starting to feel like family, for better or worse."

Gabe pulled into the Windstrom farmyard, feeling curiously like he'd come home. Weird. Probably because this was the only blood relation he had left, even if they were recent acquaintances.

Getting out of his truck, he breathed in the spring air. The only snow left was in the hedgerows. The sun and wind had dried up much of the muck. Near the sheds, a row of green machinery made its appearance in preparation for spring seeding. There was something about spring—the budding greenery ready to pop open, the returning birds flying overhead, the promise of life, and the air of hopefulness.

This wasn't his home. Born and raised in Texas, winter weather was foreign to him, as were the people he'd met here. Despite being strangers, they'd welcomed him into their midst, made him feel a part of things.

Even Emma, who had no blood ties to him, After their shaky beginning, she'd welcomed him, and seemed to enjoy his company. Had he misread things, mistaking her rural hospitality for something more? She was a hard woman to read.

Movement caught his eye by one of the tractors. Blair was greasing a John Deere 9520 tractor. Now *this* was something Gabe understood. Machinery. Stuff you put your hands on, stuff that either worked or didn't, and when it didn't, Gabe knew how to handle it.

He walked over to where Blair worked. "Hey, want a hand?"

Blair's head came up to look at him, then returned his attention to the filter he was about to remove. "Never turn down the offer of help."

The tractor's manual lay open on the toolbox, the servicing steps outlined. It was easy for Gabe to see which task Blair was on, so he moved on to the next one. The two brothers worked in silence for the next hour, speaking only when Gabe needed to know where a certain tool or lube was kept.

Finally, Blair stretched, the joints in his

shoulders popping audibly. Grabbing a rag, he wiped some of the grease off his hands. "I gotta get to the house. Told Beth I'd make supper. It's almost ready, but I have to put it in the oven." He started toward the house. "Coming?"

"So what's this big secret you said I'll want to know about?"

"You're renting a house."

"I am?"

Blair nodded. "Remember you talked about maybe sticking around?"

"Yeah." It came out cautiously.

"Well, we fixed that for you. Our neighbors across the road and down half a mile are getting older—Jed's had some health problems, and his wife's diabetes isn't getting any better. Their kids want them to be closer to medical help, so the Olsons are moving to Watford. They don't like leaving their house empty, so they asked Beth and me if we knew anyone we trusted who might be looking for a place to rent." He looked at Gabe, waiting for a response that wasn't forthcoming. "So, it's done. The place is yours for a month. If you want it after that, or don't want it, you'll have to take that up with Jed."

And it was done. Looked like Gabe would be staying around, at least for a while.

CHAPTER 60

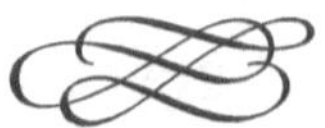

It was one thing to have a place of his own to stay, but keeping up a house wasn't enough for a guy used to putting in long hours of work.

Gabe's days quickly fell into a pattern of helping Blair ready his machinery for spring seeding, then they moved on to Reid's and Mona's farm to do the same there, then back to the Wells farm where Gabe was already familiar with their operation. Many farmers keep a notebook inside each tractor or implement, listing things they noticed that might not stop the machine from running but were signs of impending wear, or something that needed to be checked out. Gabe was on it. Once he discovered these gems, while the others continued with spring maintenance, Gabe got busy with the repairs and adjustments.

"You know," Jim Wells told him, "There are not nearly enough people around here with your skills. It takes time to run your machinery to the dealership for servicing. But many farmers would jump at the chance to have a mechanic come to their place."

It was worth some thought. That is, if he was sticking around. He had a job waiting for him back in Texas, but apart from some casual friends and his boss, what was holding him to that life? Could he carve out a new one for himself here?

That depended. Could he fit in with his new shirttail relatives? He was still feeling his way with them. It seemed reckless to throw away his life and all he'd ever known to risk tossing in his lot with these new people.

Would they want him around? And Emma. Would *she* want him around?

~

Emma looked at her phone messages.

Yesterday was the day Gabe was supposed to have arrived back in Goodrich. Lots could have happened along the way—vehicle trouble, bad weather, or anything could have delayed his arrival. Maybe he was tired from all of that driving and resting up. Or maybe he was here and just hadn't contacted her.

Emma scrolled back through the texts they'd shared the last few weeks. Sparse, compared to the volume of words that had once flown between the two of them. What had she last said to him?

Drive safely.

Technically, nothing was wrong with that, but it was something you'd say to anyone, even a stranger. Although part of her actively worked to keep Gabe at arm's length, another nonsensical part of her longed to reel him in. As if she had the power to do either of those things.

Usually, when she wanted something, she meticulously planned how to achieve her goal. The problem now was she didn't know what she wanted. So unlike her usual decisive self. The thing was, what she wanted, what she felt with Gabe, was scary. She didn't do scary. She did plans—steps to get herself where she wanted to be.

Like her career. She'd had it all planned out, and in the city, there were lots of opportunities to rise. Teaching was great, and she loved making a difference in kids' lives. But was that enough? Many people picked a grade, then taught it their entire career. Something about that seemed stagnant, yet she'd met some of those teachers, and they were happy with their choices. Was that good enough for her? How could you stand out if you did the same thing year after year, one cog amid hundreds of others doing the same thing?

She'd applied for and been accepted into grad school. But when her mom needed her, it just wasn't possible to take a leave, be a full-time student, and commute daily to be with Esther. So, grad school was on hold.

But now there was another opportunity. The university offered an extension program, where a cohort of working teachers would take classes together on weekends, summer holidays and online to get their Master's degrees.

On the plus side, she could keep her job and eventually get an advanced degree. The negative was a loss of choice. Through this cohort, only two routes were offered; one was geared toward those who wanted to become school administrators, and the other for those who wanted to attain graduate credentials in special education. Both were valid paths to do more than classroom teaching, but she'd have to figure out which would get her further.

That also depended on where she ended up. She'd need to plot her course differently if she moved back to the city than if she remained within the Goodrich school district.

Remaining here? At one time, that thought would have never entered her head; this move was just temporary until her mother got back on her feet. Her daughter relocating to a house of her own almost did Esther in, if you paid any attention to the older woman's complaints. But no one did, no one except Emma.

Esther survived this first week of living on her own without withering away. Baby steps. They were at the point now where every once in a while the two of them had an actual conversation, rather than a nitpicking fest. Maybe there was hope.

But it was lonely.

There, she'd said it, admitted it to herself. Oh, she wasn't lonely for Esther's company; in fact, it felt good to be out of that oppressive atmosphere. And no, it wasn't friends she missed; it was one friend and just that one.

Gabe. Although the man had not been around Goodrich long, he'd certainly made his presence felt. And other things felt. He aroused feelings in Emma no one else had before, things that made her almost forget all her plans, all the things she thought she needed to be successful and happy. Some of those evenings when they were together, plotting a course never occurred to her. She just was. For those hours, she relaxed and simply enjoyed.

But then things changed between them. She didn't really know him, and he didn't know her, the real her. No one did. She'd perfected displaying the image expected of her, could present the correct Emma needed for almost every situation. Except when around Gabe. He prodded. He probed, as if mining for the nugget at the heart of Emma. *That* was something no one got to see, not even her. He wanted more of her than she deemed safe to give.

And he'd backed off when she wouldn't, when she *couldn't* share more of herself.

Her phone signaled an incoming text message. She looked at the name.

Gabe.

CHAPTER 61

It was awkward at first, but slowly, Gabe and Emma worked their back to the place they had once been, to an easy closeness. They spent most evenings and weekends together, Emma carefully scheduling her hair maintenance around these times.

Now that the weather was nice out, sometimes Gabe walked Esther to Emma's house, pacing his steps to hers, allowing her to hold onto his arm. Although Esther's carping still snuck out from time to time, it was easier for Gabe to steer the conversation away from Emma's faults, with Esther not on her home ground. When her nitpicking grew too much, Gabe excused himself from the dinner table, and either settled himself in front of Emma's television with a book, or some little job that needed to be done. Emma knew that some of these jobs were made up, but she appreciated the way he removed himself from the situation and Esther's presence. Esther would soon correct herself and attempt to bring Gabe back into her orbit. Without saying anything overt, Gabe got across the message that he wouldn't tolerate criticisms of Emma.

When was the last time anyone had stuck up for her like this, Emma mused. Likely never, at least not that she could remember.

Was he such a nice guy that he'd do that for anyone? Or did he do it for just her?

No matter the reason, it felt good that someone cared.

And she learned that there were others who cared as well. Spending time with Gabe meant she was drawn into the orbit of his half-brother and extended family. Suppers and outings often included Blair and Beth, Stan and Becca, or Reid and Mona. They accepted her. Even when she simply sat quietly, they smiled at her, included her. None of the exhausting effort to always be one on top, the way it was in high school or even in college. She could just be.

Was this what it was like for other people?

~

One evening when she and Gabe were at Blair's, it seemed like a good idea to pick Beth's brain about the grad school program she was wondering about. After all, Beth had a Master's degree already.

"Beth, what do you think about the university's extension grad program? Emma asked when there was a lull in the conversation.

Gabe took his arm from around Emma's shoulders and pulled away. "Are you thinking of moving away to go to school?"

Beth answered for her. "No, they bring the program here. It's held in Watford some evenings, weekends and during the summer." She turned to Emma. "You considering it?"

She nodded. "But I'm not sure which stream would get me further."

"Depends on what you see yourself doing down the road."

"You mean you might not teach?" Gabe asked. "You're good at it. You seem to love it."

"Yeah, I do. But a person can't just stay still, you have to keep moving forward."

"Why?" asked Blair.

Emma frowned. "Well, you just do. You have to keep moving toward something."

"Who says?" Blair was stuck on this.

"It's different being a farmer," Emma tried, but got cut off.

Blair leaned forward. "Do you mean *just* a farmer? An occupation that doesn't require a graduate degree?"

"No! Of course, farmers can be ambitious too."

"What if I don't want to own the biggest machinery, or buy up more and more land? What if I just want to grow food to feed people, and create a nice lifestyle for me and my family?"

"Then, ah good. That's the right thing for you."

"But not for you?"

"I… no." How did this conversation get turned around? "I'm not a farmer. I was talking about me, not anyone else." Her voice got smaller as the sentence petered out.

Beth stepped in. "Do you have a goal in mind, Emma?"

"I'm not sure. I always planned to rise in education. There were more avenues when I taught in an urban district. If I stay here, I think to advance in my career, I'd have to go into admin or special ed. Admin would get me further, but it might be easier to get into special ed."

"You're thinking about moving back to the city?" Gabe's arms were crossed now.

"I don't know. Just looking at all my options."

"Some people take grad school classes simply because they're interested in them, or want to become a better teacher," Beth said.

"That, too, of course. But if I can get more out of it, I will."

"This sounds like the Emma I knew in high school. Always looking for ways to put herself ahead," Blair mumbled.

Emma glared at him. "What's that supposed to mean?"

Beside her, Gabe tensed.

"It means exactly what I said." Blair was not backing down.

"Blair," warned Beth.

"Is there something wrong with me trying to map out my future?" What didn't these people understand?

"Will it make you happy?"

"Happy? What does it matter how I feel? It's the results that count."

"It matters when it's at the cost of everything else." Blair's voice was quieter now. His eyes flicked between Emma and his brother.

Lights flashed through the living room window, signaling the arrival of a vehicle.

"That'll be the Adams bringing the girls home." Beth went to the door, shooting Blair a warning glance over her shoulder.

Within minutes, the room filled with the excited chatter of a teen and pre-teen talking over each other to tell their parents about their day.

CHAPTER 62

Emma said she wouldn't apologize for who she was. She insisted she had not meant any implied criticism of Blair or his life choices; she was only talking about herself.

Gabe had no problems with a woman having ambitions, who knew what she wanted and went after it. He did object if the woman was Emma, and her plans took her away from him.

But he didn't have the right to tell her that.

So instead, he sulked. Yeah, he was man enough to admit it. That's what he was doing.

During the drive home from Blair's place, they deliberately kept their conversation light and inconsequential; neither willing to tread in water that might be over their heads, nor currents that might push them to a point beyond retreat.

Still, as he lay in bed that night, Gabe could not get what she'd said out of his head. Sure, she was good at her job. With a woman as brilliant as Emma, it only made sense that she'd want to get ahead. But could she do that here?

Here. He'd begun to think of Goodrich as home. At some point, he'd have to make a decision about returning to Texas or staying here.

Was there a third alternative? Maybe. What if Emma had a different destination in mind? What if she wanted to move somewhere else to further her career? Would he follow her?

He was not a city boy, so not. He'd tried it, and although he could force himself to survive anywhere, surviving was not the same as thriving.

Was that how Emma felt about Goodrich?

He hoped not, because he was getting more enmeshed in this community. But if the only way to be with her was to leave, would he? Would she want him to?

Although the move to the city of Watford had been hard on Jed Olson and his wife, it was the right move. One episode of Olga's hypoglycemia leaving her incoherent and another of his pulse skyrocketing convinced the couple that their farming days were over. Now, not only were they renting their house to Gabe, but their land as well. They needed the income to afford life in the city, yet were not yet willing to sever all ties with their land. So, they compromised by renting it.

Gabe and Blair reached an understanding. In exchange for Gabe's labor and plying his mechanical skills on Blair's machinery and land, Gabe could use that machinery to farm his newly rented land. The two men would work together on seeding and harvesting. They'd give it a year, keeping the agreement loose, each attempting to be scrupulously fair to the other.

Gabe had more thoughts, which for now he kept to himself. There would be money coming in from the sale of Gabriella's house. *Their* grandmother's house. Since Blair absolutely refused to split the proceeds with him, maybe there was a way to run the money through the farms, benefiting them both.

But that sounded like he was putting down roots here.

Could he do that if the person who held a gigantic chunk of his heart left?

They both had a tendency to sweep things under the rug, anything to maintain peace between them. Gabe's motto had always been why shine a light on things when you can pretend they don't exist, especially things you couldn't do anything about.

But that only worked for so long. If anything was going to become of this relationship, he and Emma needed to talk, really talk, both of them without getting their backs up.

Huh. Right. Like *that* was going to happen.

He had a lot, a *lot* vested in this, so he better man up.

Don't poke the bear, he told himself. But what if that bear couldn't hibernate forever?

The bear was not Emma. It was that conversation they'd had in Blair's living room.

Did Emma look down on farmers? Because if that's what he was setting himself up to be, his wife had better be okay with it.

Wife?

Yikes. That word popped into his head of its own volition. He'd not let his thoughts get that far. Yet there it was. Yeah, that's where his heart saw this path taking him. Taking *them,* he hoped.

He had to try.

"Em, are you thinking of doing that grad school program?"

She glanced quickly at him. "I'm thinking about it. Why?"

"Just wondering. Do you have a deadline?"

"I have another two weeks to apply for the session that starts in July."

"How would you feel about giving up your summer holidays to go back to school?"

She shrugged. "The public thinks teachers have the summers off. Most spend a fair chunk of that time preparing for the class they'll teach that fall. This would just be a different focus. Besides it's part of what you sacrifice if you want to get ahead."

"That's important to you? Getting ahead?"

"Isn't it important to everyone? That's how you're judged."

Gabe's eyebrows knit. "No, you're judged by who you are, not what you do."

"Same difference."

"No, I don't think so." He turned Emma to face him. "You have intrinsic worth exactly as you are, for who you are. You don't have to accomplish anything to have value."

"Says who?"

"Oh, Emma. Someone has done a number on

you."

She stiffened in his arms. "What's that supposed to mean?"

He pulled her closer. "You are a wonderful woman. If you never did anything other than what you already have done, you would be just as wonderful.

She shook her head. "It's only results that people notice."

"Who cares what anyone notices?"

"*I* care."

"What do you think about me?"

"You in general, or do you have something specific you're getting at?"

He'd love to know how she felt about him in general, but right now was too chicken to ask. "About what I've accomplished."

"I don't know you that well…"

"Em…"

"Okay. If it's full honesty you want…"

"Yes." Even if it hurt.

"I wonder how long you're going to stick around here. You had a career back in Texas, not that I'm suggesting you should move back there. But how long can you just hang around your brother's place?"

Gabe tried to unclench his jaw before

replying. "What if I'm enjoying getting to know that brother?"

"That's great, and you should spend time with him. But what's your goal? What's your plan for your life?"

"What if I don't have my life all mapped out?"

"You should! How will you get anywhere if you don't know the steps to get there?"

CHAPTER 63

Gabe knew when to back away, so they left their conversation dangling. Both he and Emma went back to politely ignoring the elephant in the room. Even with their fundamental differences, he couldn't stay away from her.

And, he noticed that even when he gave her an opportunity, she didn't make excuses to escape his company. Even when her body posture spoke defense, her eyes pleaded for closeness, and she melted into his arms. Was there ever a woman full of more contradictions than his Emma? Too bad she wasn't an open book like him.

Although neither signed the Armistice in blood, nor even spoke about it, Emma and Blair remained civil, then edged toward being cordial with one another. Gabe suspected Beth had a lot to do with Blair's part in the truce. Emma knew how to read a room, and how to play to the people around her. He hated how that made her sound manipulative. She wasn't. For Emma, that was the way you got along with others.

They were once again at the Windstrom farm. Since Gabe worked there, Beth called Emma to join them for a barbecue this evening. Now they sat around the picnic table, stomachs full.

It was Beth who issued the invitation.

"Camping? You mean like in a tent? Sleeping on the ground?"

"Yeah, that's what camping is about."

"I've never been camping," Emma admitted.

"Really? And it's about time you did." No big deal to Gabe as they sat around the kitchen table at Blair's and Beth's house.

Seeing Emma's skepticism, Beth intervened. "Definitely join us, Emma. It'll be fun."

"And we don't even have to take a bath that night," said Randine.

"No bath?" asked Emma. "You mean they only have showers?" Public showers. She cringed.

"Nope," Blair told her. "Where we're going, it's pretty rustic and there are no services."

"What do you mean by services?" Emma asked. This was a new world to her.

Gabe explained. "Some campgrounds have services like hookups for water and electricity, and showers and bathrooms with flush toilets."

Flush toilets, wondered Emma. What other kind were there? This did not sound like her kind of outing. She used the first excuse that came to mind. "I'll have to pass. I don't have any camping gear."

"No problem," Beth told her. "We have lots—plenty of tents and sleeping bags, all the gear we'll need."

Tents? "You mean all of us would be sharing a tent?" Nope, she didn't know these people well enough, and even if she did, no one, but no one saw her at night without her makeup on.

"We have four tents," Blair told her. "One for Beth and me, the girls will share one, and you and Gabe can each have your own."

Well, that was something. But back to that shower thing Randine mentioned. "How do we wash?" Emma asked.

Beth answered. "We bring along water in a 5-gallon jug that we use for drinking, cooking, and washing. We only plan to be gone one night, so will pack food for lunch and supper the first night, and then three meals for the next day.

"And s'mores," Randine and reminded her.

"And s'mores." That was a given.

"Wait," Emma said. "What are you talking about? I thought camping was a summer sport. It's barely spring."

Gabe answered. "I wondered about that, too. But these people go *winter* camping even."

"Yeah, the first time they made us go, we thought they were trying to get rid of us," Friday told Emma. "But we survived and even wanted to go again."

"This weekend is when we planned for it. The weather's supposed to be nice," Beth said.

"Thanks for the invitation," Emma said, "but I don't think it's my thing."

CHAPTER 64

Now, here she was, against all of her better judgment, Emma thought to herself. How had she let herself get talked into this? How did she overlook that part about services and flush toilets?

There weren't any—toilets, that is. Instead, there was an outhouse; what a ridiculous name for such a structure. Not even a men's and women's one, but one shared facility.

The 4' x 4' structure held a wooden bench, and that's it. Sitting prominently on the side of the bench was a plastic Folger's ground coffee container. How odd. Who would leave a coffee container in a public place where people did their private business?

Squishing into the tiny room with her, Beth pulled off the coffee can lid, showing Emma the roll of toilet paper stowed safely within. Beside it, someone had screwed a toilet seat with its lid closed onto the bench. Beth lifted the lid to show Emma the hole underneath.

Emma wrinkled her nose, taking a step back, banging into the wall. The stench was noticeable even before they'd entered this sorry excuse for a building, but with that lid up, the odor of excrement, overlaid with sickly sweet chemicals, cloyed the air. Gross!

Pulling her backpack from her shoulders, Beth unzipped the side compartment and pulled out a jug of hand sanitizer, setting it beside the coffee can.

This was supposed to pass for hygiene?

The girls informed Emma that the rule was everyone had to set up their own tent. Emma pointed out it wasn't fair that Friday and Randine only had to do half the amount of work because they were sharing.

Friday grinned at her. "Yeah, sucks to be you.'

The competitor in Emma rose to the challenge. If those young girls could handle it, she could certainly figure out how to set up a pop-up tent and do it faster than them.

Or not.

"Want a hand?" asked Gabe, only his head and shoulders peeking out from the open flap of his tent.

"No, I've got it." These flimsy plastic rods were supposed to hold up the roof of her tent?

She did it, though. Just not fast.

Beth hushed her foster daughters' snickers when they laughed at Emma's attempts.

There was a fine line between letting herself get dehydrated, and drinking so much she would have to use that filthy outhouse. It was dark now, their circle of tents illuminated by the dancing flames of the campfire.

Nothing in Emma's life replicated the feelings of warmth, comfort, and relaxation that came from being close to a crackling fire in the great outdoors. Maybe this hadn't been such a bad idea after all.

The warmth of the fire stole the chill from the night air, making it almost cozy. The sweet, smoky aroma, the flickering flames, the gentle heat, and the sounds of popping wood burning cocooned them together. The radiant glow illuminated the surrounding area, casting shadows and creating a sense of intimacy.

The company of friends around the fire,

sharing stories, laughter, and good food, was all a new experience for Emma, one she'd cherish. At the top of her list of memories to preserve was snuggling into Gabe's arms, a blanket wrapped around their shoulders. Gradually, the conversation stilled as all six of them stared into the fire, mesmerized by the flickering flames.

The spell was shattered by giggling. Randine and Friday, armed with flashlights, ran off to use the facilities. Emma squirmed. How long could she wait until she had to do the same thing? Until daylight?

She caught Gabe watching her. "Want me to go with you?" he asked. Good grief, no. How embarrassing. If she got desperate, maybe she would tag along with the girls the next time they went to the outhouse.

They called them thermal pads. A fancy name for a mattress that, when fully inflated, was less than an inch thick. How was this any better than sleeping on bare ground? As if.

Reading her mind, Gabe explained. "They provide insulation from the cold ground. You'll be glad you have one."

An irregular thunking woke Emma. A hard slam and a couple smaller ones, a few seconds of blessed silence, then it happened all over again. That irregular pattern.

Snuggling deeper into her sleeping bag, Emma tried to catch up on her sleep. It was her bladder that had done her in. She tried to make it through the night without having to use that foul outhouse, it just wasn't gonna work. She wasted hours trying to ignore the demands of her bladder, before finally wiggling out of her sleeping bag, shivering in the cold night air. Fumbling in the dark to put on her shoes and jacket, then pulling up the zipper of her tent flap, trying to do it slowly so as not to wake anyone up, she failed.

She barely got to her feet outside her tent when Gabe was by her side, flicking on a flashlight, and pointing it at their feet. Taking her hand, he said, "Come on, I'll go with you." And he had, standing right outside the thin door of the revolting little building. It was impossible to stifle the sound of her urinating as it splashed on who knows what down in that hole.

Hard to maintain your dignity when taking a leak in the dark in the middle of nowhere with the man you most wanted to impress standing three feet away. This was *so* not the image she wanted to portray.

Thank goodness for the darkness. Gabe couldn't see the humiliation on her face, and she couldn't read what she thought of as disgust on his. With a quick, 'thanks', Emma squatted in front of her tent, eased up the zipper as quietly as she could. Trying not to point her butt into the air, she crawled inside. She was never going camping again.

Whether it was the fresh air, or the burden of embarrassment, Emma had fallen quickly back to sleep, the only sound she heard before drifting off, apart from the wind in the trees, was Gabe's retreating footsteps, then his tent's zipper opening and closing, the rustle of his sleeping bag as he slid inside it.

Voices. Giggles. Then Beth's reprimand telling the girls to keep it down since Emma was still sleeping.

"She needs to be up anyway if we're going hiking."

Hiking. Ugh. At this hour? Emma brought her wrist up to her face, the motion turning her Fitbit watch on. 6:35. This was Saturday morning, her chance to sleep in. Guess not.

"Here, I'll take her some coffee. That will get her up," offered Randine.

"She takes two creams and one sugar in it," said Gabe.

There was the sound of a spoon clanking against a metal cup. The familiar snick of her tent's zipper rising. Maybe if she kept her eyes shut, whoever was out there would go away.

No such luck. Crawling forward while balancing a cup in one hand, Randine advanced, invading Emma's privacy. Give it up, she told herself. Pushing herself up on her elbows, plastering on a smile for the young girl, Emma waited for the coffee. Coming to a full sitting position, she reached for the cup Randine held out.

Now Randine peered at her, then the girl's face cracked into a huge grin. "Friday!" she yelled. "Come here and see Emma. She looks like a racoon, all black around her eyes." She fell to her side, laughing. "Uncle Gabe, ya gotta see this! She looks so funny."

From outside came Beth's voice. "Friday, don't you take one step." The voice got closer, then Beth's head peeked through the open tent flap. She reached out her hand to grab Randine's arm, coffee mug and all. "Get out of there and leave Emma in peace." To Emma, she said, "I'm sorry.

Please forgive my daughter." She looked closer at Emma, then hid her own grin. "Come out whenever you're ready."

CHAPTER 65

Minutes later, an arm snaked through the partially opened tent flap.

Beth. "Here, have some coffee. It makes everything better."

Despite her humiliation, the aroma of the rich, earthy and slightly smoky brew penetrated her senses, and Emma reached for it with a quiet "Thanks." The steam swirled in the cool morning air and she sniffed. One sip and she was hooked on the strong, full-bodied cup of caffeine.

Sitting cross-legged in her sleeping bag, she cradled the tin cup, letting the warmth and the aroma wash over her. Pine needles, clean air, and campfire. Thank goodness the wind was blowing away from that despicable outhouse, or that stench would override everything else.

Randine was probably right, and she did resemble a racoon, but Emma was afraid to look. When was the last time she'd gone to bed without first removing her makeup? Probably never; well, maybe that one time when she was a little girl, but she'd learned her lesson fast. Not only did she always cleanse her face properly, but she followed a five-step system that included moisturizers and eye cream. Always. Except for last night.

She had her creams in her toiletry bag occupying one compartment of the two suitcases she'd brought along on this trip. Gabe had laughed when she emerged from her bedroom with not one, but two totes in hand.

"You do know we're only going for one night, don't you?" he'd asked.

"I know that. What I don't know is what I'll need, so I have to be prepared." If there was one thing Emma excelled at, it was planning. If you covered every eventuality, you wouldn't be caught off guard.

But here she was, off guard. And mightily embarrassed. Sure, it had only been a ten-year-old girl who saw her looking such a mess, but that child attended the same school where Emma worked. She had an image to uphold, one she'd just blown.

How had she forgotten the nighttime ritual of cleansing her face? She was so out of routine, so out of her element. She remembered sitting on a log around the campfire, sharing a blanket with Gabe, his arm around her shoulders, keeping her tight to his side. The laughter, the easy camaraderie of Beth's family, the teasing between Blair and Gabe, almost as if they truly were brothers. The shrieks from the girls at Blair's ghost stories, each one more outlandish than the last. Her head had fallen on Gabe's shoulder, and she dozed, content.

The next thing she'd known was Gabe helping her to her feet. "You can't sleep here," he told her. "You'll appreciate the warmth of your sleeping bag once this fire dies down." He'd opened her tent, and helped her inside, settling her bag on top of the mattress. Rummaging around in her things, he'd produced her toque, plunking it on her head. "Beth says to sleep with this on; it'll help keep you warm."

She hadn't even heard him back out of her tent, nor the zipper sliding closed. The fresh air, the food, the company all worked together to push her into a dreamless sleep.

One where she wore her makeup.

The damage was done now and she couldn't go back. How to move forward, though?

She drank deeply, her coffee already half gone.

From around the fire, she listened to the voices.

"Why won't you let *me* wear makeup?" a child asked.

"Didn't you just see a good example of why *not* to wear makeup?" Blair replied.

"Blair!" Beth elbowed her husband.

"Sorry," he said. "The real answer is that you don't need it. You're beautiful the way you are."

That might be true for Friday; she was a cute kid.

"Look how gorgeous Beth is; she doesn't need to hide behind anything, and she doesn't put gunk on her face." Blair kissed Beth's cheek.

"I do, sometimes," Beth said.

"Yeah, but not when we're camping." Blair's tone was dry.

No one said anything. There was a thunk as someone threw another log on the fire, and the snap and pop as water evaporated from the wood.

Gunk. Hiding. Is that how they saw her? Did other people think that about her?

But she'd seen her face in the mirror before and after applying makeup. There were reasons beauty products were a multi-billion-dollar industry. It enhanced features, smoothed out uneven skin tones, hid overly large pores, and called attention to eyes.

Who wouldn't want to look their best?

Beth, that's who. Emma chided herself for that unkind thought. Yes, Beth was a pretty woman, but she could be so much more with the right kind of sculpting to bring out those cheek bones. Some smoky shadow would emphasize her blue eyes in contrast to her dark hair. Emma could share some tips with her. That is, if Beth wanted.

Did Beth feel that she'd already snagged her man and didn't need to worry about looking her best? Now, that was just a plain nasty thought, Emma chided herself. Nothing about Beth implied that. Beth didn't pretend. She was who she was, and Blair seemed to appreciate her for exactly that.

What might that feel like? To be loved for yourself, without any enhancements, to be good enough?

Beth wasn't perfect. Last night's supper proved that—burned bacon, toast with some black parts and some barely warmed parts, over-easy eggs under and overdone, some sticking to the cast iron frying pan, one falling into the fire, four boxes of Kraft Dinner tossed into a pot of boiling water, then mixed with packets of orange powder. No apologies for the quality of the meal, just laughter, and teasing, and everyone's forks scraping their plates clean.

Blair, Friday and Randine loved and approved of Beth even when she let her flaws show through. Last night around the campfire, the breeze constantly blew Beth's hair all about, obviously hair without benefit of extra-hold hair spray. Did the woman look her best? No, but her smile was radiant as she sat within the circle of Blair's arm, grinning at their foster daughters.

What would it be like to be so comfortable with yourself, to know you were valued just as you are? Unbidden, that tingly sensation inside the bridge of her nose warned her to take her thoughts elsewhere. Too late. Twin tears rolled down her cheeks.

Could her makeup get any worse?

CHAPTER 66

Was it possible to remain inside this tent all day? For the rest of her life? Emma was doubtful her bladder would tolerate that. But she could stay put at least until there was nothing left in her coffee cup.

Emma wiggled out of her sleeping bag. The slippery material made it impossible to do this silently, so the others around the campfire would know she was moving around.

First, her face.

Doing what she absolutely should have done last night, Emma dug out her makeup removal pads, the protective paper crinkling in the morning air, as she brought the moist paper to her face. And scrubbed.

She stopped. No! That was not how she treated her delicate skin. Gently, Emma brushed the towelette over her face, beginning at her neck, using an upward motion so as not to invite gravity to take over. A separate pad removed the stains on her eyelids and the mascara from her eyelashes. At least she hoped it did. Without a mirror to verify the kind of job she was doing, who knew? All she could do was mop up the best she could.

Stowing the soiled pads in the sealable plastic bag she'd brought along for that purpose, Emma debated applying fresh makeup. Again, without a mirror, how would that work?

What if she didn't? Could she just ignore the whole ritual and go out there barefaced? Never since middle school had she left her bedroom without makeup on.

Beth would be out there, almost assuredly, sans any sort of makeup at all. Was Beth the benchmark she wanted to hold herself to? The old Emma would scoff at that, but now she wasn't so sure. What would it be like to be so self-assured, like Beth, to not care what people thought of you?

Was that fair? Did Beth really not care about the opinion others had of her? Beth took pride in her work. While she was neat and tidy, was it just her appearance and other's reactions to it that Beth didn't think about?

Beth had Blair, secure in his love, so maybe she didn't worry about such things.

But *she* didn't have that. Or did she? Was there a chance that Gabe might like her anyway, even when she didn't look her best? Esther would say no, and that it wasn't worth the risk. Esther wasn't here, though, and sometimes Emma wearied of her mother's voice in her head.

Maybe she couldn't have her morning shower, but applying deodorant and combing her hair were things she couldn't skip. Pulling on fresh underclothes, socks, jeans, a t-shirt and a sweatshirt didn't take long. She finger-combed her hair into a low ponytail and secured it with a clip.

Dare she go out looking like this? Was it worth the risk?

Impossible to do this quietly, Emma raised the zipper of her tent. It's not like she could sneak out; they'd see her as soon as her head popped out of the fly.

Okay, Emma, you're made of stern stuff. You can do this.

She bared her naked face to the world.

Blair was there first, helping her to her feet, then with an arm around her, led her to the fire pit, seating her beside his brother. Gabe's arm awaited her, and he placed a kiss on the side of her head. Beth brought over the coffee pot, offering to refill her cup.

"Thanks. Morning, everyone." She gave a half-smile to the group gathered around the fire, not quite meeting anyone's eyes.

"Morning, beautiful," said Gabe.

Emma's eyes flew to his face. Was he being sarcastic? No, that was not the message his eyes sent. She relaxed into his side.

"The black's gone," commented Randine.

"Randine! We don't make personal comments about people," admonished Beth.

"But it's true," the girl replied. She squinted at Emma. "Mostly," she added.

Emma willed her hand not to fly to her face. "Hard to do a good job without a mirror."

"Why do you put that stuff on your face?" Randine asked.

"You idiot," her sister said. "To look good. Everyone knows that."

"How does it make you look good?"

Everyone waited for Emma's response.

"People use makeup to enhance their features, and to hide flaws."

"Why?"

"Well, to look their best."

"Why do you care?"

Beth tried to stall the child. "Randine, enough. Leave Emma alone to enjoy her coffee in peace."

"But I want to know. You don't go around looking at yourself in a mirror all day, so you can't see how you look."

Friday, a little older and wiser, answered. "It's about how other people see you."

"Why does it matter how other people see you?" Randine would not let this go.

Maybe the child had a point. "To be honest," Emma said, "I'm not sure. Maybe it doesn't matter, not nearly as much as I once thought it did."

That seemed to satisfy Randine. Or maybe the squirrel chattering at them from a tree branch snagged the girl's attention, but the conversation moved on.

Blair stood, tossing the dregs of his coffee into the fire. "Anyone up for this hike?"

"Sure, but I need a potty break first," said Beth. "Girls? Anyone else?"

Emma followed her, as did her daughters,

while Gabe and Blair dowsed the fire with water, scattered the ashes in the sand, and made sure the surrounding rocks were in place.

"Sorry again about this morning," Beth whispered to Emma. "Kids are unpredictable and you never what's going to come out of their mouths."

"It's all right, and maybe I've been a little too hung up on my appearance." She hated feeling this vulnerable. "I didn't bring a mirror with me. Do I look okay?"

"Emma, you look lovely, as usual. Maybe even more so today. Fresh, and well-rested."

Emma studied Beth's face. Was she telling the truth? There seemed no guile there.

CHAPTER 67

Her muscles loosened the more they walked. Dappled sunlight filtered through the pine needles of the trees around them. Roots and twigs littered the path, making it essential to watch the ground, yet with each step, something in the scenery snagged the eye. A tiny cerulean flower, soft green moss, mushrooms glistening in the morning dew.

Emma drew in a deep breath. How had she never before experienced the scents of an early morning in the forest?

Beside her, Gabe used their clasped hands to pull her closer, then to slow them down as they brought up the rear of their little group, placing a kiss on her knuckles. “I’m proud of you.”

"How so?"

"I know how tough this morning must have been for you."

"Yeah, well, kids, you know."

His gaze said he wasn't buying it. "You do look beautiful, you know."

She looked away, resisting the urge to cover her face with her hands.

Gabe stopped them on the path, Randine's voice drifting back to them. The child rarely stopped talking.

Letting go of her hand, Gabe cupped her face in his palms, running his thumbs up and down her cheeks. "You *are* beautiful. Just as you are, inside and out."

"Gabe…."

"Emma, believe me. Somehow, you come across as so strong and confident, but I don't think you see what I do when I look at you."

She had to ask. "What do you see?"

"I see the most incredible woman I've ever met. One who's smart and lovely, talented and dedicated not only to her students, but to her family. Someone who would champion any cause she believed in and not stop until she'd accomplished what she set out to do." He paused. "Someone I love."

Emma's breath hitched. Had she heard him right?"

"Emma, I love you." He searched her eyes.

She closed hers. It was too much.

"Emma?"

She brought her palms up, resting them on his chest. His warmth came through his sweatshirt. She raised her eyes to his.

"Em, everyone has something to fight for, but not everyone has someone to fight for them. I'd like to be that someone for you. That is, if you'd let me."

Tears filled her eyes, then overflowed.

"Emma, say something. Are those good tears, or have I scared you off?"

"I..." She swallowed and tried again. "No one has ever said such a thing to me. I've never really had someone in my corner before." It was true. Even though she'd had loving parents, they'd never made her feel that she was enough. Their approval was contingent on her trying harder, being the best. It was exhausting.

Could she trust this man? She thought of what Beth and Blair had, Becca and Stan, Greg and Aggie, Mona and Reid. Was such a thing possible for her?

"Babe, don't leave me hanging here."

Emma relaxed into him, her face buried in his shirt. "I love you, too."

"What? I didn't hear that."

She raised her face, the tears still coming, her smile tremulous. "I said I love you, too."

"Oh, thank God." He gathered her to him, swaying them gently from side to side. "Emma Lowry, would you marry me?"

Against his shoulder, she nodded.

"Em, I need words."

She raised her head. "I love you, and I'd love to marry you."

Gabe's whoop could be heard for miles. "She said yes!!!"

From up ahead came Blair's "Why the big surprise? Knew she would." His statement ended with an oomph as Beth elbowed him in the gut.

"Congratulations!" Beth yelled, covering up her husband's complaints about her ill treatment of him.

Hollers and hoots from the girls. Then Beth telling Friday and Randine, "No, you can't go see them right now. Give them a few moments alone together."

ONE MONTH LATER

Do events simply fall into place on their own or are they matters planned out long beforehand?

Either way, things came together.

Now, with a permanent stake in the community, Gabe approached his landlords. Rather than simply renting the Olsen's land, he put in a bid to buy all four sections. If the deal went through, that would mean his land base would match Blair's, a more fitting partnership.

The sale of Gabriella's house finalized. Once the legal, accounting, and other expenses were taken out, along with money set aside for the final taxes, there was a generous chunk of change left over. No matter what Gabe said, the incredibly stubborn Blair adamantly refused to accept any of the money.

So, with Emma's help, Gabe came up with a plan. Doubling their land base would put a strain on Blair's machinery, no matter what kind of foolish hours a two-man team attempted to put in.

Upgrading one of the Blair's tractors to a newer, higher horsepower model would allow it to pull larger equipment. Moving from a 45-foot air seeder to a 60-foot unit would make seeding faster and smoother, with fewer breakdowns than would be expected with the current, older equipment. Replacing the combine harvester with a newer, larger model would help get the crops off faster.

Agriculture was a risky business. Every spring, farmers invested hundreds of thousands of dollars getting seed into the ground, with no guarantee they'd make a profit come harvest time, or break even. Blair pointed this out to Gabe; *being* a farmer was a lot different from simply working *for* a farmer or rancher.

Gabe had no idea that the stubborn jut of his chin mimicked that of his brother.

"Don't say I never warned ya," Blair told him.

Using Blair's machinery as trade-ins brought

the cost of buying new equipment down to something manageable. With the combined money from the sale of Gabriella's house, plus Gabe's mother's home, he had enough in the bank to cover the new machinery, pay off most of the purchase of the Olsen land, and have enough left over to tide him through the first year of farming and living expenses, until he got a crop harvested in the fall.

But before any of that happened though, Gabe conferred with Beth to determine just how much it would cost a person to get a master's degree, then down the road, a doctorate. He had a feeling his ambitious wife-to-be would eventually turn her thoughts in those directions, and he wanted to make sure that money was not something that would stand in her way. Although he knew that his Emma would always find a way, this was one gift he could give to her.

CHAPTER 68

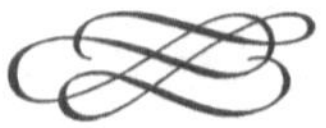

Alvin was better. After staying with his grandparents for nearly a week, he recovered from his respiratory illness and was back home with his parents. Aggie was almost fully recovered from her accident and her breathing no longer labored.

"I can't thank you enough," Aggie told Emma on the phone. "Without the heads up from you, I might have caught Alvin's virus. My doctor says that could have had serious implications for me."

"Glad it all worked out fine and that you're recovering."

"*I'm* recovering, but Greg is having a tough time getting over it. His hovering drives me nuts. But you know who didn't do too badly?

Alvin. For an autistic kid who doesn't take well to change or the unexpected, he handled the whole thing much better than we'd anticipated. And we owe a large part of that to you, with your understanding and help in supplying visuals."

"I just made up some stuff quickly. I can do that anytime you need it, or I can show you how to do it yourself."

"Alvin starting school was a big deal for us; we were terrified. He weathered kindergarten, but we were really worried about how Grade 1 would go. It's more structured and different. But it's been great, thanks to you. We can't tell you how much we appreciate the way you've gotten Alvin's school life off to such a good start."

"Thanks. I just did my job."

"It was more than that, far more, and we thank you. Our only regret is that he won't have you next year."

"I've started some visuals for him on transitioning to the next grade. Want to see what I've put together?"

Emma thought about her conversation with Aggie. Although teaching Grade 1 had been new to her, and lots of prep work, she'd enjoyed the challenge. And Alvin, especially Alvin, and a few other students who had extra challenges. They made the job rewarding.

Transitions were tough for all kids, but especially those on the autism and similar spectrums. They thrived with consistency and routines; adjusting to new ones took a toll on them, their families, and the educators. Learning their way around a new classroom and coping with a different teacher was tough for them.

Did it have to be that way?

"Are you sure, Emma?" Wayne Tait, the school principal, leaned back in his chair, steepling his hands. "This is rarely done, and with good reason. You know how much work it was preparing to teach Grade 1 when it was new to you this year. Most teachers like to sink into that, keeping to the same grade for a number of years, getting comfortable with that curriculum without the onerous task of building lessons from scratch. I appreciate what you're saying about how it would make things easier for the students if they had you again in Grade 2, but have you thought about the amount of extra work you're adding to your plate if you switch grades yet again?"

How could he ask such a question? Did he think this was some impulsive whim? That was *so* not her. "Yes, I'm aware of what this would mean for me as well as for the students."

"Laura Peel talked to me a while ago. While it's inevitable in a small school with only one classroom per grade that eventually a parent will teach their own child, Laura said that if there was any way she could avoid having her daughter in her Grade 2 class next year, she'd jump at the opportunity to switch grades." He rose from his chair. "Why don't you think about this overnight and let me know tomorrow? If you still want to move up with your students, I'll talk to Laura about trading grades with you for the fall."

~

Gabe might be *her* guy, but he was still such a guy. After he moved into the Olsen's farmhouse, he did nothing to the place other than stow away his clothing, and buy a few groceries. The house really needed to be brought into this century. The way 70-year-olds decorated the place might've been fine when they first did it decades ago, but if Emma was going to live there, the place needed to see changes.

And she needed to get on with those changes now. Summer would be busy with the wedding, taking her first grad school class, and preparing to teach Grade 2.

Methodically, she started with one room at a time, removing the doilies, then the stained, saggy furniture from the living room. Enlisting Gabe's and Blair's help in removing 50-year-old carpet revealed pegged wooden floors with decent potential. Now, with those floors stripped, sanded, coated, and buffed, they gleamed.

Learning from Beth, Becca, and Mona about flooring upkeep in farm homes, the entryway and kitchen now had ceramic tiles underfoot.

While she worked her magic indoors, Gabe, Blair, and the cousins tore off the rotting timbers from the outside deck to build a new, multi-level outdoor entertainment spot. Blair held a beam in place while Beth used a drill to put in the screws to hold it. Emma came out of the house with her new purchase—a neon pink cordless drill.

"Would you look at that," said Beth.

"Every time I bring over a tool and set it down, Gabe grabs it, and it's gone." Emma gave her fiancé a scowl. "So I bought myself a pink drill. That should tell everyone it's mine and to leave it alone."

"Yeah, like that's going to work," muttered Blair., and went back to fitting the next joist.

"Thanks, babe," Gabe told Emma, reaching for her drill. "The battery's nearly dead on mine, and I need another one. Perfect timing."

Blair built a table that followed the angles of the outdoor seating area that would hold 15 people for a meal. He told them that was their limit; they were not allowed to have more guests than that at one time.

The table was a hand-crafted thing of beauty, an early wedding present, and this was its inaugural christening. Friday and Randine took charge of Mona's and Reid's son before the child was even unstrapped from his car seat. Now Mona and Reid, Blair and Beth, Becca and Stan, and Robin and Keith lounged around the table.

And Esther. A smiling Esther. Exiting the kitchen, she carried a tray stacked with steaks and sausages out to the barbecue and hollered for her son-in-law to be. "Gabe, get over here. Emma says it's time for you to start cooking."

The table was set, the salads waited in their fridge, and loaves of freshly baked garlic bread warmed in the oven.

The rest of the group sat around the table, throwing out advice and criticisms at Gabe and Blair on their grilling skills.

"Esther, I can't thank you enough for the

alpaca wool knitting that you have done," said Becca. "We were really struggling to keep up with inventory to sell in the store, but you've made a difference."

"Glad to help, and I think the exercise has even done these arthritic hands of mine some good."

Robin looked at Becca and Mona, who gave her nods. "Esther, I've been meaning to ask you something else. The girls and I have been talking. We're struggling at the store. Mona is the only one of us working there full time, and with Becca and me putting in shorter hours, some days we never get lunch or a break."

Becca took over. "Here's what we were wondering. Do you think you might be willing to come in and work for a few hours a day?"

At the look on Esther's face, she added hastily, "It doesn't have to be every day even just once a week would make a difference, but you could increase that if you wanted."

Mona weighed in. "If you would work two or three hours around lunch time, that would help us out so much. Even just one hour, if that's all you felt you can manage."

Before Esther could answer, Keith broke in. "For crying out loud, Robin. Couldn't you have asked a man? Now you've just added another female into the mix. That's four of you against me. And I thought I didn't stand a chance before." He flinched at the kick under the table from his wife. "Oh, no offense, Esther, to you, or your gender. The girls are right. We could really use some more staff and we'd appreciate it if you would consider helping us out."

Esther's hand was at her throat. "But I've never worked in a store like yours before. I have no idea how to run those electronic cash registers and payment machines.

"Oh, don't worry about that," Robin assured her. "If Keith could learn the system, anyone can."

"Hey!" Keith looked to Stan and Reid for help. They studiously looked off into the distance.

"Steaks are ready," yelled Gabe. "Let's eat."

Do they go through with it?

Yep, Emma and Gabe marry.

Would you like a front row seat at their wedding?

Read all about it in this bonus chapter at https://BookHip.com/KCQBNMP

(Plus you'll also learn about the new direction Esther's life has taken).

~

You can see all of the books in this series at http://www.amazon.com/dp/B0B5VJQV5V.

MORE ABOUT THE AUTHOR

Dr. Sharon A. Mitchell lives on a farm, with her nearest neighbor several miles away. Does that seem like a setting to spark the imagination? It does for her.

She takes long walks with her hundred-pound German Shepherd dogs, Pickles and Dill. (She didn't name them - don't blame her).

Her current projects are writing more books in the series The Farmers of Goodrich County - clean and wholesome romances with down-to-earth heroes, and heroines who are more than their match.

She's also working on her eighth psychological thriller novel for the *When Bad Things Happen* series.

In addition to short stories tied to that series, she's written six other novels, each featuring an autistic child or young adult. Two nonfiction books accompany that autism series.

Sharon's been a teacher, counselor,

psychologist and consultant for decades and continues to teach university classes on kids who learn differently to soon-to-be teachers and administrators.

She loves to hear from her readers and always responds. Email her at sharon@sharonmitchellauthor.com.

Follow her to be notified of her next books on any of these social media links:

BB bookbub.com/authors/sharon-a-mitchell
facebook.com/DrSharonAMitchell
twitter.com/AutismSite
instagram.com/autismsite
pinterest.com/mitchellsha3047

www.ingramcontent.com/pod-product-compliance
Lightning Source LLC
LaVergne TN
LVHW041055080826
845145LV00007B/1586

* 9 7 8 1 7 3 8 9 7 5 5 6 3 *